# Stay Over

### KINCAID BROTHERS BOOK ONE

*NEW YORK TIMES* BESTSELLING AUTHOR
# KAYLEE RYAN

Copyright © 2022 Kaylee Ryan
All Rights Reserved.

This book may not be reproduced in any manner whatsoever without the written permission of Kaylee Ryan, except for the use of brief quotations in articles and or reviews.

This book is a work of fiction. Names, characters, events, locations, businesses and plot are products of the author's imagination and meant to be used in a fictitious manner. Any resemblance to actual persons, living or dead, or actual events throughout the story are purely coincidental. The author acknowledges trademark owners and trademarked status of various products referenced in this work of fiction, which have been used without permission. The publication and use of these trademarks are not authorized, sponsored or associated by or with the trademark owners.

The following story contains sexual situations and strong language. It is intended for adult readers.

Cover Design: Book Cover Boutique
Photographer: Regina Wamba
Editing: Hot Tree Editing
Proofreading: Deaton Author Services
Paperback Formatting: Integrity Formatting

# Chapter 1

## BROOKS

I'M STANDING IN THE BACK of the room, watching as my little cousin smiles up at her future husband. I admit that Deacon and Ramsey together is not something I would have predicted. He's ten years older than her. The same age as Orrin, and Ramsey, she lands in the middle of Archer and Ryder. I never saw it coming, but to see the two of them together, no one questions the love they have for each another.

The crowd, and by the crowd, I mean most of my brothers, chant for them to kiss as they stare lovingly into one another's eyes. Deacon wraps his arms around her, pulling her into his chest, and drops his lips to hers. The moment is so intimate I have to look away, feeling as though I need to give them privacy.

My eyes land on Palmer, and the smile that lights up her face as she watches her brother and her best friend kiss can only be described as pure joy. She radiates happiness for them, and I'm sure there's a little bit of pride there as well. She's the one who got them together, and I've heard her boast about it many times. Even though she brags about setting all of this in motion, she can't hide her happiness for the couple.

"When I get married, I'm not doing any of this engagement party shit," Maverick, one of the twins and the babies in the family, says, stepping up beside me.

I huff out a laugh. "Trust me, my man, when you feel like that"—I point to where Deacon stands with his arm around Ramsey's waist, holding her close to him while they talk to his parents—"about someone, there likely isn't much you wouldn't agree to."

"How would you know?" my little brother challenges.

He and his twin, Merrick, just turned nineteen, and they have so much to learn. "Call it a hunch," I tell him.

He's quiet for a few minutes, and when he speaks again, his words surprise me. "You ever been in love, Brooks?" His voice is softer than it was previously.

"Love like that?" I point to our cousin and her fiancé. "No. There has never been anyone to hold my interest long enough." It's true. I've dated here and there but never anything or anyone serious. Not because I'm against the act of falling ass over heels in love. It's the opposite, in fact. I grew up watching my parents and the love they have for one another. I'll never settle for anything less than what they have.

"Dad's always preaching about working hard and loving harder, yet all of us are still single. I mean, Merrick and me, we're the babies, but the rest of you, well, except for Orrin, are still single."

"Love takes time, kid," I tell him.

I feel a slight punch to my arm and grin. He and Merrick both hate it when we call them kids. "It took Orrin thirty-two years to find the one, and Deacon too. They're the same age. But they found it. We will too. Besides, you're too young to be thinking about settling down."

"I'm not. Not really. I just… you know, these things make you think, and the way Orrin fell so fast for Jade, I was just curious if it would be like that for the rest of us."

"Honestly, I don't know. I think that sometimes it's fast and others it's like a slow build. There is no timeline you have to follow."

"Yeah," he agrees as Rushton, the middle brother of the nine, joins us.

"What are you two talking about all serious?" His eyes bounce from me to Maverick.

"Mav was just telling me that when he gets married, he's omitting the engagement party," I tell him.

Rushton nods. "You might be on to something, little brother."

After draining the last of my beer, I hold up the empty bottle. "I'm grabbing another. You want one?" I ask Rushton.

"Nah, I'm set." Rushton holds up his bottle of beer.

"I'd love one. Thanks for asking," Maverick quips.

"Yeah, not happening. Mom would hang me up by my toes." Mav grumbles, making me smile, as I turn away from them and make my way to the bar. If we were at my place or one of the others, I'd let him drink, but this is a different setting, and like I said, Mom would be pissed, and if there is anything that me and my brothers hate, it's when our momma is pissed at us. All nine of us are Momma's boys and damn proud of it.

Reaching the bar, I raise my bottle at the bartender before setting the empty on the bar. I'm just about ready to turn around and do some more people-watching when I feel a shoulder bump into mine. Turning, I see Palmer standing next to me.

"I do good work, huh?" She smiles up at me. Her emerald eyes are sparkling.

"Are you ever going to let them live that down?" I ask her, nodding at the bartender, who places a fresh ice-cold bottle in front of me. "What are you drinking?" I ask her.

"Oh, a beer is fine." She smiles kindly at the bartender, and the woman actually blushes. Palmer turns her attention back to me. "And no, probably not. I have to keep it up so that I have a good case for them to name their firstborn after me."

"I don't know if the world can handle more than one Palmer Setty," I tease.

"Hey, I won't be Setty for long," she fires back.

"Really? I didn't know you were seeing anyone." I take a pull of my beer as the bartender places Palmer's in front of her and quickly scurries away.

"Oh, I'm not. However, I know I don't want to be some

spinster cat lady. I believe that there's someone out there for all of us. I just haven't found mine yet."

I hold my beer up, and she taps hers to mine. "Maybe Ramsey needs to get involved, so you don't hold this over her head forever."

"Oh, I'm so going to regardless." Palmer laughs. "She's my best friend, and she's marrying my brother. I set them up. That's lifetime bragging rights, my friend."

"Good to know. I guess my brothers and I can take credit for Orrin and Jade since we all helped him get ready for their first date."

"That gives you like a year, maybe. I mean, I set them up, I planned it, and now they're getting married. Lifetime." She grins, bumping her shoulder into mine once again.

"Savage. I like it."

She nods before turning to face the crowd, resting her back against the bar. I mimic her stance and survey the room.

"Orrin and Jade seem happy." She nods to where my oldest brother has his girlfriend, Jade, wrapped in his arms, swaying back and forth on the dance floor.

"Yeah. Things are getting serious, I think. At least they are for him." I realize that Jade is one of Palmer's good friends and is her sister Piper's best friend, and I might be freely giving information that I should be keeping to myself.

"No, for her too. She's really into him."

"Good." I nod even though I'm not sure she's looking at me.

"We're probably going to find ourselves at one of these with those two as the guests of honor sooner rather than later."

"You're probably right. My momma will be thrilled. Two weddings and the chance at more grandkids. Declan moved to the top as her favorite when Blakely was born."

"Stop." I turn to look at her to find her smiling up at me. "Your momma is too damn sweet to have favorites."

"Oh, that's not true. Blakely is by far her favorite."

"Am I sensing some jealousy from you?"

"Nah, she's cute as hell. Besides, when she was born, it kept Mom from asking the rest of us when we were going to give her grandchildren. Now that Orrin is in a serious relationship, it's only a matter of time before she starts asking again. Hell, she might already be."

"Carol would never." She places her hand that's not holding her beer over her heart and acts offended on my mom's behalf.

"Oh, she would. In fact, let's place a bet."

"I thought you left the betting to your brothers," she teases.

"We do, but this calls for one anyway."

"All right, big man. What are the terms?"

"If I win, you have to... you have to be my dance partner for the rest of the night." I don't know where that came from, but I can't take it back. Besides, Palmer is beautiful, and she looks sexy as hell in her little black dress. I could think of worse ways to spend the rest of my cousin's engagement party.

"And if I win, you have to come to my shop and help me put together a new bookshelf I bought for the lobby to display framed photos and store albums of my work. The one I had was too small."

"Done." I hold my hand out for her to shake. She slides her much smaller hand into mine, and a zap of something I can't name hits me out of nowhere. I quickly drop her hand and search the crowd for my brother, pretending that touching her soft skin didn't feel as though I was being electrocuted in the best way.

"Moment of truth," I tell her, nodding to where Orrin and Jade are standing on the opposite side of the room, still swaying back and forth in each other's arms.

"Let's do this." She grabs my hand, and that feeling hits me once again. This time she stops and stares up at me and back to our joined hands before shaking her head and pulling me across the room to my brother and her friend. "Hey, guys," she greets them, dropping my hand.

"What are you up to?" Jade chuckles.

"Who me?" Palmer places her hand against her heart just as she did earlier, feigning innocence.

"Yes, you." Jade smiles at her.

"Well, we"—Palmer looks over and points at me before turning back to Jade and Orrin—"have a little wager going, and the two of you hold the answer."

"This should be good," Orrin chimes in.

"I bet her that Mom has already been asking you when you're going to give her more grandchildren now that you two are getting serious," I tell them.

"Oddly enough, she hasn't mentioned it," Orrin confesses.

"Hah! I win!" Palmer wiggles her hips in that tight-ass dress of hers, and my cock twitches in my jeans.

"Well, not exactly," Jade speaks up.

"Please tell me my mother isn't harassing you about grandkids." Orrin's tone is pleading. His eyes are closed, and his head is tilted back as if he needs the gods of patience to rain down on him.

"Well, she's not harassing me. However, she did mention it last week at Sunday dinner."

"Damn, I missed it." I'm a registered nurse by trade, and I work at the Willow River General Hospital Emergency Department. My hours change in varying stages of twelve-hour shifts, and that includes working every third weekend.

"I'm sorry," Orrin says sincerely. "I'll talk to her."

"No. Don't tell her I told you. She was really sweet about it, and it didn't bother me."

"So we both win." I grin over at Palmer.

She shrugs. "As long as I get my shelf put together, I'm good."

"What did you win?" Jade asks me.

"This one"—I point at Palmer—"has to be my dance partner the rest of the night. I've been avoiding your cousin Jackie all night, and Palmer is my excuse to keep doing so."

"She's... a lot to take on," Jade agrees. "She means well, but she has zero subtlety."

"Subtlety? Is that what you call her grabbing my ass and telling me I owe her a dance?" I ask.

Jade, Palmer, and Orrin all crack up laughing at my expense. "Laugh it up, assholes. I'm telling you, those talon nails of hers bit into the skin even through my jeans."

"Prove it," Palmer challenges, and if I knew it wouldn't send my cousin or my mother into orbit, I'd pull my pants down now to show her.

"How did she get an invite anyway?" I ask them.

"Is that a serious question?" Orrin asks. "Deacon invited what seems like all of Willow River. He's shouting from the rooftops that Ramsey agreed to marry him."

"She's changed him," Palmer says. I turn to look at her, and she has a soft smile on her lips as she watches Deacon and Ramsey where they're talking to Mayor Hanson.

"Damn, he really did invite the entire town." I laugh.

"Well, I guess I have a debt to pay. You think you can manage taking me for a spin out there?" Palmer indicates to the dance floor behind us.

I drain my beer and set it on a nearby table. Palmer takes a hefty drink of hers and then hands the bottle to Jade. "Finish this for me, will you? Hot beer tastes like cat piss." As soon as Jade takes the bottle, Palmer finds my hand and leads me to the dance floor.

She stops and turns to face me, and the song turns slow. Sliding my arm around her waist, I pull her close and begin to sway.

"You're not half bad at this," she says, peering up at me under long lashes. Her hands that have been resting on my chest move to wrap around the back of my neck. The action causes her tits to press tight against me, and I have to make a conscious effort to keep my hardening cock from pressing into her belly.

"Not half bad?" I scoff. "I could dance circles around everyone on this dance floor," I announce with confidence.

"You're going to have to wait until another night for that, big guy." She runs her fingers through the back of my hair. "I'm in the middle of paying my debt."

"Are you saying you can't hang?"

"Oh, I can hang, but these heels are killing my feet."

"Take them off."

"What?"

"You said that the heels were killing your feet, so take them off."

"The floor is probably dirty and sticky, and just no."

"Good call. We can sit," I tell her. "I don't want you hurting yourself just to fulfill a silly bet."

"I'm good, Brooks. Just don't expect me to go dancing circles around everyone here." She winks, and I feel the action in my chest, a tightening that I've never felt before.

I chalk the feeling up to my dry spell. I've been picking up a lot of hours the last few weeks to cover for another nurse who was on maternity leave. That hasn't left much social time. I need to do something about that. I make a mental note to call a few of my brothers so we can hit the town. Maybe head over to Harris and hit a bar there for the night.

"Let me know if you need a break," I tell her.

"Trust me. I will." We're both quiet for a few minutes, just swaying to the slow beat, when her eyes connect with mine. "You know, you could be missing out on a lot of fun by not giving Jackie that dance." She nods behind me, a grin plastered on her face. I twirl us around so I can see what she's talking about.

I have to bite down on my cheek to keep my laughter contained and not draw attention to us or the situation. Jackie is standing between my two baby brothers, and they're all three grinding on each other like they're at a strip club and not the small manor on the outskirts of town.

"They better hope our momma doesn't see them," I say for Palmer's ears only.

"They're young, and a hot older woman is showing them attention. Let them live it up."

"I'm not breaking that up. I'm not going anywhere near that clusterfuck, but they better hope that Mom doesn't see it. She'll drag them both away by their ears."

"There is so much to be learned from Momma Kincaid." She laughs. "I can only imagine the chaos of raising nine rowdy boys in one house."

"It was all kinds of loud, but it was also fun. My parents let us be kids, and honestly, I'm not sure how we didn't drive them batshit crazy."

"Love."

"What?"

"Love. That's why you didn't drive them batshit crazy."

"You're probably right," I agree. My parents have a love for one another that surpasses anything I've ever witnessed before. And that love they have for each other spilled over to all of us kids. There was never a day growing up that I didn't know that my brothers and I were the most important people in their world. That's how it should be and why I'm still single at the age of twenty-nine. Sure, that's not old by any standards, but I'm also not getting any younger. One day I'll find her. I'll find the woman who tilts my world on its axis and makes me feel whole at the same time. When I do, I'm never letting her go.

## PALMER

I'M DANCING WITH BROOKS KINCAID.
*Brooks Kincaid!*

Brooks's older brother Orrin was best friends with my brother, Deacon, growing up. Orrin usually had a brother or two with him when he came to visit. Most of the time, it was Declan or Brooks. That's where my crush started. In fact, I can tell you the exact date that my young heart fell for him.

I was eleven the day Brooks Kincaid became my hero. Deacon was twenty-one and home from college. He invited Orrin and some other people over, and as always, Orrin brought Declan and Brooks. I was eleven and starving for my brother's attention. Not that he didn't give it to me, but Piper was the one who got the majority of his time. Now that I'm older, I get it. She was closer to him in age. At sixteen, she wasn't the nuisance of a little sister that I'm sure I was. I know I'm a lot to handle. I own that.

Anyway, I was missing my big brother and was acting out to get his attention. He and his friends, along with Piper and a few of hers, were sitting outside around the fire. The sun was just starting to set, and I knew that my mom was going to tell me it was time to come inside soon. I was jealous of my sister and how she got to hang out with Deacon. So my eleven-year-old mind thought it would be a great idea to climb the tree near the fire pit. I thought for certain I would climb to the top and call out to Deacon, and he would be so proud of me for how high I made it.

I'm sure I don't have to tell you that my plan was a disaster. I climbed about halfway up and made the mistake of looking down. I'd been in my treehouse before, but that was with the ladder my dad and brother had built. Once I looked down, my knees started to wobble, and my palms became sweaty. I called out for my brother, but he didn't hear me. I started to cry as fear washed over me. I just knew I was going to fall to my death. Yes, a little dramatic, but I was eleven and upset.

It just so happened to be my lucky day. Brooks walked away from the fire to take a leak and heard my cries. He wasted no time climbing up in the tree and bringing me down with him on his back. I clung to him like he was my everything, and that's when it all started. Over the years, I've run into him, more so when his cousin Ramsey and I became best friends.

Never once have I acted on this silly crush, though. Never in my life have I ever even breathed that he was someone I was interested in, not until the night my brother proposed to my best friend, and Ramsey made us all voice our choice of men in attendance. Never once have I touched him with more than just a teasing punch or elbow.

That changed tonight.

This is the third straight song we've danced to. My feet are killing me, but that's not going to stop me. I wanted to squeal with excitement when he said his prize was me being his dance partner for the remainder of the night. I knew it was only to keep Jade's cousin Jackie at bay, but it was time with him. His hands on me and mine on him. No way in hell was I passing that up. I pretended to be excited that I won when in reality, I never wanted to lose anything so damn bad in my entire life. When Jade spoke up and changed the outcome of the bet, I was all too eager to drag Brooks's fine ass out onto the dance floor.

I know that our dancing doesn't mean anything. However, it's almost like a childhood fantasy come true. For one night, I get to have all of his attention, and that's enough for me. It's not like I'm in love with him. He's just my childhood crush, and I'd be lying if I said that eleven-year-old Palmer wasn't screaming from excitement.

Hell, I would have been happy to spend my evening with any of the Kincaid brothers. Even the twins that were making a Jackie sandwich earlier out here on this very dance floor. They're all sexy as hell. It's more than their looks, though. They are genuinely good guys, hard workers, and even though Orrin, so far, is the only one showing signs of settling down, they're not man-whores. They don't blow through women like it's their job. At least, I don't think they do. They do a pretty damn good job of hiding it if that's the case. Willow River is a small town, and word travels fast. I've never heard anything but great things about the Kincaid brothers or the Kincaid family in general.

Carol and Raymond Kincaid raised nine good men. I think they deserve the right to ask about more grandchildren. Before I know it, a smile pulls at my lips, thinking about Carol giving her sons a pouty lip and asking for grandbabies.

"What's got that smile lighting your face?" Brooks asks.

I move my gaze from the crowd back to him. "I was just thinking about your mom and her giving you and your brothers a pouty lip and a sob story to match asking for more grandkids."

"That's pretty accurate." He nods. "What's even funnier is that none of us have said we're never having kids. In fact, I'd say coming from such a large family, we'll all end up with a kid or two. What my mom and dad, by association, fail to realize is that it's their intense connection and the way that they love one another that's held us off this long. I'm pretty sure that I speak for all of my brothers when I say if we can't have that, we don't want it at all."

I want to ask him about Blakely's mom and Declan. We all know she passed away as the result of a car accident not long after Blakely was born. There have been rumors, but I'm sure most of it is small-town gossip. Not to mention, it's none of my business.

Instead, I go for, "So do you want kids one day?"

"Yeah." He gives a slow bob of his head. "I couldn't imagine not having a loud, chaotic home. What about you?"

"There were only three of us, but yeah, one day." The song turns to a fast one, and I inwardly curse the deejay. Just as I move to step away from Brooks, he manages to grip my waist and turn me so my back is to his front. He points in front of us, and I lose it. My head falls back, resting against his shoulder as my laughter takes over. In the middle of the dance floor are Maverick and Merrick, his twin brothers. However, instead of Jackie, they're dancing with their mom. They're making the silliest of dance moves, and Carol's face is beet red. She's also smiling from ear to ear. My eyes move past them to find Raymond shaking his head and laughing at his two youngest sons while they dance like loons around his wife.

"I bet there was never a dull moment in your house growing up." I glance over my shoulder to find Brooks's eyes already waiting on mine. I swallow hard at the nearness as his hot breath brushes across my cheek.

"Never." He mouths, "Chaos," and I nod, definitely understanding what he means.

Instead of releasing me, Brooks slides his hands to my hips, and we begin to move to the beat. I'm glad that the lights are turned down low. I'm sure my face is as red as a tomato. Before I know what's going on, my best friend and the lady of honor steps in front of me, my brother at her back, holding her much like Brooks is holding on to me. Ramsey grabs my hands, and the two of us let loose. We ignore the men behind us, at least that's what I try to do, and just enjoy dancing and acting a fool with my best friend. Eventually, Brooks and Deacon have to let us go because we're jumping around and being silly, much like Maverick and Merrick. When the twins appear, each one taking one of us by the hand, Ramsey and I don't hesitate to follow them to the center of the dance floor and join them in their silly antics, taking Carol's place. I glance around and find her in Raymond's arms. They're both wearing matching smiles.

Merrick is my partner, and he moves in behind me, aligning

his body with mine. His hands are on my hips as we gyrate to the music. As the youngest of the Kincaid clan, these two sure know how to throw down some moves. I can't help but wonder if that's a trait they learned from their older brothers or if that's just their own swag. I'm sure they were a hit at their high school dances.

Merrick turns me in his arms and holds me close as we rock to the beat. "You know," he says, his lips pressed close to my ear, "we started this to fuck with Deacon. He gets all kinds of jealous anytime, anyone, even us, puts their hands on Ramsey."

"That's cruel." I smile up at him, shaking my head.

Merrick shrugs. "Yeah, but it's our job as Ramsey's family, to mess with him. What I didn't plan on was getting a two-for-one deal."

"Well, thank you for the pleasure of your company, good sir," I tease him.

He nods. "You're right. It's a triple deal." I raise my eyebrows in question. He's totally lost me now. Merrick flashes me a cheesy grin before lowering his lips to my ear once again. "We get to fuck with two of Deacon and my brother, and I get to dance with you."

"Your brother?" I ask confused.

Before he has time to answer, I get to make my own assumption when Brooks appears, laying a heavy hand on Merrick's shoulder. "I'll take it from here, Mer," he tells him. The entire time his eyes are locked on mine. There is an expression on his face that I can't name.

The breath stalls in my lungs as Merrick chuckles but steps back, and Brooks takes his place. I could be imagining it, but his grip on my hips feels tighter, and the set of his jaw more prominent. I don't even realize I'm doing it until I feel his stubble beneath my palm as I lay my hand against his cheek.

"You okay?"

He pulls me closer and nods. His jaw is still tight; I can feel it twitch, and I tense, not sure if it's me who's upset him. "You have a debt to pay, Palmer," he reminds me.

"Oh. I'm sorry." I don't really know what to say because it was a dance with his little brother, and I was already dancing with Ramsey, and he didn't seem to mind. My hand drops from his cheek and lands on his shoulder.

Brooks shakes his head, expels a heavy breath, and grabs my hand, resting it back against his cheek. "You have nothing to apologize for. I'm just... tired, I think. You didn't do anything wrong, Palmer." Deep blue eyes will me to believe him.

"We don't have to keep dancing. It was just a bet," I remind him.

His hold tightens even further. His head bends as he once again places his lips next to my ear. "I want to dance with you."

I can't even formulate a reply, reeling from the huskiness of his voice, when Jackie steps up beside us.

"Hey, Brooks. Got a dance for me?" she asks. Her voice is high-pitched, her dress cut way too low, and she bats her eyelashes about five hundred times in a minute, all while sticking out her bottom lip in a pout.

Does that usually work for her?

"No can do," Brooks says smoothly. "Promised all my dances tonight to my girl." He wraps his arms all the way around me, causing me to do the same.

His girl? Eleven-year-old Palmer is jumping around and acting a fool at his words. The adult Palmer knows he's just trying to get rid of her. Doesn't mean I can't relish how it sounds to have him call me his. Words I definitely never thought I would hear coming out of his mouth.

"Oh, well, you won't mind, will you, Palmer?" Jackie asks.

Brooks stiffens in my arms.

"Sorry, Jackie." I rest my head on his chest. "He's all mine." A thrill shoots through me when I feel his cock harden at my words. I get it. He's a man, I'm a woman, and we're holding one another so close there's not even any room for air between our bodies. It's a natural reaction, but it still causes a spike in my adrenaline that it's me he's holding and reacting to. Then again, that might just be my hormones.

"I didn't realize," she mumbles before turning on her heel and walking away.

The song is a fast one. Some catchy beat I've never heard before, so I try to pull away, but Brooks's arms are locked around me so tight I can't move.

"Thank you," he whispers. And then he goes and changes the entire course of the night when he presses his lips to my neck, just below my ear. "I owe you one," he says, his voice low and deep.

I don't respond, and if I'm being honest, it's because I can't. Even if I knew what to say to that action, my mouth won't cooperate. Maybe it's my brain. Whatever the reason, I can't speak. So instead, I rest my head on his chest as the song changes again to a slow, sultry tune. Brooks doesn't lessen his hold, so neither do I. Instead, I hold onto him and pretend that just for tonight, for this one moment in time, he really is mine.

When the song changes to "Girls Just Want To Have Fun," I feel a hand on my shoulder. Lifting my head, I see Jade standing there smiling. I take a step back from Brooks, and this time he lets me. Ramsey appears on my other side, sliding her arm through mine, and Piper shimmies over as well.

"We have to dance to this," Jade says, tugging me and the others to the center of the dance floor.

I can feel my face heat because, for a few minutes, I forgot where we were. I forgot that this is my best friend's engagement party. My best friend who is marrying my brother. Everything around me ceased to exist but the man who held me in his arms.

Brooks Kincaid is too damn sexy. The man literally had me lost in the moment from being so close to him. I need to latch myself to my friends for the remainder of the night and let him off the hook. Let myself off the hook. I'm not sure how many more dances I can take without begging him to take me home with him. I'm not ready for that level of embarrassment, so avoiding him is my best bet.

I manage to do just that over the next couple of hours. I also down more shots than my normal allowance, but the girls and I are having fun, doing our own thing. Every once in a while, I'll glance over at my brother, who is talking to Orrin, Brooks, and Sterling, with a smile on his face. I never let my eyes land on Brooks. I don't trust myself to not run and throw myself at him.

However, the crowd starts to thin, and it's just us girls on the dance floor and a handful of others milling around. My brother steps up and swoops Ramsey into his arms, and Orrin does the same with Jade. I watch as Rushton holds his hand out for Piper, and she takes it easily. Taking that as my chance to grab a drink, I turn only to step into a broad chest.

"You've been giving away my dances." Brooks smiles down at me, and I realize the shots were a bad idea. I don't have the strength or the brain capacity to come up with a reason to flee.

"One more, Palmer," he says softly, not giving me a chance to say no as he tugs me into his arms. He holds me like I'm his and like he's mine, and I can't resist the pull to snuggle into him. His hands gently stroke up and down my spine, and I have to mentally remind myself he's not in fact mine.

When the song finally ends, I lift my head to stare up at him. His dark blue eyes hold something I can't name, and before I know it, words are tumbling past my lips before I can stop them. "I like pretending to be yours."

A slow smile tugs at his lips. "This night definitely turned out better than I had anticipated."

"You ready, Palmer?" Deacon asks from beside us. He has a sleepy Ramsey in his arms. "This one is ready to crash."

"Yes." I glance back to Brooks. "Thank you for the dances."

Not saying a word, he nods as I loop my arm through Ramsey's, stealing her from my brother and leading her out to the parking lot to his car. This night has been all kinds of amazing, and odd, and just… everything I never thought it would be. No matter how much alcohol I've had, I know this will be a night I'll always remember.

## BROOKS

GROCERY SHOPPING IS ONE OF my least favorite things to do. However, I hate eating out all the time. Not to mention, eating all that junk is counterproductive to my workout regimen. My brothers and I all work out. A couple of them have physical jobs and they don't have to hit the gym as often. I like to stay fit and healthy, hence the reason I must go grocery shopping today.

I just finished a three-day stint of twelve-hour shifts and I'm drained. All three of those twelve-hour shifts turned into fourteen plus, and I'm fucking exhausted. I'd rather chill around the house and catch a few more hours of sleep, but I've got adult shit to do that's not going to do itself. So after a quick shower and a protein bar, because I have nothing else in my kitchen, I hop into my truck and head to the store.

I'm almost into the corporation limits of town when I see a familiar black Hyundai and dark head of hair that I'd love nothing more than to wrap my fist around. Checking my mirrors, I turn on my signal and pull in behind her.

Palmer's eyes are wide and worried until I step out of the

truck, and she recognizes me. Willow River doesn't have a lot of crime, but a woman all on her own on the side of the road is never a good thing, not in my eyes.

"Brooks." She breathes my name as if she prayed for me and I was delivered to her. "Deacon," she says into the phone pressed to her ear. "Brooks just stopped." She gives me a relieved smile. "I don't know," she tells her brother.

"What's going on?" I ask.

"I don't know. I was driving, and it just lost power. The radio went, and all the gauges, and just nothing."

"Sounds like the alternator."

"That's what Deacon said. I tried to call my dad, but he's not answering, so I'm waiting for Deacon to come and get me."

"I can take care of it. He's working today, right?" Deacon's a lawyer in Willow River and used to work more than anyone I know, that is until he met and fell in love with my little cousin, Ramsey. She's helped him find a work-life balance that he desperately needed.

"Are you sure?" She takes in my cargo shorts and T-shirt. I'm certain she was expecting to see me in my scrubs.

"I'm sure. I'm off the next two days."

"Thank you, Brooks." Her shoulders slump with relief. "Deacon," she sighs, "Brooks says he can take care of it." She pauses, rolls her eyes, and hands me the phone. "He wants to talk to you."

I chuckle at her annoyance but take the phone from her hand and place it to my ear. "What's up?"

"Are you sure you don't mind helping?" Deacon asks.

"Positive. Today's an off day for me. I was just running errands. I'll take a look, and if I can't get it to work, I'll call Declan and have him dispatch one of his guys with a tow truck."

"Thanks, Brooks. I owe you one. I'm getting ready to head into court, and I was just going to call a tow and send Ramsey to pick her up."

"It's all good, man. I'll shoot you a message later letting you know what the turnout is."

"Thanks." There's relief in his voice.

"No problem," I reply and hand the phone back to Palmer.

"Hey." She's quiet while she listens, and I pull my own phone out of my pocket to text Declan.

> **Me:** Hey. Just found Palmer stranded just outside of town. I'm going to take a look but from what she described sounds like her alternator.

His reply is immediate.

> **Declan:** Let me know if you need me to send the truck.
>
> **Me:** Thanks.

I slide my phone back into my pocket in time to focus back on her conversation. "Yes, I feel safe with Brooks. Don't worry. Thank you, and good luck in court." She ends the call and slides her phone into her purse, draped across her shoulder.

"Everything good?" I ask.

A slight blush coats her cheeks as she rolls those big green eyes. "Yes. He's just worried. The consequences of being the baby of the family."

"My guess is that he would have the same worry for Piper."

She nods. "You're right. We're lucky to have such a great big brother who cares about us."

"You are," I agree. "All right, toss me the keys, and I'll take a look." She hands me her keys, and I slide behind the wheel, adjusting the seat to accommodate my large frame. Turning over the starter, nothing happens. Everything is just dead, which leads me to believe my suspicion about the alternator is correct. "I think it is the alternator."

"Damn. How expensive is that?"

"Couple hundred bucks. Declan will take care of you." I climb out of the car, hand her the keys, and pull my phone out of my pocket.

> **Me:** Send the truck.

I follow it with a message telling him the general area where we're located.

**Declan:** Got it. Gus is on his way.

"Declan is sending one of his guys with the tow truck. Let's grab whatever you need out of your car and put it in my truck. Where were you headed?"

"The grocery store. I have an anniversary session later tonight, so I needed to knock a few items that need to get done off my list."

"That's where I was headed as well. I can take you, then drop you off at your place."

"Thanks. I need to figure out how I'm going to get to this shoot tonight and to work the next couple of days."

"As long as he can get the parts, I'd guess Dec will have you all fixed up tomorrow. You can take my truck tonight. Just drop me off at my place after we get groceries."

"I can't ask you to do that."

"You didn't ask. I offered. I'm off the next two days, and other than grabbing groceries and mowing the yard, I have no plans." Even if I did have plans, I would have offered my truck.

"Are you sure? It will just be tonight. I'll see if I can borrow Ramsey's car tomorrow, and she can ride to work with Deacon."

"I'm sure. And don't bother her. You won't need it all day. Just keep my truck until Declan tells you that yours is ready. Swing by and pick me up, so we can pick yours up. It will be less than twenty-four hours if I know my brother. I'm telling you it's fine."

Her eyes soften and, if I'm not mistaken, mist with tears. "Thank you, Brooks. You're saving me."

I pretend to ignore the way I want to pound on my chest when she tells me that. I'm also going to pretend that I haven't thought about her body pressed to mine last weekend at the engagement party. I. Will. Not. Think. About. That.

I also won't think about how I wanted to strangle my little brother because he was dancing with her. I don't understand; therefore, I'm keeping that shit locked tight in the box labeled *don't go there* in my mind.

"Let's grab whatever you need. Don't leave anything valuable just in case. Declan has cameras all around his shop, but better safe than sorry."

"Just me and my purse. I haven't stopped at the studio to load up any of my equipment. Yet."

"We can do that on the way back from the store as well so that I can help you."

"You don't have to do that."

"I know. I want to. Grab your things. We can wait in my truck until the tow gets here." I want to stand and wait for her but think better of it. Instead, I head back to my truck and climb inside, making sure the doors are unlocked for her. A couple of minutes later, she's pulling open the door and climbing inside. She settles in and smiles over at me, and something weird happens in my chest. It grows tight.

"Thank you, Brooks."

"You're welcome. Besides, I strongly dislike grocery shopping. Maybe going with someone else will make it less dreadful."

"Do you like to cook?" she asks.

"I don't hate it," I reply, and she chuckles.

"I enjoy it, but I don't do it often with just me. Usually, I make something like chicken and rice or spaghetti and eat it for a few days. It's hard to cook for just one."

"I do a lot of grilling in the summertime. I meal prep year-round, which makes packing lunch for work a hell of a lot easier. I make big portions and divide them up into multiple containers that last me for the week. Usually, that's one of my days off, meal prepping."

"Look at you making me feel like an underachiever," she teases.

"I mean, I'm pretty damn good at meal prep. I've got that shit down to a science."

"Do you get tired of eating the same thing?"

"Not really. I mix it up each week with different spices and vegetables. I can't remember which brother—I'm guessing it was

Orrin since he was the oldest. He started working out and eating healthier, and the rest of us just followed suit. Now it feels like that's all that I know. The only times I ever really veer off is when I make it to Sunday dinner at Mom and Dad's or have wings at the Willow Tavern."

"Wings aren't bad."

"They are when they're deep fried, but that shit is so good." I rub my belly thinking about them. I need to call one of my brothers so we can hit up the Tavern on one of my nights off.

"Your mom is such a good cook," she moans, and my cock stirs behind my zipper.

I ignore my cock and answer the woman. "She is. That's why Sundays are always a free to cheat day. Not to mention, my momma would kick my ass if she slaved over a stove all day and I showed up and didn't eat."

"She knows you're all health nuts, right?" She laughs.

"Well, I wouldn't call us health nuts. We try to eat well, and we do work out often."

"That's how you got these," she says, reaching over and giving my bicep a squeeze.

The spot where her hand meets my flesh feels as though it's burning. "And lifting patients all day." I pretend like the fact that her hand is still resting on my arm or the fact that she noticed that I work out doesn't affect me. I'm not vain, but I also work hard to stay fit. The fact that the woman who's consumed my thoughts for the last week took notice makes me want to stand a little taller.

What is it about Palmer Setty that pulls this kind of reaction out of me?

"How often do you work out?" she asks, pulling me out of my thoughts.

"Honestly, not as much as I used to. I try to get in a few workouts a week, but sometimes my schedule just doesn't allow it, and then sometimes on my day off, I don't want to do shit."

"You work crazy long hours."

"I do, but I enjoy it. There's always something new every single shift."

"What made you want to be a nurse?"

I usually don't open up to women. In fact, it's always superficial. None of them have ever inquired to get to know me. They're always throwing themselves at me or asking me to help set them up with one of my brothers. It's exhausting. I don't feel that right now with Palmer. She's Ramsey's best friend, and Ramsey is as close to a sister as I will ever get until my brothers decide to get married.

"When I was fourteen and the twins were four, they came down with pneumonia. They were in the hospital for over a week, and during that time, their nurses were incredible. I remember the day a male nurse walked in. I was shocked. In my fourteen-year-old brain, all nurses were women. Anyway, he was so good with the twins and doted on my mom and all of us, really. He joked around and lifted everyone's spirits. The twins took to him right away, and he was one of the only nurses there who could convince them not to freak out if they were passing meds or whatever. One night it was my turn to stay with Mom and the twins. We all insisted that we take turns so that she was never alone. Dad had to work, so we stepped up. Anyway, one night, Mom ran down to the cafeteria to grab some food. Merrick started having a seizure, and I freaked out. I didn't know what to do, so I just went to the door and yelled. Alex, that was his name, was sitting at the nurses' station and came running. He was so calm and knew exactly what to do. He sat on the bed and moved Merrick to his side, all while talking calmly to me, getting me to chill the hell out." I laugh, thinking about how scared I was that day. "By the time Mom got back to the room, all was well. Alex explained that it was likely the high fever that caused the seizure, and he had such a way that you clung to his every word, and you believed him when he said that everything was going to be okay. I decided that day that I wanted to be just like Alex. I wanted to be able to help my family like that if they ever needed me."

She smiles softly, and I see something in her eyes, something I can't name, but they soften, and have me leaning in just a little closer to her.

"What about you? Why photography?"

"Nothing as profound as your career choice. But when I was ten, my parents bought me a Polaroid camera for Christmas. I ran through the three boxes of film that came with it by the end of the day. I was obsessed. The next year I got a digital camera for Christmas. I took pictures of anything and everything. I don't know. I just fell in love with being able to capture a moment. To be able to capture the emotions of the people for them to look back on at a later time."

"Like the blind-date photoshoot with Deacon and Ramsey?"

"Exactly. I was behind the lens. I could see the chemistry before they even considered it. I knew that the two of them would be great together. Took me months to figure out how to set them up without them knowing or thinking that I was actually setting them up."

"I have to admit that was smooth."

"Thank you. Make sure you remind them of that. That helps in my quest for them to name their first born after me." She flashes me a wide grin.

I shake my head, a smile pulling at my lips. "You keep saying that." I chuckle. "Good luck with that endeavor. Rams can be hard-headed."

"Oh, I know. And I don't really expect them to. I just like teasing them. I couldn't be happier that the two of them have found each other and are now each other's forever."

Before I can ask her about her forever, and if that's even something she wants, Gus pulls in with the tow truck. It's a good thing too. I don't need to dig deeper into this beautiful woman sitting in the cab of my truck. She's already all I can think about over the last week, and learning more about her just makes this sudden obsession I have worse.

"I'm going to go talk with him. I'll be right back."

"Brooks." She calls my name as I'm reaching for the door handle. I turn to look at her over my shoulder. "Thank you for taking care of me."

So many different replies flash through my mind. *I'll always take care of you. Give me a couple of hours alone in my bedroom, and I'll show you how I can take care of you,* just to name a couple. Instead, my reply is simple. "Always." I toss her a wink and climb out of the truck. I take a quick second to adjust my hard cock behind my zipper before approaching the back of her car, hoping to hide what she does to me, while I explain to Gus what I know about what caused her to breakdown and telling him to call me if he has any issues.

By the time Gus has the car loaded, my cock is back to normal, so I turn and head back to the truck. "We're all set. He's going to tow it to Declan's shop, and they'll let us know what's going on. I didn't have your number, so I told them to just call me." I hand her my phone. "Add yourself in there, and I'll text it to Dec, so he has it."

She takes my phone and tries to open it. "Uh, I need a passcode," she says, trying to hand it back.

"123456."

"Brooks! That's like the easiest code ever."

"I know, but I hate the damn thing. The only reason I have a code on it at all is because when I'm at work, it's in my scrub pockets, and I end up calling random people when it's not locked."

"I guess that makes sense. But still, you need to make it a little harder. What if someone found your phone?"

I shrug. "I've had a phone for years now and never lost one. Although, I guess there is a first time for everything. Go in and change it for me."

"What? No. You should do that. You don't want me to have your code."

"Why not? Are you going to steal my phone?"

"No."

"Then make me a new code and tell me what it is."

"When's your birthday?"

"August ninth."

"0809," she mumbles as her fingers fly across the screen. "There. Done." She places my phone back into the cupholder.

"Thank you. Now, we've got some groceries to buy." Checking my mirrors, I pull out onto the road and head to my original destination. I wasn't expecting her today, but I'd be lying if I said I wasn't happy with how the day turned out.

## Chapter 4

### PALMER

BROOKS PULLS INTO THE DRIVEWAY of his house and puts his truck in Park. "I hate that I'm taking your wheels," I tell him. We spent over an hour in the grocery store. He followed me around the store like a lost puppy, and since I didn't know what he needed, I made sure to stroll up and down every aisle. It was surreal, and much to my surprise, enjoyable. I had a good time grocery shopping with the hottie, but I'll take that with me to the grave.

"Palmer, it's fine. Trust me on this. I'm going to pack in these groceries, do some meal prep, and I'll sleep in tomorrow, which basically means sleeping until like seven because my body is used to getting up early for work. Besides, I want to mow the lawn before the hot June sun is high in the sky, and just chill. It is my day off, after all."

"I know, but it sucks to not have your vehicle."

"I'll be fine." He's quick to reassure me.

"Well, let me help you carry everything inside."

"You don't have to do that."

"I do." I climb out of the truck and open the back door to start grabbing his groceries.

"You think you're going to be all right driving this thing?" he asks, taking the majority of the bags and shutting the door with his hip.

"Yeah, I'll be fine. I've driven my dad's and Deacon's several times." I follow him into the house and place the bags on the counter as my phone rings. Digging it out of my back pocket, I answer, "This is Palmer." I listen to the caller, my client, for this evening. "Oh, I'm sorry to hear that. Sure, just call me when you're ready to reschedule." We say our goodbyes, and I end the call.

"Everything okay?" Brooks asks.

"Yes. That was my client for this evening. They had to cancel. She's sick. Bronchitis."

"Bummer," he replies.

"Well, I guess I don't need your truck now."

"Nah, take it anyway. Just come and pick me up tomorrow on your way to grab your car. It's all good, Palmer."

"I guess I should get my groceries home. Are you sure you don't mind?"

"I'm positive." He smiles, and I feel that smile and its effect on me all the way to my toes.

"What are your plans for tonight now that you're off the hook from your shoot?"

"Probably nothing. Unless you don't mind me out hot-rodding in that truck of yours," I tease.

"Why don't you take your groceries home and then come back?" He looks shocked himself that he asked. It's on the tip of my tongue to decline and let him off the hook, but he keeps going. Selling his case. "I'm meal prepping, and I can show you how I do it."

"I'm sure you don't want me here cramping your style." I wave him off.

"I asked you to come back, Palmer. That means I want you here." There's something in his tone, it's laced with confidence and assurance, and it's impossible for me to say no.

"What can I do? Do I need to bring anything? Pick anything up that you might have forgotten?"

"No. Just you, Palmer." His eyes are dark blue pools of something that I can't name, but I damn sure wish I could.

"Okay. Well, I guess I'm going to run home, and I'll be back. Um, you have my number now, so if you think of something...." My voice trails off.

"Drive safe. I'll see you soon." He nods and begins to unbag all his groceries.

My arms are loaded down with bags, because I'm that person who will overload herself to the point of falling over to prevent making more trips. Why, I have not one single idea, but that's how I've always done it. My cell phone rings, but by the time I get all the bags untangled from my arms and hands, it stops, only to start again.

I dig it out of my back pocket and swipe at the screen. "Hello," I say breathlessly.

"Hey. How's your car?" Ramsey asks.

"Brooks thinks that it's the alternator."

"Are you at Declan's shop? Do you need me to come and get you? I got held up earlier, but I could slip away now."

"No. Thanks though. Brooks let me have his truck." I'm greeted with nothing but silence. Pulling the phone away from my ear, I check that we didn't get disconnected. "Ramsey?"

"I'm here."

"Oh. I thought that I lost you."

"Did you just say that Brooks let you have his truck?" Her tone does nothing to hide her shocked reaction.

"I did."

"That's his baby." I can hear the surprise in her voice.

"Men are crazy about their trucks around here. I asked him several times, and he insisted it was fine. Wait, do you think he's just trying to be nice because you and I are besties, and it's really driving him insane right now that I have his truck?"

"Palmer, I… no. If I know anything about Brooks, hell, any of my cousins, they're honest people. He would have told you he'd drive you if he had an issue with it, or he wouldn't have offered at all. I'm just shocked, I guess. He loves that truck."

"It's not like I'm going to be out tearing up cornfields with it. I'm actually just driving back to his place tonight, and then I'll come home and wait for Declan to call me, telling me my car is ready. I'll go pick up Brooks and take him to the shop with me so he can get his truck back when I pick up my car."

"Wait. Wait. Wait. Hold up. You're going back to Brooks's house tonight?"

"Yeah. We went to the store together, and my client canceled, and he invited me back to show me this meal prepping he does." I try like hell to keep the excitement out of my voice. The thought of spending more one-on-one time with Brooks has me giddy, but I won't let that show. Not even to my best friend.

"Am I dreaming?" Ramsey asks.

"What?" I laugh.

"This is just… wow. So you and Brooks went grocery shopping. Together?"

"We did. Let me back up. So, my car broke down, as you know. When I was on the phone with Deacon, Brooks drove by. He stopped and told me he would take care of it and to tell Deacon not to worry. He talked to Deacon, and they said, well, whatever it is they said, and then he texted Declan while he was at the shop, and after he looked at the car, he realized it was nothing he could fix there on the side of the road, so Declan sent a truck. Then Brooks was headed to the grocery store, and I was too, needing to get some things done before my shoot tonight. So we shopped together. Then he drove us back to his place. I helped him carry in his bags, and I got the call that my client had canceled while I was there. When we were shopping, I questioned him about this meal prepping he does, and he invited me back to watch and learn how he does it."

"And you're going back?"

"Yeah. I came home and unpacked my groceries, and I'm heading back over in a little while."

"In his truck?"

"Yep." I can't see her, but I know my best friend. Her mind is spinning, trying to determine whether this little impromptu get-together means anything. There isn't a single angle she can analyze in that head of hers that I haven't already thought about. The conclusion? Brooks is just being the nice guy that he is. That's all this is. Sure, I'd love for it to be more, but that's not what tonight is about, and I'm okay with that. I'd just be sitting at home editing images or maybe reading a book or binge-watching a new series. No way in hell am I passing up an opportunity to hang out with Brooks Kincaid for any of that.

Pulling out of my thoughts, I realize there is nothing but silence greeting me on the other end. "Rams?"

"I'm still here."

"It's not a big deal. We were talking about cooking for one, and he said that he meal preps, and I'd like to see how he does it." And spend more time with him, but I don't let those words escape.

"You chose him," Ramsey states.

"What?"

"The night that Deacon proposed, the reopening for the Willow Tavern. You, Piper, and Jade were talking about the guys, and when I asked who had your eye, Jade said Orrin, and you said Brooks."

Shit. "I had to pick one of them. You insisted."

"Palmer." Her tone tells me she's not buying the shit that I'm selling.

"Fine. Yes, I chose him. It's nothing. He's a nice guy who helped me out today and offered to teach me how to do this meal prepping he's so fond of. That's it."

"Why, Palmer? Why does that have to be it?"

"Because he's Brooks Kincaid. He's gorgeous and nice and has a good job. He has his shit together and could have any woman that he wanted."

"And yet he invited you to come back to his place."

"He was just being nice."

"Let me tell you something about my cousins. They are good men, fiercely loyal, and they don't play games. That means that they don't invite just anyone into their homes. That's not how they operate."

"But I'm not just anyone. I'm your best friend, and like his cousin, you are the closest that clan has to a sister."

"This is going to be fun."

"What are you talking about?"

"Oh, nothing. So, you're good? You don't need me to come and get you? You don't need to borrow my car?"

"I'm good. Declan should have my car fixed tomorrow, and I'll be able to give Brooks his truck back, and then all of this will be like it never happened."

"Uh-huh." She chuckles. "Call me when you get home tonight."

"I'm fine. I've driven big trucks before."

"That's not why I asked you to call me. I want details."

"There are no details. Unless you and my brother plan to start meal prepping."

"Just call me, Palmer."

"Fine."

"Love you," she singssongs.

"Love you too, brat."

Her laughter fills my ears as I end the call and finish putting my groceries away.

After everything is put away, I run to my room, brush my teeth, and freshen up a little. I blame my best friend for putting thoughts that shouldn't be there in my head, but here I am, letting a little piece of her assumption take root in my soul.

Locking up my house, I hop back into his truck and head back toward his place. I drive slow, slower than I need to, not because I'm worried about driving his beast of a truck, but because I need to clear my head and get Ramsey's suggestions to disappear.

Pulling into the driveway, I curse when I see a black Tahoe I know that vehicle. His brother is here, and even though it shouldn't be, this feels like it's going to be all kinds of awkward.

Climbing out of the truck, I stand tall and make my way to the front door. I knock once when a deep voice calls out for me to "Come on in." Grabbing the handle, I turn, pushing open the door. I set my purse, phone, and keys on the small table in the foyer and follow the voices.

"Hey." I wave. My eyes find Brooks, and he smiles. I then move to Declan and smile at him, and then my gaze travels to his adorable daughter, Blakely. "I love your pigtails," I tell the sweet little girl.

"Thanks. My daddy makes them." She offers me a toothy smile. "Hims does awright, but Rams and Mamaw's are better," she says, matter of fact.

"Well, I think your daddy does a great job," I tell her, my eyes finding Declan's. He shrugs and grins. "Thank you for taking my car on," I say.

He nods. "I should have it done tomorrow sometime."

"Thank you."

"That's what I do." He gently tugs on one of his daughter's pigtails. "You ready to go, squirt?"

"I's hungry."

Declan chuckles. "You're always hungry," he teases.

"Uncle Brooks, you's got any snacks?"

"You know where they are," Brooks answers.

Blakely nods and races to what I see is the pantry as she opens the door. On the bottom shelf, there appears to be an array of snacks. "Teddy's!" Blakely exclaims.

"You're going to spoil her dinner," Declan grumbles.

"You know I can't say no to her," Brooks counters. "I buy them for her."

"You all spoil her. Do you realize how bad it's going to be when she's a teenager? Uncle Brooks, I need a manicure. Uncle Brooks, Dad says I can't get my hair done. You better start learning now. That shit's about to get expensive."

"Daddy, bad word," Blakely announces as she hands Brooks the small pack of Teddy Grahams for him to open for her. He does with a smile, handing them back to her.

"What do you say?" Declan asks her.

"Tank you." She smiles up at Brooks, and he bends over, picking her up in his arms and kissing her cheek.

"Who's your favorite uncle?" he asks her.

"You are."

Declan laughs. "You do realize she tells all of you that you're her favorite, right?"

"Blakely." Brooks gasps, placing the hand that's not holding her over his heart. "Are you playing me?"

She's smiling up at him, and you can see how close they are. Brooks's eyes are smiling, and the sight of his strong arms holding his niece has my ovaries screaming. What is it about a man doting on kids, whether they are his or not, that's so damn hot?

"You's my favorite rights now," she tells him.

"My girl." I hold my hand up for a high-five, and she doesn't disappoint, slapping her little hand against mine. "That's how it's done."

"You're as bad as they are." Declan shakes his head. "Come on, squirt. We need to get home and get you some dinner."

Blakely shoves a Teddy Graham into her mouth and grips the bag before holding her arms out for her dad to take her. Declan's features soften as he pulls her from Brooks and settles her on his hip.

"Now who's spoiling her?" Brooks teases.

"I'm her dad. I'm allowed."

"Uh-huh." Brooks laughs.

"I'll see you two tomorrow." He waves and Blakely does as well, and then they're gone.

"She's adorable."

"Right?" Brooks responds.

"I wouldn't be able to tell her no either."

"It's tough. If it was something that was going to hurt her, I would tell her no, but it's a snack." He shrugs.

"Speaking of snacks, are we still doing this meal prep thing?"

"Yes, but I'm starving. Have you eaten?" he asks.

My stomach answers for me as it growls, the sound filling the kitchen. "No."

"How about we go grab something to eat, then we can come back here and start the meal prep?"

"Are you sure?" He wants to go out to eat with me? What is this life?

"I'm positive. I might wither away otherwise. What sounds good?"

"Anything, I'm not really a picky eater."

"You need to get home at a certain time?" he asks.

"Nope. My client canceled. I'm all yours."

His eyes flash, and I can feel my face heat from embarrassment.

"Let's hit the food trucks over in Harris."

"Is that today?"

"Yeah, and it sounds damn good right now. We'll have lots of options."

"I'm game."

"Perfect." He swipes his phone from the counter and shoves it in his pocket. "You driving?" His lips pull into a grin.

"I think I'll claim shotgun for this adventure."

He chuckles. "Let's go." With his hand on the small of my back, he leads me to the front door. I grab my purse and phone and hand him the keys to his truck. "Thanks." He guides me out to the porch, and when he drops his hand to lock the door, I keep walking to the truck, needing a little distance.

I didn't think about his long-ass legs, though. He catches up with me, and his arm darts out in front of me, pulling open the door. "You don't have to do that."

"My momma would kick my ass into next week if I didn't." I think it's more than that. Carol and Raymond Kincaid raised their boys with manners, and it's just who he is. It's easier to blame his momma. My brother is the same way. Momma's boys hiding behind their sweet mommas, making them seem vengeful if they forget their manners.

"You should be ashamed of yourself," I mock scold him once he's behind the wheel and we're pulling out his driveway.

"Why's that?"

"Putting the blame on your mom."

A boyish grin lights up his face. "It's not a lie. She would be disappointed, but you're right. I just wanted to get the door for you." He shrugs like it's no big deal. Like his words don't have my heart thumping in my chest like the procession section of the high school marching band.

I shake my head because I don't have words. Well, I do, but I can't seem to find them right now. Just when I thought today couldn't get any better, Brooks Kincaid calls another audible and renders me speechless.

## BROOKS

"WHEN DO YOU WORK AGAIN?" Palmer asks from her seat in the passenger side of my truck.

"Friday. I'm off again Saturday and Sunday, then go back Monday, off Tuesday, Wednesday, and Thursday, and then back for my weekend Friday, Saturday, and Sunday."

"Yeesh. That's a lot to keep up with."

"You get used to it. I work every third weekend. That's always a three-day stretch Friday, Saturday, and Sunday. I work twelve hours shifts. My schedule alternates. There really is no rhyme or reason to how I'm scheduled except for the fact that I'm guaranteed every third weekend shift. The other days always vary. They always give me two days off a week. They just might not be consecutive."

"Do you hate that? Not knowing exactly when you're going to work?"

"Nah, I'm used to it. I have my schedule a month in advance, and I work with some great people. We all switch shifts for each other. Those who have kids often have events or games, and everyone is always switching. I don't mind it. It's nice to have a day off during the week to do things like dentist appointments and grocery shopping. I loathe going, so it's nice to go when most everyone else is working."

"You seemed okay today."

"I had good company." I don't glance over at her. I keep my eyes trained on the road in front of me, but I can imagine that light pink blush coating her skin. I grip the wheel tighter to keep from turning to see if it's there. However, I need to get us there safe, and getting lost in the flush of her creamy white skin isn't a good plan.

"What about you? I can't imagine you have normal nine-to-five hours."

"Not at all. I have to be available when my clients need me. Tonight, for example. They both work but wanted anniversary photos done, and they're leaving to go out of town this weekend. So I scheduled them for an evening."

"Lots of weekends too, I'm sure."

"Some. I try to do no more than two if I can. However, I have to be ready when the work is there. I'm usually at the shop most days, working on edits and being there to handle any foot traffic. Wednesdays are my half days. That gives me the afternoon to run errands. You know when my car doesn't take a shit on me." She laughs, and the sound washes over me like waves lapping on the shore.

"Dec's good. He'll have you all fixed up."

"I appreciate that. And you. Thank you for today and for letting me borrow your truck."

"It's not a problem, Palmer. You've already thanked me." I want to reach over and place my hand on her thigh. Instead, I continue to keep both hands on the wheel. Ten and two like a fucking sixteen-year-old. That's what this woman does to me.

What I don't understand is why all of a sudden she's all I can think about. Why am I bending over backward to help her? Why am I grasping at straws, thinking of ways to spend more time with her? She's not the first gorgeous woman I've had pressed against me on the dance floor.

Why now?

Why Palmer?

I pull into Sunflower Park, and my stomach grumbles just seeing all the food trucks set up. "I'm starving."

"What are you going to get?" Palmer asks.

I glance over at her just in time to watch as she licks her lips as she stares through the front window at all the trucks. "Everything." My voice is gravelly, but I can't seem to stop it. Watching the tip of her tongue trace those pretty pink lips is like leading a man to water in the middle of a drought in the desert.

"There's like ten trucks here." She pulls her eyes from the trucks to look at me.

"Did you miss the part where I said I was starving? I think I could eat an entire cow right now."

She tosses her head back in laughter. "Well, come on then, hungry man. We don't want you withering away to nothing." She reaches for the door handle and effortlessly hops out of my truck.

I do the same, rushing to the front of the truck to catch up with her. I rub my hands together. "All right, where are we starting?"

"How about we divide and conquer? Meet back here at the truck, or if we can find a picnic table?"

I point an index finger at her. "I like the way you think, beautiful." The endearment slips off my tongue without thought. It's true. Palmer is beautiful. This time I get to see her flush, and my cock lets me know he appreciates the pink hue of her cheeks as well.

She clears her throat. "I want pulled pork for sure."

"Yep." I nod. "I'm going to need some of that."

"French fries too."

"Get a big bucket, and we can split it."

"Done."

"Corn dogs?" I ask.

"Is that even a question?" she challenges, making me laugh.

"How about this: You take the left side, I'll take the right, and we'll meet back here, and if we can't find an open picnic table, we'll drop the tailgate?"

"I'm in."

I turn to walk away. I wasn't bullshitting. I'm starving.

"Wait." She reaches out and grabs my arm. My skin tingles where her hand still grips me. "Drinks are on my side. Sweet tea or lemonade?"

"Both. Get the large, and we can split them."

"I don't think I can carry all of this." She laughs.

"Okay, we might have to do this in shifts," I tell her. "Grab the drinks, and anything else, maybe the bucket of fries. They have a handle. I'll grab what I can carry. Then we'll either have to go back for more or eat, then go back for more."

She holds her hand out in front of her, and I laugh as I place mine on top of hers. "Readyyy break!" she calls out before turning on her heels and making her way to the lemonade booth.

My chest is shaking with laughter as I watch her walk away. When a loud grumble sounds, I realize my stomach won't let me stare much longer. The sooner I get our food, the sooner I can be next to her again. I turn and move to the pulled-pork booth first. My mouth waters as I stand in line.

I manage to grab us both a pulled-pork sandwich, two corn dogs, an order of onion rings, and an order of mozzarella cheese sticks. My arms are full of food as I make my way back to the truck. Palmer is already there with the tailgate dropped. Two large drinks, a huge bucket of fries, and something else I'm not sure what it is, is next to her.

"What's that?"

"Deep-fried pickles," she moans. "So good."

Ignoring the way my cock twitches against the zipper of my cargo shorts at the sound, I start unloading my hands with her help before hopping up and taking a seat, the food piled between us.

"How in the world are we going to eat all of this?" Her eyes widen as she takes in the food.

I point to my chest. "Entire cow."

"I thought you were exaggerating."

"I'm a growing boy." I smirk.

"Well, you better save room for funnel cake because I'm not passing that up."

"Don't worry. I've got this."

We both dive into our spread, not bothering to keep the conversation flowing. I'm too hungry to talk right now. I do, however, watch her from the corner of my eye. She's eating, and I love that. So many times, women I've dated think they can't eat or be who they really are with me. That's just wrong on so many levels. You have to eat to live. I'm thrilled to see that she's enjoying this as much as I am.

"So good," she says, covering her mouth while she chews. She swallows, takes a hearty sip of the sweet tea, and smiles. "This was the best idea ever. I'm going to have to do this again sometime."

It's on the tip of my tongue to tell her she can't come again without me, but I don't let the words out of my mouth. Instead, I nod, grab a deep-fried pickle, slide it through the cup of ranch dressing, and take a huge bite.

"I'm so full," she says, finishing off the last bite of her pulled-pork sandwich.

"Oh, no, you've got funnel cake to eat."

"You're going to have to roll me home," she says dramatically.

"Come on, you. You said you want funnel cake, and we're not leaving here without it." I jump off the tailgate and begin to gather our trash. I toss it in the nearby trash can before going back to her.

"Fine," she mutters. She might be full, but she wants this.

Stepping closer, I place my hands on her hips and lift her from the tailgate. I know I shouldn't, but I let her body glide down mine before her feet finally hit the ground. My cock is now hard, and my body is heated, but I ignore it. Instead, I lace my fingers with hers and lead her toward the funnel cake truck.

"Oh, God, they smell so good," she moans again, and I shift my stance to alleviate some of the evidence of what she does to me. She turns to look up at me. "Can we share one? I really don't think I can eat it all by myself, and I'm going to want to, so I need you to help me. I need support, Brooks. This is a dire situation."

I chuckle at her dramatics. Leaning down, I place my lips next to her ear. "I've got you, beautiful." She shivers, an action she can't hide, and it makes me want to pull her into my arms and kiss the hell out of her. Who am I kidding? Everything she does makes me want to kiss the hell out of her.

Someone bumps into her, and I slide my arm around her waist to steady her. "I'm so sorry," a woman with two small kids says to us.

"You're fine," Palmer says. "You need some help?" she asks the woman. She's holding one kid on her hip and one by the hand while trying to dig in the bag draped across her chest.

"Do you mind?" the woman asks.

"Not at all. I'm Palmer." She reaches for the little girl in the woman's arms. "And who are you?" she asks the cherub.

"This is Nora, and this is Nicholas." The woman points to the little boy next to her.

"Nicholas, are you excited about a funnel cake?" she asks him.

"Yeah!" The little boy, who looks to be about the same age as Blakely, tosses his little arm in the air and jumps with it.

Palmer laughs, a sweet melodical sound, and it's not the least bit fake. "Me too." She points at me where my arm is still around her. I can't seem to let her go. "My friend here is going to help me eat mine. I've already had too much."

"I have to share with my sister," he tells her.

"Sharing is important."

"That's what my mom says."

"Well, she's right. You know moms usually are."

"Even when I have to wash my hands after I potty?" He tilts his little head to the side and stares up at Palmer as if she holds the answer to every question his little mind can dream up.

"Especially then."

"Aw, man." He kicks his foot, and I have to bite my tongue not to laugh out loud.

"Thank you." The woman wads the money she just pulled from her wallet in her hand and reaches for her daughter.

"Why don't you go ahead and order? I'll hold her and walk her to wherever you are sitting."

"I can't ask you to do that."

"You didn't. I volunteered." She glances over at me.

"I've got us covered."

She nods and turns back to the woman. "See, it's all good. Besides, I just ate my weight in food. I could use a little more time for it to settle."

The woman gives Palmer a grateful smile, and my chest expands with air. Palmer Setty is a breath of fresh air. Few will go out of their way to help a complete stranger. Palmer did it with kindness and grace, and it endears her to me even more.

She's beautiful, smart, driven, funny, kind, and sexy as hell, but all that makes her even more so. She's a unicorn in my world, and I don't know what to do with that information. I've never met anyone like her, and that's both terrifying and exhilarating all at once.

The little girl in her arms smiles at me, and I can't help but smile back at her. "You're a cutie," I tell her, tapping her nose with my index finger. She rewards me with baby giggles, which takes me back to when Blakely was this little.

"Thank you again. We're set up on a blanket, just over there." The mom points to a quilt positioned in the shade beneath an old oak tree. There is a stroller and toys littered all around her. "My husband was supposed to come with us, but he got called into work. I didn't want to disappoint them." She huffs out a breath. "Thank you for helping me."

"Anytime." Palmer looks at me. "I'll be right back."

"I'll meet you at the truck." She nods, and I have the strongest urge to bend and press my lips to hers. I have to remind myself that Palmer's not mine, and that's not what this is, but the yearning to feel her lips against mine is strong. For the second time since we arrived, I find myself standing still to watch her walk away.

"Next!" the lady running the truck calls out.

I shake out of my Palmer haze and step up to order her a funnel cake. "One, please," I say, handing over some money.

"Your wife is great with kids," she comments as she counts out my change.

It's on the tip of my tongue to tell her she's not my wife, to tell her she's not my anything, but "She is," comes out instead. The woman smiles kindly, passes me my change, and then slides a huge funnel cake covered in what appears to be half a pound of powdered sugar. I smile as I walk away. Palmer is going to enjoy the hell out of this, and I'm going to enjoy the hell out of watching her eat it.

Placing the funnel cake on the tailgate, I hop up to take a seat. From where we're parked, I have a perfect view of Palmer and the mom with her two kids. Palmer is currently spinning in circles with the little girl on her hip while the mom gets her son settled with a juice box on the quilt. I can't hear her laughter, but I don't need to. The sound is already in my head, and it's one I don't know if I'll ever be able to forget.

When she starts heading this way, I should avert my gaze, but I can't seem to do it. I can't look away from her. Once she's reached the truck, she hops up on the tailgate and immediately eats a piece of the funnel cake. "Why is this so good?"

"The sugar," I manage to reply.

"Reminds me of being a kid at the county fair. I always had to have a funnel cake and cotton candy." She takes another bite.

I'm still staring at her, but now it's at the dusting of powdered sugar that rests at the corner of those pink lips I want to taste. Before I can think better of it, I reach out, swiping at the sugary powder with my thumb, and place it in my mouth. Her eyes widen, and she licks those lips like I wish I could. That light pink once again coats her cheeks, and I discover something about myself in this moment.

I have more willpower than I ever knew I possessed. Because the second thing I learned, I'd give anything to kiss Palmer Setty.

Clearing my throat, I try to maintain control of myself and the situation. "Now that I'm an uncle, and I see what sugar does to kids firsthand, I don't know why my parents ever let us have anything with sugar in it," I tell her.

"Right? It's a rite of passage, though. I mean, you have to experience childhood with cotton candy, funnel cakes, deep-fried Oreos, candy apples, all the things, Brooks."

"I'll remember that when the Willow River County Fair comes along later this year. I'll make sure you get your sugar fix."

She points her long, manicured finger at me. "Don't tempt me with a good time, mister." Her smile is radiant, and the urge to kiss her once again washes over me.

"Not a threat," I reply, my voice thick. "A promise."

She visibly swallows at my words and averts her gaze. "You better eat some of this."

Knowing I need to do something with my mouth before I decide to throw caution to the wind and kiss her, I tear off a piece of the cake and pop it in my mouth.

## PALMER

"THANKS FOR INDULGING ME," BROOKS says in the truck on the way back to Willow River.

"It was fun and so good, but I ate way too much." I place my hand over my too-full belly.

"It was fun." He glances over with a smile on his handsome face, and I have to work extra hard to breathe normally.

The sun is starting to set, and I realize the majority of my day was spent with him. "I took up most of your day."

"Nah, I got everything done that was on my list. And had great company while doing it."

Does he not realize that when he says things like that, it makes my heart flutter in my chest? It almost feels like a bird is caged inside, trying to take flight.

"You can just take me home," I tell him. "I can call you when Declan calls me or call Ramsey. She can take me."

"Do you want to go home?" he asks.

Damn it. "No."

"Good. Besides, we have some meal prepping to do."

"You still want to do that?"

"Yeah, I mean if I don't do it now, I have to do it tomorrow since I work again on Friday. I told you I'd show you."

"That was before you took me to Harris for the food trucks."

"You got plans tonight, Palmer?"

I want to lie. Not because I don't want to spend time with him, but because I crave time with him, and I know this can only end one way for me. "No."

"Then we meal prep." He says it so simply, as if spending more time with me isn't a big deal. I guess to him, it's not, but to me, it's everything. So much so that my teenage heart that's still buried down deep is starting to resurface. It's risky, but no way am I saying no. I'll take all the time he's willing to give me.

"So, what are we making?" I ask him.

"Chicken, rice, black beans, and broccoli."

"I'm feeling pretty guilty right now about all the junk I just ate with you listing off all of those healthy options."

A deep throaty laugh reaches my ears. "It's fine to indulge, Palmer."

*I'd like to indulge in you.* "Two words, Kincaid. Funnel cake."

"You loved it."

"Oh, I'm not debating that. I enjoyed the hell out of it."

He turns onto his road, and my cell phone rings. Digging it out of my purse, I see Ramsey's smiling face on my screen. "Sorry," I tell him before swiping at the screen and placing the phone to my ear. "Hello."

"You didn't call me."

"I said I would when I get home."

"Where are you?"

"We just pulled into Brooks's driveway."

"The plot thickens," she says.

"Stop it." I chuckle.

"Tell me what's going on? Where were you?"

"Nosey Nell," I tease her.

"Damn right. And this is payback. You were all up in my business with Deacon when we first got together. Hell, you still are. You're convinced we should name our firstborn after you."

"I mean, I did get the two of you together," I tell her. She laughs, as does Brooks from his spot next to me as he guides his truck into his driveway.

"Is that Brooks with you? You're still with him?"

"Mmhmm. I just told you that I was."

She squeals. "Okay, well, call me when you get home. I don't care how late it is. I need to know everything."

"You sure about that?"

"Yes! What kind of question is that? Now I want to know even more. I mean it, Palmer, you better call me."

"Yes, Mom," I jest.

"Tell Brooks I said hi."

"Will do." I end the call, dropping my phone back in my purse. "Ramsey says hi."

He nods. "You ready for this?"

"Let's do it." Together we exit the truck and make our way inside.

"Make yourself at home," he calls over his shoulder after kicking off his shoes and walking toward the kitchen.

Shrugging, I do the same and follow along behind him. He's already reaching into the refrigerator and pulling out what we need. "What can I do?"

"There's a pot beneath the island. Grab it to boil the rice. I'm going to go fire up the grill."

"Got it, boss," I joke, doing as he asks. "Do you always grill?"

"Usually. Even in the wintertime. I just pull the grill to the edge of the garage and open the door. Grilling is faster and easier for such a large quantity."

Over the next fifteen minutes or so, he explains what we're making and his process. "I'm going to go put these on the grill."

I move to the stove and watch as the rice boils and the broccoli steams. "He needs a rice cooker," I muse.

"Had one. I wore it out," he says from behind me. He grabs the spoon and moves in closer. One hand lands on my hip while the other dips the spoon into the pot with boiling bags of rice and pushes them under the water.

The heat of his body pressed to mine reminds me of last weekend when we were dancing. I've thought about that night more times than I care to admit this past week. I work on keeping my breathing even. What would be more embarrassing than Brooks realizing that him being near me causes my breathing to turn labored and my heart rate to spike? Yeah, I need to keep that on lockdown.

"I think this is just about done."

Is it just me or is his voice huskier than normal? "I've got this, Kincaid. I know my way around a kitchen. I've just never meal prepped before," I sass, attempting to hide my desire for him.

He squeezes my hip. "The chicken is almost done." The words are barely out of his mouth before he steps away, and I miss the warmth of him instantly. Shaking out of my Brooks haze, I get busy removing both pots from the stove and draining them. Brooks enters the patio door and places a huge plate of grilled chicken on the counter.

"Ready?" he asks.

"Yep."

"I'm going to cube this chicken. Can you take the containers and add a spoonful of rice and a spoonful of broccoli? Oh, and this." He walks to the cabinet and pulls out two cans of black beans. "Can opener is in the top drawer to the right of the stove."

"This all smells really good."

"Thanks, it's the seasoning. It's your dad's, actually."

"Really? How did I not know that?"

"I don't know."

"How did you get it?"

"Deacon. He had some at his place one night, and he got your dad to give me a container. I actually need to hit him up for another. That man is a genius."

"He won't tell us what's in it. He claims it keeps us kids coming back to see him."

Brooks nods. "It's worth it. Not that you wouldn't go visit your parents, but this seasoning he makes is definitely an added incentive."

I start dishing out the broccoli and rice, then move on to opening the two cans of black beans while he cubes up the chicken breasts. "All set," I tell him.

"Perfect. I'm going to add the chicken, and then we just scoop a little of the black beans and a spoonful of salsa over the rice, and we're good to go."

"This looks really good. No wonder you're okay with eating it all the time."

"I sometimes do steak and cooked carrots. I do mix it up, but it's always the same for however long it takes me to eat through this. I'm usually too damn tired after a twelve-hour shift that turned into an even longer one to cook. I can shower, pop this in the microwave, and call it good. Same thing for packing lunch. I can sleep a little longer being able to just pull one of these from the fridge."

"You've got the bachelor life down to a science," I tease.

"Blame Orrin. He started it. The rest of us just went along with it because it's a genius plan. The only one that differs a little is Declan because he has Blakely. She does like most foods, but she's also a kid and loves chicken nuggets shaped like dinosaurs, and macaroni and cheese."

"I mean, it's a dinosaur nugget. Kid's got good taste."

"Right? I keep a bag in the freezer for her."

"You really do spoil her, you know."

"Yeah." He nods. "We all do. She's our only niece, and she's a hellcat, that one. Some of the things she comes up with." He shakes his head as if he can't believe the adorable little girl is capable of the personality that she rocks.

"Nothing wrong with a little spoiling. As the baby of the family, I speak from experience."

"I can imagine. We do the same with Ramsey, and she's our cousin and has only been in our lives for more than a quick visit for a couple of years now."

"I'm happy for them. I know I give her and my brother hell for me getting them together, but that's just to rile them up. I knew instantly they would be perfect forever. It just took me a while to get my workaholic brother to slow down and convince Rams to do me a favor."

Brooks points at me. "That was sneaky but a good move. He's good for her."

"She's good for him."

"So, what about you? No leading man in your life?"

"Does my camera count?"

"Nope. Must be human," he teases.

"Nah. I'm always working it seems, and well, when you grow up with everyone in a small town, it's hard to find someone you don't remember picking their nose and eating it in elementary school."

Brooks grimaces. "Nice visual. I understand what you're saying, though."

"What about you? Just living your best life as a bachelor?"

"For now."

"For now?"

"Yeah. One day I'll find her."

"Find her."

"Yeah, the one that will make me want to change her last name."

"Brooks Kincaid, are you a closet romantic?" I jest, because the talk is getting a little deep, and it's on the tip of my tongue for me to blurt out that I volunteer for the position.

"Nah, I wouldn't say that. Do I plan on being a bachelor for the rest of my life? No. I'm not in a hurry either."

"So you're just living your best life? Is that what you're trying to tell me?" My tone is light, hiding that deep down, I want to know the answer.

"Maybe." He laughs. "But I look at it more as I want to settle down, but I don't want to settle, if that makes sense?"

I let the meaning of what he's saying sink in. "Yeah, it makes perfect sense, actually. Should I add 'words of wisdom' under the things I've learned about you today?"

"Only if you promise not to tell my pops. Those are his words. Raymond Kincaid is full of life lessons. For as long as I can remember, he's taken all of us on camping and fishing trips. We load up and leave Mom at home, giving her some time without all of us kids. Some Mommy time we used to call it. Anyway, we fish, camp, and play flashlight tag, and just goof off and expel all the energy that's created with nine boys so close in age. We still play now, even as adults from time to time. At night we sit around the campfire, and Dad always has something to say. Some type of wisdom for us."

"I love that," I say softly. I can't help but wonder if that's a tradition he'll carry on with his own kids.

"Yeah, his favorite is work hard and love harder. I've heard that one more than any of them."

"Sage advice."

"It is. Don't tell him I said that. He'll get a big head, and then we'll have to hear all about it." His voice is laced with humor and causes a tightening in my chest. The longer I'm here with him, the more I learn that the crush I thought was that of a teenage girl claws its way to the surface.

"Your secret is safe with me."

He winks, and my belly flutters.

"What else can I do?"

"That's it. We're all done. I need to put the lids on these and then load the dishwasher."

"You get the lids. I'll load the dishwasher."

"You don't have to do that."

"Hey, I was a part of this mess. I don't mind. I have nowhere to be." I'm stalling. I'm not ready to leave. I'm exhausted. It's been a long, tiring yet happily unexpected day. I know I need to go home and get some sleep. I have a newborn and her two-year-old brother coming into the studio in the morning, so I need to get rested, but I don't want the day to end. I don't know if I'll ever have him like this again.

All to myself.

We work in comfortable silence, cleaning his kitchen and

packing up the meals that we just made for the week. "Keep one of those out," he tells me.

"You can't seriously be hungry?" I blurt, making him laugh.

"No. I'm not, but you can take it with you for lunch tomorrow."

"Oh, no, Brooks, you don't have to do that."

"I know, but I want to. Take one. See if you like it. You can hit your dad up for some of his seasoning." He winks.

"I'm telling you he's taking that with him to the grave."

"Maybe, but I'm pretty sure all you have to do is bat those long-ass lashes and those big green eyes, and he'd give you anything you asked for."

I swallow hard. "He's immune. Piper and I have tried," I tell him. I'm proud of myself for keeping my voice even and not letting him see how his words affect me. I don't let him see that the things he says lights a fire in my soul.

"Huh" is all he says.

"It doesn't work on Dad. Well, it doesn't for most things, but it does work on Deacon. How do you think I talked my big bro into doing the blind photoshoot with Ramsey?"

"And he met the love of his life."

"Funny how that happens."

"I've known Deacon a long damn time. Drank more than a few beers with him. We've all been close since we were little, and there isn't a better man for my baby cousin."

"Who are you calling baby? Ramsey and I are the same age, old man."

"Old man?" His hand clutches his shirt right over his heart. "I'm not even thirty yet."

"Yet," I goad.

"Baby," he mutters.

"Hey!" I punch at his arm. Not hard, but enough to get my point across. "I just turned twenty-three. There are only six years between us."

"So if I'm old...." His voice trails off, and I give him an exasperated look that has us both cracking up.

"Shut it, Kincaid."

"I'm just messing with you. I like to see the fire in those green eyes of yours." He reaches out and tucks my hair behind my ears.

"I should get going. It's late."

"You good to drive? You could stay over. I have two spare rooms with beds that my brothers usually use."

He's offering to be nice because that's who Brooks Kincaid is. He's the nice guy. That one who it's impossible to hate and the one who makes it impossible not to fall for him. I speak from experience.

"I'm good. Thank you again for letting me use your truck." I smile up at him, and he leans in just a little closer. My pulse begins to race. If I didn't know better, I'd think he was going to kiss me.

I really want him to kiss me.

"Drive safe, Palmer." He reaches around me and grabs the meal container and hands it to me. "I'll walk you out." With his hand on the small of my back, he guides me out to his truck.

"I'll call you tomorrow as soon as I hear from Declan.'"

"That works."

"Thank you for today. For helping with my car, the truck, the trip to Sunflower Park, and meal prepping. All of it. I had a good time."

"Me too."

I give him an awkward wave before climbing behind the wheel and pulling out of the drive. Today is a day I'm sure to never forget. I just wish I knew how to make another one happen, and soon.

## BROOKS

I TOSSED AND TURNED ALL night long. Every time I closed my eyes, there were a pair of emerald-green ones staring back at me. As the sun peeks over the horizon, I know I need to get up and get moving. Lying here in bed thinking about my friend's little sister isn't doing me any favors. Grabbing my phone from the nightstand, I put up a message in the group chat I have with my brothers.

**Me:** Headed to the gym.

**Declan:** Headed to the shop.

**Orrin:** I'm in.

They're the only two who reply, but that doesn't surprise me. Usually, we go in the evenings because we all work, and getting motivated to work out at 5:00 a.m. so that you still have time to shower and head to work isn't exactly our idea of a good time. However, sometimes on my days off, I go in the mornings.

I toss off the covers, and my feet hit the floor, and that's when I remember I don't have a truck. "Fuck," I mutter, running my hands through my hair. I debate on what to do and settle for calling Orrin.

"What's up?"

"I need a ride to the gym." I close my eyes, waiting for the inquisition to start.

"Where's your truck?"

*There it is.* "Palmer has it." I'm greeted with nothing but silence on the other end.

"Palmer?"

"Yeah, you know Palmer, Deacon's little sister, Ramsey's best friend?"

"Why does Palmer have your truck?"

"Her car broke down. She needed wheels while Dec fixed hers. I was off today, so I offered."

"How did you get involved?"

"Does it matter? Can you pick me up or not?"

"Yes, and yes. My girl is going to want to know all the details, so I've learned to ask these things."

"Stop hiding behind your girlfriend." Orrin and his girlfriend, Jade, have only been dating a short amount of time, but my oldest brother has conformed to being in a serious relationship with ease. I don't give it long before he's dropping to one knee, asking her to marry him. I like Jade. She's sweet, and she's good for Orrin.

"I'm not. I'm simply being a good boyfriend. Trust me, one day, you'll understand."

I ignore him. "I'll be ready."

"I'm heading out now."

I end the call and drag my ass to the bathroom to brush my teeth and get ready for the gym. In the kitchen, I mix us both up a pre-workout shake, grab my phone, and go to wait for him on the front porch. It's not two minutes later, he's pulling into the driveway.

"Here." I hand him the pre-workout shake through his window before making my way over to the passenger side and climbing in.

"Thanks. Talk."

"There's nothing to say. I was driving by and saw her broken down on the side of the road, so I stopped. She was on the phone with Deacon. He had court. I was off, so I offered to take a look and ended up texting Declan to tow her to his place."

"And now she has your truck. Your baby."

"She does."

"And you're chill as hell right now. Spill it."

"There's nothing to spill." I barely avoid rolling my eyes. "She needed wheels. I was there, I was off today, and it made sense. Declan will have her car fixed today. She'll call me when it's ready to swing by and get me, and we'll go to Dec's place to pick hers up."

"Aren't you just the good Samaritan," he jokes.

"Can we not do this?"

"Fine," he quickly concedes. "What's wrong with her car?"

I sigh heavily, letting my head drop back against the seat. "Her alternator."

"Easy fix."

"That's what I just said."

"What did you get into last night?"

"I went to Harris for dinner and did some meal prepping."

"Who went with you?"

I grit my teeth. "Palmer."

Deep belly laughs come from my oldest brother, and if he wasn't driving us, I'd probably punch him. Not to hurt him, but maybe in the arm so he knows he's annoying as fuck right now. "Why is that funny?"

"Because it is. It's like pulling teeth to get information out of you. Why can't you just admit you're into her?"

"Who said anything about me being into her? We've been friends with Deacon for years. She's Ramsey's best friend, Deacon's little sister. Why wouldn't I stop to help her? I'd like to think... no, I know for a fact that if it were Deacon who was driving by, and it was Ramsey, he would have stopped."

"Of course he would have. That's his fiancée."

"You know what I mean, jackass. If they weren't together, he would have stopped and offered to help."

"Do you think he would have given her his truck and taken her to dinner?"

I shrug. "Probably."

"So, the two of you went to Harris for dinner, the next town over. I just want that to go on the record, and then what? She drops you off at your house and takes your truck?"

I should have stayed home and in bed. "No. She came inside for a while."

"Wait until I—" he starts, but I turn to look at him. I'm glaring at the side of his face, and I know he can feel me.

"No." My voice is gruff and a tad bit menacing. "You will not run and tell your girlfriend anything. I was helping her out. We went to dinner. She stayed to watch how I meal prep, and then she went home." I don't tell him how my cock was half-mast most of the night or how I offered her to stay over. I never let women stay over. Hell, I never bring them to my place. I'm not one of those guys who has a new woman every weekend. I've had the occasional hookup, but they're never at my place. Other than Ramsey, my mom, and Jade, my house is a woman-free zone.

Until last night.

Until Palmer.

"Relax, I'm just busting your balls."

"Well, don't."

A few minutes later, he's pulling into the gym. He parks but doesn't turn the engine off right away, which tells me he's got something to say. I wait, knowing he's not going to rest until he says what's on his mind.

"Look, Brooks. You're my brother, and I love you. There is nothing wrong with liking Palmer. Deacon doesn't have a leg to stand on. He's engaged to our little cousin who is ten years younger than him."

"She's the same age as Palmer."

"Yeah, but you're a few years younger than Deacon. There's what? Seven years between the two of you?"

"Something like that."

"I say if you're into her, you pursue it."

"It's nothing, Orrin. Can we just drop it? I was being a nice guy, and you're trying to marry me off because of it."

"I'm not trying to marry you off." He chuckles under his breath. "I'm just telling you that you never know when you find the one."

"You saying that Jade is the one?" I turn the tables on him, only it backfires. My big bro is all too willing to talk about his girlfriend and how he feels about her.

"Yes." There is not one single second of hesitation in his reply.

"I'm happy for you, man. But Palmer and me, it's not like that. She's beautiful, I won't deny that, but we're just friends." A friend that I can't stop thinking about. A friend who is the sister of another friend, and the best friend of my little cousin. That's all kind of twisted and complicated, and I don't like complicated. I get enough drama working in the ER for a lifetime.

He nods. "All right, I'll drop it. For now." He kills the engine, grabs his keys, and reaches for the door.

We haven't even made it into the gym, and I feel like I've been worked hard. Lack of sleep and your brother digging into your nonexistent love life will do that, I guess.

After the gym, Orrin dropped me off at home. It was just after eight, and I decided to mow the lawn before the heat of the day really hits, and I was already a sweaty hot mess anyway. That was hours ago. I'm starving, so I head to the kitchen to heat up one of the meals we made last night when my cell rings.

I try to fight it, but I can't contain the smile that lifts my lips when I see Palmer's name on the screen. The last thing I want is my brother riding my ass, bragging that he was right. "Hey," I answer.

"Hey. Declan just called, and my car's ready."

"Great. I'm finished with everything I wanted to get done today, so I'm ready when you are."

"I'm starving. I was going to heat up the meal you sent home with me, and then I'm headed your way."

"I'm getting ready to do the same. Why don't you save yours for tomorrow, and I'll heat you up one of mine?"

"Brooks, I can't eat all of your food."

"You can. Besides, I'm off this weekend and will more than likely be eating out with one or more of my brothers and then having dinner at my parents' Sunday night. They're only good for a week, so you'd be saving me."

I'm not making it up. Sure, I could eat two most days, but I'm not telling her that.

"Okay. Let me lock up the studio and put a note on the door, and I'll be right over."

"I'll have everything ready and waiting." I place my phone facedown on the counter and rub my hands over my face. I wish I knew what it was about this woman that has me doing things I've never done before.

Shaking out of my thoughts, I pull two containers from the refrigerator and pop them both in the microwave. While they're warming, I gather forks, napkins, and two bottles of water. The microwave dings after three minutes, and I realize that I started them too early. It's a good ten-minute drive to my place from her shop. I leave them alone for now. When she pulls in, I'll heat them for another minute to make sure they're warm before serving.

I stop and think about my current situation, me worrying about heating up lunch for my friend's little sister, and I laugh.

Out loud.

It's official. My cock has taken over. It's either that or I've lost my ever-loving mind. This isn't me. Orrin was right, even though I'd never tell him that. A soft knock on the door pulls me back to the present.

"Come in!" I call out. Moving toward the microwave, I hit the one-minute button and turn to face her.

"Hey." She smiles and waves, and I have the sudden urge to pull her into my arms and kiss the breath from her lungs.

Instead, I reply in a similar fashion, lifting my hand for a wave. "Hey." The microwave beeps, and I'm grateful for something to do. Grabbing one container at a time, I set them on the island where I have two places set up for us.

"Dig in." I nod toward her container, and just like I knew she would, she picks up her fork, removes the lid, and takes a big bite.

"This is so good." She covers her mouth with her hand. "Don't tell my dad I said that. It will go to his head."

"Your secret is safe with me." I force myself to turn to my own food and not watch her eat. For one, it's rude as hell, and two? Well, she's sexy as hell, and I'm not going there. I can't go there. She's already taking up too much space inside my head.

"How's your day been?" she asks in between bites.

"Went to the gym with Orrin this morning, mowed the lawn, and that's about it. Yours?" I ask politely.

"I had a shoot first thing this morning. Two adorable kids. A walk-in that wanted boudoir images for her anniversary next week. I'm shooting her later today."

"Boudoir?" I almost choke on the word.

She nods as if my cock isn't straining against my zipper, thinking about her lying in skimpy lingerie across the bed.

My bed.

"Yeah, I've done a lot of them. Wives like to do them for their significant others. Husbands too."

"No. Men do that?"

"They do. Some do it for the comedic side of things though some are... sexier. The women always choose sexy. That's usually their goal, but some of the men want it to be a joke."

*Don't ask her, man. It's none of your business.* "What about you?" The words seem to take on a life of their own. "Have you ever been the one in front of the lens instead of behind it?"

"No." She laughs. "Not because I don't want to. I just haven't had the time, and well, I'm the only one who would see them." She points at her chest. "Single pringle over here."

I'll take one for the team. I'll look at them. "Suddenly, I feel like I might have chosen the wrong career path." This makes her laugh.

"I don't know about that. Most of my clients, the women at least, are relieved it's another woman taking their pictures when they are open and exposed like that."

*I want you open for me.*

*I want you exposed to me.*

"I can't imagine that their husbands would love the photos as much if they knew a man was behind the lens."

I nod. "I would guess that you're right about that." I know for damn sure if it was my girlfriend or wife, I'd feel a hell of a lot better knowing it was a woman. The thought of another man getting to see her, whoever she might one day be, is unsettling. That says a lot considering I'm single with no current attachment.

"I should convince Rams to do a shoot for Deacon. Oh, and Jade for Orrin."

"I don't need to hear this."

"What? Why?"

"That's my sister and future sister you're talking about. I don't need to picture either of them like that." I shake my head as if I can literally shake thoughts out of my mind.

"Ramsey is your cousin, and Jade and Orrin aren't even engaged yet." She waves me off. "Besides, you were fine when it was me who was in front of the lens."

"If you were mine, I wouldn't be fine with it. Behind the lens or in front of it, not unless it was only with me and for me." I wipe my mouth with my napkin, tossing it on the now-empty container.

She takes a drink of water and pushes her empty container away from her. "What are we talking about here? You wouldn't be fine with the shoot? With a man being the photographer? Or would it bother you that your brothers see or just got the mental image?"

I growl. Fucking growl at her. I swallow hard and take a long pull from my bottle of water before answering her. Setting the bottle on the counter, I turn in my chair to face her. Unable to help myself, I rest my palm against her cheek. "Palmer, if you were mine, I'd be jealous as fuck if it were a man behind the camera. I'd be jealous as fuck if any other man got to see you like that, and I sure as hell wouldn't want my brothers to have that image in their heads. No way."

Her emerald eyes widen, and I can't resist tracing just below the beautiful orbs with my thumb. Her breathing has picked up a notch, as has mine. I don't know what the fuck is happening, but I can't stop it either.

I lean in. Her lips are calling to me like a siren. They look soft and sweet, and I need to find out for myself. I crave the knowledge and fear I'll never be able to find out. Before I can do something that I can never take back, she speaks.

"Well, all right then." There is a light tone to her voice, but it's also a little shaky.

Letting my hand drop, I stand and gather our dishes, tossing them in the sink, then gathering our trash and tossing it as well. "We should get going if you need to get back to the studio."

"Yeah. Yes. Right. The studio." She stands, and I can't be certain, but her legs look a little unsteady. Good, that's how she makes me feel every time I'm in her presence, at least since the night of Ramsey and Deacon's engagement party.

"Come on, beautiful. Let's go get your car." I offer her my hand and pull her to her feet. I don't want to let go, but I know that it's best if I do. She's too damn tempting, and my resolve is weak where she's concerned.

## PALMER

LIFTING MY SEX ON THE beach to my lips, I take a hefty swallow.

I need it. Hell, I've earned it after the way things in my life have been going recently. Girls' night is exactly what I need.

The last two weeks have been insane. It all started when my car broke down, and the sexy Brooks Kincaid stepped up to be my knight in shining armor. He stopped by my studio and put my shelf together, and I admit that I ogled him the entire time. Then there was a water leak at my studio. I rent the space, so my landlord had to deal with it, but still, it was a pain in the ass. I had plumbers in and out for a few days and then a construction crew to fix the ceiling. Luckily it was in the small break room. No images or equipment was ruined.

Then this week, I've had a full schedule, and I swear every pissed-off kid in the tri-state area was on my schedule. Usually, I can pacify them with toys, and with the help of the parents, we get the shoot in. Let me add that I love kids—I do—but this week they've been holy terrors. Every last one of them. So, yeah, I've earned this sex on the beach and the three before it. Or was it four?

"Okay, ladies, I have a confession," Ramsey says, draining her cranberry and vodka.

"Let's hear it," my sister, Piper, tells her.

"I don't want a big wedding." She bites her lip like she's waiting for us to scold her.

"Then you don't have a big wedding."

"But isn't that what people expect?"

"It's your wedding, Ramsey. You make it about you and Deacon. As long as the two of you are happy with your choice, no one else matters," Piper says gently.

"I keep hearing my father demanding I have this huge extravagant event, one to impress the masses, and I don't want that. Honestly, we could go to the courthouse or to Vegas, and I would be happy. I just want to marry Deacon and start the rest of our lives."

"Aw." Piper, Jade, and I all say at once.

"Stop." Ramsey shakes her head at us.

"We want you to be happy. Your families want you to be happy," Jade chimes in. "You do you, and we're going to be here cheering you on."

"You don't think Deacon will be upset?"

"You mean my brother, Deacon? The one who was a workaholic until you stole his heart? No, he's not going to care at all. If I know my brother, he's going to want a ceremony. He's going to want to marry you in front of his closest friends and family, but it doesn't have to be this big over-the-top event. It's your day, babe." I slide my arm around her shoulders from where she's sitting next to me in the booth.

"Okay, well, since we're spilling confessions, I have some news," Piper whispers.

"Are you going to tell us?" I ask, leaning over the table. Ramsey does the same, with my arm still around her shoulders.

Jade grins, which tells me she already knows. "Hey." I point to my chest. "I'm the sister."

"Best friend." Jade points at herself and sticks her tongue out at me, being silly. She knows I love her.

Piper's eyes flash around the Willow Tavern before leaning over the table. Jade does the same, and I can imagine how ridiculous we look in our little girls' night huddle in this booth. "Heath asked me to be his girlfriend." The confession rolls off her tongue, and the smile that lights up her face tells me she had a good time without me having to ask.

"When did this happen?" Ramsey asks.

"I stopped in here Monday night for some wings to take home for dinner. He was eating at the bar. We started talking, and he asked if I wanted to get together. I said yes."

"And?" I prompt her. "Where did you go?"

"You won't believe me when I tell you." Piper's being coy and we all know it. She's crazy about Heath, and he's crazy about her.

"Spill," Ramsey urges.

"We drove to Harris and had dinner at this cute little pizza place I'd never been to. Then we went to the movies, and after we went to Sunflower Park and there was an ice cream truck there. We sat at one of the picnic tables and just talked for over an hour."

I'm so proud of myself that I'm able to keep my composure when she mentions Sunflower Park. I will never be able to go there or even hear about that place and not think of Brooks. Here I am two full weeks later, and I'm still thinking and obsessing over the time I got to spend with him.

Every. Single. Second.

"Tell them the rest," Jade says.

"He dropped to one knee, holding up a sunflower to me. My heart stopped, but his teasing smile told me it wasn't going to be a marriage proposal. He asked me to be his, and I said yes."

"You picked him," Ramsey says, sitting back in the booth.

My arm falls from her shoulders, and I wring my hands together under the table. I think I know where my best friend is going with this. She and I had a very similar conversation.

"What?" Piper asks, raising her eyebrows in confusion.

"The night Deacon proposed." Ramsey holds up her hand and wiggles her fingers, making her engagement ring sparkle even in the low light of the tavern.

"I picked him?" Piper asks to clarify.

"Yes. You were all staring, and I told you to pick. Jade picked Orrin, and we know how that's working out. You said Heath, even though the two of you had already been on a date, you still picked him." She turns to face me. "Palmer picked Brooks."

"That's right." Jade laughs. "I got my man, you two got yours." She points at Piper and Ramsey. "You"—she points to me—"have some catching up to do."

"She's right." Piper keeps her eyes trained on me. "What about you, little sister?"

"What about me?" *Deny. Deny. Deny.*

"You picked Brooks," Piper reminds me, as if I need a reminder.

"We were all just talking. Rams insisted I pick." I shrug. "So I picked."

Ramsey turns in the booth to face me. I finish off my drink and turn to look at her head-on. My features are schooled. "So," she says dramatically, "you're telling me that if Brooks walked in here right now and asked you to dance or hell, get out of here with him, you'd turn him down?"

I open my mouth to reject her claim but quickly close it. "No. I wouldn't turn him down," I confess.

"That doesn't count as your confession." Piper calls me out. "We all already knew that. You have to give us something else."

"Seriously?" I ask her.

My sister smirks. "Yep."

"I'll go next to give you some time," Jade volunteers. She takes a drink of her cocktail and then blurts out her confession. "We had unprotected sex."

"Are you on the pill?" Ramsey asks her.

"Yes, but still."

"Orrin is solid," I tell Jade. "He's a stand-up guy. If you were to ever get knocked up, he'd be there."

"He'd drag you down the aisle." Ramsey laughs. "I've never seen Orrin with anyone the way he is with you."

Jade's eyes mist with tears. "I just... I don't want to lose him."

"You won't." Ramsey reaches across the table and places her hand over Jade's. "He's in this with you, Jade. I promise you. If you're worried, talk to him."

"I will. Thanks." She picks up her drink and downs it.

"Sister." Piper raises her eyebrows at me.

"Fine. I've never been able to orgasm with oral sex." I roll my eyes because they made me give them something.

"He's doing it wrong," a deep masculine voice says from beside our table.

I don't turn to look. I don't need to. I know that voice. I've spent the last two weeks thinking of nothing but the man it belongs to. I lift my glass for another drink, but it's empty.

Shit.

"I need a refill. Anyone else?" I ask, sliding out of the booth and ignoring the fact that Brooks, my brother, and Orrin are all standing there.

Right. There.

My face is hot. The need to flee is strong. "No? Good. I'll be back." I turn on my heel and make my way to the bar. I stand here forever waiting to be served, but part of that could be that I'm scrolling on my phone and not making eye contact. I'm also not looking at a damn thing on my phone. I can't focus. My mind is fuzzy. I never wanted Brooks or Orrin to hear that about me. And my brother... Nope. I'm not thinking about it. I'm just going to pretend it never happened. I'm going to stand here and pretend I'm waiting on a drink I have not ordered. Then again, maybe I need to order two. I need to get shitfaced, and then maybe I can forget this entire night ever happened.

I feel a hand on the small of my back, and I know it's him. I can feel his presence. "Hey," he says, his hot breath fanning across my cheek.

"Hey." I don't bother turning to look at him. I can't without him seeing it all over my face that I want him.

"You all right?"

"Yeah. Just waiting on a drink."

"Palmer, you've been standing here for way too long to just be waiting on a drink."

Busted. "I'm good. Promise." This time I take a quick glance over my shoulder, and he's standing close. So damn close. Breath rushes from my lungs at my body's reaction to him. The goose bumps that break out across my skin and the way heat pools between my thighs.

"Let's dance." It's not a request. It's a demand.

"No one else is dancing."

"Yes, they are."

This time I have to turn to look to see if he's telling me the truth. Sure enough, the girls are all on the floor with their men. Heath is here, which I didn't notice when I sprinted off toward the bar.

"Dance with me, beautiful."

"Brooks, I…" I don't even know what to say. I'm humiliated. That's not me. I am a go-with-the-flow kind of girl. However, I've never spilled intimate details about my sex life to my brother and his friends either.

"Palmer, dance with me." He laces his fingers through mine, and the warmth of his touch has me dropping my defenses and letting him lead me to a dark corner of the dance floor.

He pulls me into his arms without a care in the world who is watching. I rest my hands on his chest, but he's not having that. With a gentle touch, he lifts my hands and places them around his neck before he wraps his arms back around my waist. We're close, so close I can feel his hard length pressing against me. My eyes widen, and I seek him out.

He nods. "That's all for you, Palmer."

"For me?" I croak.

"Yes. It's all for you. Do you really think I can hear you talking about oral sex and orgasms and not get hard?"

"Ummm, yes?"

"No." He mutters something under his breath that sounds a lot like "Not with you." But I don't question him about it. I'm too speechless to ask even if I wanted to.

"I'm sorry?"

He leans forward, resting his forehead against mine while his body shakes with silent laughter. I close my eyes and relish the feel of being this close to him. When he finally lifts his head, he's regained his composure, but his eyes, his dark blue eyes, are full of heat, and need, and desire.

For me.

Seeing that, I can't resist running my fingers up the back of his neck and burying them into his hair. He groans, but it's a good groan, a needy groan, so I don't stop, and he doesn't ask me to.

"Let me show you." His voice is gravelly.

"Show me what?" I ask, tilting my head to the side to study him. His eyes are intense as he pins me with his steady gaze.

"Let me show you how it feels."

"How what feels?"

This time he leans in, so his lips hover next to my ear. "Let me show you what it feels like when a man eats your pussy. Let me show you what that kind of orgasm feels like." He nips at my ear and a shiver of desire races down my spine.

"You want to? You want to do that?"

"More than anything."

"How would that work?"

"Palmer, if you don't know how that works, then it's no wonder you've never had an orgasm when a man is going down on you."

"No. I mean, with us. We're friends. We're connected in so many ways." My eyes flash to where my brother and Ramsey are dancing close, not caring about anything or anyone around them. For once, I know how that feels.

"Nothing wrong with a little benefits between friends." His words, I think, are meant to be playful, but the look in his eyes is feral.

My heart is racing, and my hands have a slight tremble. I wonder if he can feel them shaking? "So you're proposing a friends-with-benefits arrangement?" I need clarification.

"Yeah. Something like that."

He has no idea that I've crushed on him my entire life. Thirteen-year-old me used to write Palmer Kincaid in my diary that I hid under my bed. I don't know if my heart will survive this kind of arrangement with him. Then again, this is my childhood fantasy come true. I can't say no. This is Brooks we're talking about. And to top it all off, he's a good guy. I know he would never do anything to intentionally hurt me. I just need to keep feelings out of it. He's offering sex, well, at least oral sex, and this shot to experience something like this with him.

I can't say no.

"We keep this between us." I need for him to agree to this. I don't want whatever this turns out to be when it ends to also end lifelong friendships in the process. We hide it, and I keep my heart on lockdown, and we're golden.

"If that's what you want." He shrugs like he couldn't care less if our friends and family know about this arrangement he's proposing.

The Weeknd's "Earned It" plays over the speakers, and I can't hide my smile. This song is sexy, and considering our conversation, I think it's rather fitting. "Okay," I agree before I can think better of it and change my mind.

"Tonight?" His voice is soft, yet he rushed to get them out.

I swallow hard. "Tonight?"

He applies gentle pressure to my back, which has me stepping in even closer. He's hard, and there's no use denying that I'm just as turned on as he is. "How?" I ask.

"When we leave here, you come back to my place."

"My place is closer."

"You can park in the garage at mine."

"Good point."

"Tonight?"

I nod. "Okay."

I'm shocked when he leans in and kisses my cheek. "I can't go back to the table like this. Can you walk in front of me toward the hallway?" He points to the long hall where the restrooms are located just about five feet from where we're standing.

"Do you want another drink?"

"No. I'd rather you not have another either. I want you to be coherent enough to remember this."

"I'm not drunk." I was buzzing, but his offer sobered me right up.

"I'd like to keep it that way."

"I'll grab a water," I concede.

"I'll take one of those too. Now, lead me to the hallway." Turning in his arms, I grab his hand and lead him toward the long hallway. I don't stop, deciding I could use a few minutes of my own to freshen up.

"I'll meet you at the table." I don't wait for his reply. I drop his hand and push open the bathroom door. I freeze when I see Ramsey standing at the sink washing her hands. "Hey." My voice is wobbly. That was too close.

"Hey. Are you okay? Your face is all flushed."

"Yeah, it was hot out there on the dance floor, and I think all of those sex on the beach drinks are finally catching up with me. I might head home soon."

"We're heading out too. We can drop you off at your place."

"Oh, yeah, that would be great." Fuck. I didn't think about the fact that I didn't drive here, and even if I did, I can't drive to his place after I've been drinking.

"We'll wait for you by the door."

I wave, and as soon as she's gone, I move to a stall and dig my phone out of my back pocket to text Brooks.

>   **Me:** I didn't drive here.

**Brooks:** Ride with me.

**Me:** That's not hiding this.

**Brooks:** Fine, I'll come and get you.

**Me:** Then you'd have to take me back home.

**Brooks:** You could stay over. I can take you back in the morning.

**Me:** I don't think that's a good idea.

No way can I sleep all night in his arms and be able to keep my heart on lockdown.

**Brooks:** Your place?

**Me:** Yes. Just park in the back of the lot. It's late. No one will notice.

**Brooks:** How are you getting home?

**Me:** Deacon

**Brooks:** Okay.

I debate on asking him for a time, but I don't. He's here. He'll know when I'm leaving, and if he shows up, great, and if not, well, this either doesn't happen or gets rescheduled. Taking a deep breath, I exit the stall and walk straight out of the restroom to find Ramsey and my brother. I find them by the door just like Ramsey promised. However, I wasn't expecting Brooks to be there too.

"Hey. Are we ready?"

Deacon nods. "Brooks offered to take you home since it's on his way. You good with that?" Deacon asks.

I bob my head. "Oh, yeah, for sure. That makes sense. You two are on the other side of town." I don't look at Brooks, afraid I'll give us away. Sneaky bastard.

"Yeah, and since I picked you up, we don't have to worry about getting your car to you." Ramsey is grinning like a fool. I know what she's thinking. That this is my chance. I picked Brooks, and she has it in her head that I'm going to get the same happy ending that she's getting. If she knew that Brooks is only looking for a fling, I imagine her smile wouldn't be so wide, if it was there at all.

I nod. "I'm in." If they only knew how in I was about to be.

## BROOKS

SHE WON'T LOOK AT ME. That's probably a good thing. I'm not sure I'd be able to hide my desire for her right now if she did.

It's been three weeks of nothing but this girl in my head. Then the day her car broke down, something else happened. She's suddenly in everything I do. At work, there was this cute little boy who came in with strep. He was four and had the best personality. He told me I was his hero, and don't ask me why, but I wanted to pick up the phone and call her to tell her all about it.

Then there was the grocery store. I can't go there and not think about her. And meal prepping in my kitchen, forget about it. She's wormed her way under my skin, and while sleeping with your friend's sister is frowned upon, I can't help it. I've never been that guy. The one to put a woman above my friendships or my family, but she's burrowed her way inside me, and this is the only way I know how to get her out.

She's taken over my life and my mind. I just need to satisfy my craving for her, and then life can go back to normal for both of us. I see it in her eyes that she wants me too. She's on board with this, as long as we keep it between us. Honestly, I'm at the point of wanting her so damn bad I don't really care who knows. Friendships be damned, but I know it's better this way. This isn't us falling in love. This is me showing her what it's like when a man who knows his way around a pussy cherishes hers.

My fingers twitch to touch her, which is why I blurted out to Deacon that I could take her home. It's not a lie. She is on my way, and he's on the other side of town. I was being a good friend and a bad one at the same time. I'm about to devour every inch of his little sister, and I want her so bad after craving her for the last three weeks. I can't seem to find it in me to care that I'm breaking the bro code.

Steeling my resolve, I turn to look at her. Her green eyes show me so much. She's cautious about what we're about to do, but she wants it just as much. "You ready?" I manage to ask without letting the desire I feel for her shine through.

"Yes." One word, with that look in her eyes, tells me everything.

She wants this.

She wants me.

My cock is as hard as steel, and I know the time to flee is here. I can't let anyone see me like this, or our cover is blown. I slide my hands into my pockets for two reasons. One, I'm hoping it will hide the fact that I'm hard for her. The other? It keeps me from reaching for her. It keeps me from sliding my fingers between hers or placing my hand on the small of her back. It keeps me from slipping my arm around her shoulders and pulling her into my chest.

I've never had this raw need for a woman before.

Only with Palmer.

Deacon and Ramsey push open the door to the Willow Tavern, with Palmer and me right behind them. As soon as we're outside, I pull in a lungful of fresh air. Slowly, I exhale, attempting to calm my ass down.

"Palmer, I'll call you tomorrow," Ramsey calls out as they walk toward Deacon's truck, and we walk toward mine.

Palmer lifts her hand in a wave but doesn't stop moving toward the passenger side of my truck. I want to race after her and open her door, but that would be too obvious, right? No, that's not true. My momma raised me to be a gentleman, but before I can make a choice, she's already tugging the door open. She slides inside and stares straight ahead. Opening my door, I take my spot behind the wheel.

My hands grip the wheel so tight that my knuckles are white. Starting the engine, I reverse out of the parking spot and pull out on the road. A glance out of the corner of my eye, even in the dim lighting of the cab, I can see her wringing her hands together. Not able to resist, I reach over and lace her fingers with mine.

"We don't have to do this, Palmer."

She takes an audible breath. "Did you change your mind?"

"No."

"Okay."

"Okay." I keep her hand in mine while we drive to my place. Sure, we could have gone to hers, but I don't want questions as to why my truck was sitting in the lot longer than it takes to drop her off.

It's more than that, though. Over the last three weeks, most recently, the last two, since the day we hung out at my place, I've wanted her there. I imagined her in my space again. I've imagined her in my bed, in my shower, on the kitchen island, and, well, every other surface in my house. It's weird for me because I've never wanted a woman there. With Palmer, it's a need. It's more than an itch that needs to be scratched.

It's indescribable.

The remainder of the drive is silent. Her hold on my hand never wavers, and that gives me hope that she's not going to regret this. I know I'll never regret this night with her. Whether it's just tonight or a series of nights, I know without a doubt I could never regret any of them. Not with her.

"Do you want something to drink?" I ask Palmer as we make our way into the house from the garage. I went ahead and pulled my truck inside. I don't need any of my brothers stopping by to annoy me. I don't want anything to come between us tonight.

"No, thank you."

She's stiff, and that worries me. Dropping my keys to the counter, I pull her into my arms. Mine are wrapped around her in an embrace. I hug her until I feel her body relax into mine. "We don't have to do this, Palmer." I'll be disappointed, but I'd never force her.

She tilts her head back to look at me. "I want to."

I study her, looking for anything other than the absolute truth in her eyes, but find nothing. I want to lift her to the counter and devour her, play out one of my many fantasies where she's concerned, but this is our first experience with this new benefits plan we've agreed to. I think my bed is the best place for us to start. Not to mention, I've lain awake for more hours than I care to admit wishing she lay there with me.

My bed it is.

"This way," I murmur. I offer her my hand, and she takes it without hesitation and allows me to lead her down the hall to my room. Pushing open the door, I guide her inside. The moon is bright tonight, giving off a light glow. Enough that I can see her but not make her uncomfortable. This is an all-new version of Palmer. It's one that I'm not used to. She's usually more forward with what she's feeling.

I wrap my arms around her again, and she does the same. She's no longer stiff, and that's a win in my book. "You hold all the control here, Palmer. If you want to stop, or hell, not even start, that's your call."

"Always the gentleman, Brooks Kincaid." Her tone is light and teasing and more like the Palmer I know.

"If you could read my thoughts right now, you might not consider me so gentlemanly," I say, my voice gruff.

"You might be thinking dirty thoughts, but you'd never cross a line I wasn't willing to cross. If I didn't believe that with all that I am, I wouldn't be standing here with you right now, wondering when you're going to make your move."

There she is.

Slowly, I slide my hands up her back and beneath her long hair. Gently, I grip her neck, bringing her closer. "Can I kiss you?" I whisper the words, my lips barely a breath from hers.

"Finally," she mutters.

A deep rumble of a laugh escapes my chest as I press my lips to hers, tasting her for the first time. Her lips are as soft as I imagined them to be and even sweeter. I trace at them with my tongue, asking for entrance that she quickly grants. Her tongue glides against mine as the taste of alcohol and something that is uniquely Palmer assaults my senses.

I can't get enough.

Removing my hand from the back of her neck, I trail my fingers down her arms. I gently grasp her wrists and place them around my neck. "Hold on." She does as I ask and squeals in surprise when I grip the back of her thighs and lift her into my arms. On instinct, she wraps her legs around my waist. She rocks her hips, and the sound of "Oh, God" falling from her sweet lips has me barely maintaining control.

My feet begin to move on their own accord. When her back is pressed against the wall, I fuse my lips with hers and kiss her as if I'll never get another chance to do so, and honestly, I'm not sure if I will. I hope like hell that I do, but just in case, if tonight is it, I'm going to make it one to remember for both of us.

Her hands are buried in my hair, and her legs are locked around my waist. When she rolls her hips, rocking her pussy over my cock, we both groan at the contact. "I want you." Her confession is whispered between her pants of breath.

"We'll get there," I tell her, trailing kisses down her neck.

"Why wait?" She tilts her head to the side, giving my lips room to roam.

"This all started for a specific reason," I remind her.

"We can work our way up to that."

"Beautiful, there's something you need to know about me. You come first. Always." She emits a whine, and I'm pretty sure it's of protest.

"Where are these skills you were boasting about, Kincaid?"

"You sure this is what you want? Once I taste your pussy, there's no erasing that. No take backs."

"We've already agreed to the terms, Brooks. I'm here in your room, grinding on your dick, and you're trying to what? Change my mind?"

"No. I don't want to change your mind, but I'm giving you an out if you want it."

"I don't want it."

I don't reply. Instead, I step back from the wall and place her back on her feet. She sways a little and has to reach out to grip my shirt to steady herself. "Strip."

"You don't want to do it for me?" she asks, a hint of that Palmer sass in her tone.

"No." Reaching behind my head, I grab the neck of my T-shirt and toss it on the floor. "You're behind, Palmer." That jumps her into action as she pulls her shirt over her head, and it too lands on my bedroom floor.

She's wearing a white lace bra that does nothing to hide her hard nipples, the tight peaks begging for my mouth. I lick my lips. I'll get to that. First, I need to remedy a little something for her. She's never had an orgasm from oral sex, and I'm about to be her first. Just the thought has me wanting to stand taller and square my shoulders as if the world can tell that I, Brooks Kincaid, am the first man to ever make this beautiful woman's pussy sing with his mouth.

Fuck, I'm leaking. I'm so ready for her.

I make quick work of my jeans and underwear, my eyes never leaving her body as more and more of her is exposed to me as she strips out of her clothes. I've seen her in a bikini several times over the years. It's an altogether different experience when it's a bra and panties, especially when I know they'll soon be on my bedroom floor with the rest of her clothes.

I grip my cock, stroking slowly as I watch her reach behind her and unclasp her bra. She teases me as she drops each strap slowly before letting the garment fall to her feet.

"You got me naked, Brooks. Now what are you going to do with me?" she asks in her sexy-as-fuck voice. It's raspy with desire and does nothing to help me control this raging need I have for her.

"I'm going to need you to work with me here."

"Tell me what you need." No hesitation on her part. She has no idea what I'm about to ask of her, but she's ready and willing all the same.

Fuck me, that's hot.

"Stand on the bed."

Her eyes widen, but she does what I ask and makes her way to the bed. I follow her, offering her my hand to help her climb up. "Now what?"

I don't answer her right away. Instead, I run my palms up her calves and over her thighs. I lean in and place a kiss on her quivering belly. I'm still gripping the backs of her thighs. "You're beautiful." She doesn't reply, but that's okay. I don't need her to. My touch moves back down to her thighs, and I bend down. Lifting one leg, I toss it over my shoulder. She laughs and buries her hands in my hair for balance. I repeat the process with the other, keeping a hand on her back to steady her. Then I stand.

"Brooks." She's breathless as I turn and move us back to the wall. "What are you...?" Her voice trails off as her back hits the wall.

"Hold on, babe. Keep your legs locked."

"Brooks?"

My hands rise to rest on her hips, holding her where I need her as I swipe my tongue through the folds of her pussy.

"Oh, fuck!" she screams out, and I chuckle before continuing to explore her with my tongue. "This is a little dramatic for the job, right?" She poses it as a question that tells me she's not sure. It also tells me any fucker before me hasn't given her his all. Assholes. I don't know how many there have been, and I don't want to know. Right now, it's me, and that's all that matters. I'm the one doing this for her. I might as well be the first. No one before me counts.

My reply to her question is to suck on her clit. I hear a thump and peer up, never taking my eyes off her to see her head resting back against the wall. Her eyes are closed tight, and she's biting down on her bottom lip. Her cheeks are flushed, this time from pleasure and not embarrassment.

That fuels my need to devour her. To give her this feeling, this moment in time where she feels the waves of ecstasy crashing through her veins, just from my mouth.

My. Mouth.

Sucking, licking, and nipping, I hold nothing back. Her legs tighten around my neck as they start to tremble. She rocks forward, and I groan. The vibration of the sound against her clit causes her to emit a moan that rivals mine.

"B-B-Brooks," she breathes.

I suck harder. I want her there. Keeping one hand on her waist to steady her, the other explores until I find her breast. I roll her hard nipple between my thumb and forefinger, and it's as if that move alone is a trigger to her pleasure. She tugs at my hair, her grip tight as she calls out my name.

I don't stop until her legs and her hands in my hair relax. When I know she's wrung out from pleasure, I stare up at her. Her eyes are already watching me. I can't see the green orbs, but I don't need to. I have the color memorized. I've thought of little else these past few weeks.

"How do you feel?"

"Blissed out."

"Hold on tight." She wraps her arms around my head, and I move us to the bed. I bend down, and she falls back onto the mattress with a soft laugh that fills the room. It not only fills the room, but it's as if that sound reaches inside me and squeezes my heart causing a tightening in my chest. It's not a feeling I've ever had with a woman, but it doesn't surprise me that it's happening with Palmer.

She's different from anyone before her.

"Thank you," she says, smiling up at me. The glow of the moon illuminating her smile. The one that's just for me.

"Don't. Don't ever thank me for our shared pleasure."

"But you gave me something."

"And what? Do you think I got nothing out of that? Do you honestly think that I didn't enjoy the hell out of eating at your pussy, with your hands in my hair and those sexy tan legs of yours wrapped around my head? Trust me, beautiful, I got just as much out of it as you did."

"But you didn't get off."

"Don't you worry about me. This was for you."

She sits up, climbing on her knees, while I still stand beside the bed. "What if I said I wanted this?" Her small hand grips my cock. She strokes lightly, teasing me, and dammit, I'm going to let her. I'll never stop this woman from touching me.

"I'll give you anything you want." Those words have more meaning than she realizes. Hell, more than even I realize.

"I want you."

I hold my arms out at my sides, letting her know she can do whatever it is she's thinking about in the beautiful head of hers. "Here I am."

She chuckles. It's a lighthearted, happy chuckle that has my lips tilting up in a grin. That grin quickly falls away and molds into a curse when she wraps those pretty pink lips around my cock. With each stroke, she takes me deeper, her hand working in tandem with her mouth. My arms hang at my sides, and my hands curl into fists. I want to bury my hands in her hair, but I can't lose control. Instead, I stare down at the beauty that is Palmer and watch her swallow my cock over and over. She shifts her position, and I have a feeling she's just as turned on as I am. She cups my balls with her small soft hands and takes me to the back of her throat.

"Palmer," I grit out. "I'm close. You have to pull back." I say the words, but she keeps going at me like I'm her favorite meal. "Palmer." I push her hair back out of her eyes, and she peers up at me under long lashes. "I'm going to come down your throat if you don't stop now."

She doesn't stop.

It takes one more swipe of her tongue along the underside of my cock before I'm spilling into her mouth, all while cursing her name. I want to close my eyes and just soak in the feel of my release, but I force my eyes to stay open and watch as she swallows every last drop.

My knees are weak, so I move to sit on the bed next to her, pulling her into my lap as I do. I hold her close as I try to calm my breathing. She feels good in my arms. So good, in fact, the feeling has me opening my mouth to change the rules.

"Stay over?"

She's quiet for a long time before lifting her head to look at me. "I should really go home. I have a lot to do tomorrow."

Is that… disappointment that I feel? I know we said this was benefits only, but I'm having a hard time letting her go, even though I know I have to. "All right," I begrudgingly agree. "Let's get dressed, and I'll take you home."

## PALMER

I'M AVOIDING MY BEST FRIEND. I know, I know, it's a shit thing to do, but I'm a terrible liar, and she's going to see right through my bullshit. I needed a few days to get my head wrapped around my night with Brooks. Okay, fine, a few days has really been a week. It's been a week today since her cousin, my brother's friend, rocked my world, and I'm still reeling.

I'm standing in the kitchen of my small one-bedroom apartment, staring at my phone as if it were the devil. There's a message from my best friend, and I can only imagine what it says. She's been asking to grab dinner or meet for drinks since last Sunday. It's Saturday morning, and I know if I don't agree, she's going to end up on my doorstep. In fact, I'm shocked she's not here beating down my door already.

My phone chirps, letting me know there's a message waiting. Taking a deep breath and mentally pulling up my big girl panties, I grab my phone and swipe at the screen.

**Ramsey:** Stop avoiding me.

**Ramsey:** Palmer!

**Ramsey:** I'm on my way over. You better answer the door.

I laugh because Ramsey and I are so much alike. I would have said the same thing. I would have caved earlier than she did, but we are one and the same. A knock sounds at the door, and I know my best friend has a key, so she shouldn't be knocking. This is her way of making me let her in. Not just into my apartment but into what's been going on in my head this past week. She doesn't know something happened with Brooks, but I'm sure she's got a pretty good idea that my mood has something to do with him.

Plastering a wide smile on my face, I pull open the door. "Hey, I just got your messages." Not a complete lie since I just read them.

"Just now?" There's skepticism in her voice as she enters my apartment.

"Yeah, I've been up to my eyeballs in editing." Also not a lie. I've had a lot of shoots recently, and I've been editing for hours each night. I don't mind it. I love my job, and it kept my mind busy.

She eyes me, looking for signs that I might not be telling her the truth. I focus on keeping my features schooled and my breathing even. "You've been avoiding me all week."

"No. I've been working all week. Big difference." I turn and lead her into the small kitchen. "You want something to drink?"

"I'm good, thanks. So, what are your plans for today?" she asks.

"As of an hour ago, nothing. Unless you count laundry and the grocery store." Just the thought of the grocery store has Brooks coming to the forefront of my mind.

"That." Ramsey points at me. "What was that look? Something is going on with you."

"Nothing is going on with me. I'm dreading going to the store on Saturday. It's always packed on the weekends. I usually try to go on my Wednesday afternoons if I can to avoid the crowds."

"Well, I'm yours the entire day. Let's go grab some breakfast, and we can brave the store together."

"Do we have to?" I whine.

"No. You can starve or eat out this week."

"Neither sound appealing."

"Why don't you get what you need to do the meal prepping that Brooks taught you."

"It's basically just making a bunch of food and putting it into containers."

"Don't tell Brooks that." She laughs.

"Fine. Let's get moving, but I want real breakfast. We're going to Dorothy's Diner. I want French toast and bacon. Lots and lots of bacon."

"Done." She waves for me to follow her.

Sliding my feet into my flip-flops, I grab my purse, keys, and phone, and we head out the door. "I'll drive," I tell her.

"How's your car doing? Any more issues?"

"Nope. Declan fixed me right up."

She smiles at that. I can see the pride she has for her cousins, who are more like brothers to her.

"How was riding home with Brooks last weekend?" She waits until we're in the car and on the road to drop this question on me, and to be honest, I'm grateful. I have to keep my eyes on the road, which means I don't have to look her in the eye.

"Fine. I'm glad it kept you and Deacon from having to drive to my side of town."

"You should let him know you're interested."

"Ramsey. No. We are not doing this today."

"But you picked him, Palmer."

"Not this again. We were hanging out. I was trying to distract you from what was about to happen. You told me I had to pick. My eyes landed on Brooks, and he's who I chose."

"Liar."

"Fine. You're right. I picked him. You said I had to choose, and if I had my pick, it would be Brooks. That's not reality, Ramsey. I know that you and my brother are in this perfect bubble of love, but that's not me, and that's not me with Brooks. He's not interested."

"You don't know that."

"Don't make me turn this car around," I say in what I hope is my best impression of my mom's voice.

Ramsey bursts out laughing. "I bet your mom, and I can guarantee Aunt Carol said that a million times over the years."

"Together, I'd say you're right."

"I won't keep pestering you about it. You have to understand you convinced me to go out of my comfort zone and do that photo shoot. You knew that Deacon and I were good for each other before we did. You helped us find one another, and now look where we are. He's my future, and I want you to have yours. I have this feeling in my soul, much like yours, that Brooks is that person for you. He's your forever, Palmer."

My heart squeezes in my chest. She has no idea how her words are affecting me. She doesn't realize that I'm trying like hell not to fall for him. She doesn't know that we got intimate last weekend and that I've packed my phone with me like it's a third limb since that night, hoping to hear from him.

We agreed not to tell anyone at my insistence. This exact scenario is why. If Ramsey had any idea of what happened between Brooks and me, she'd be all over both of us to give this a real shot, and as much as I'd love that, I know that's not where we're headed.

"I believe that if it's supposed to happen, it will. Can we just leave it at that?"

"Fine." I know my best friend, and I know she wants to say more, but her ringing cell phone cuts her off and saves me more of her speech. "Hey, babe. You're on speaker," she answers.

"Are you with Palmer?" my brother asks.

"Yep. We're doing her grocery shopping, and then I don't know what we're getting into."

"Let's have people over to swim. It's hot as hell."

"It is hot today. Palmer?"

"Sure." I shrug as I hit my signal to turn into the lot of the grocery store. "I'm always up for a swim. What are we doing for food?"

Deacon answers, "Let's just do burgers and hot dogs. Some sides, maybe."

"Do we have the meat in the freezer, or do I need to grab it while we're here?" Ramsey asks my brother.

"Go ahead and get more; what we have is frozen."

"Will do. I'll pick up some sides and dessert."

"I planned on having you for dessert," my brother says, his voice changing to something deep, sexy, and disgusting because eww, that's my brother.

"Hey!" I say loudly. "Your sister is in the car, and I can hear you," I remind him.

"Sorry, baby sister, but I'm not going to change how I talk to my wife just because you can hear me."

"She's not your wife yet," I say to fire him up, and it works just as I knew it would.

"See that bright sparkly thing on her left hand? That's my ring. She's my wife."

"Last I checked, her last name wasn't Setty," I tease.

"Rams?"

"Yes, dear?" she asks sweetly. She's barely controlling her laughter. My brother is over-the-top ridiculously in love with his fiancée.

"We need to set a date."

"I told you. I'm ready when you are. I don't want a big fancy wedding. I just want to marry you."

"Fuck," he mutters as if her words hit him deep in his chest. "You sure? Baby, I want you to have everything."

"And all I want is you."

I melt a little and feel like I'm witnessing something personal that maybe I shouldn't be, but they know I can hear them.

"This weekend. We're deciding when and where this weekend. You hear that, little sister?" Deacon asks. "She's going to be my wife."

"I know, Deacon." I smile, my heart full of nothing but love for the two of them. "The real question is, when are you going to make me an aunt?"

"As soon as she'll let me."

"I'm ready now," Ramsey says as if we're discussing the weather. Silence greets us on the other end of the line. "Deacon?"

"I fucking love you, Ramsey."

My best friend, who is going to be my sister very soon, smiles. It's more than just a smile. Her entire face lights up. "I love you too. We're at the store. We're going to grab what we need, stop by Palmer's, and then we'll be there."

"Be safe. Both of you. Love you both," he says, and the line goes dead.

"Come on. Let's get this over with so we can get you home to your man."

"No rush," she says, climbing out of my car.

"You're good for him."

"And I know someone you would be good for." She lets the words hang between us as we walk into the store. We each grab a cart and begin filling them up. She doesn't bring it up again, but what she doesn't know is that she's watering a seed of hope that's already been planted.

"Remind me to tell my brother what a genius he is," I say to Ramsey. We're currently sitting around the pool at the house that is now hers as well as my brother's. The sun is shining, and we're blissfully soaking up the rays. After we finished at the grocery store, we unpacked all of mine at my place before I grabbed my bikini, and now here we are in her backyard, lazing the day away.

"Oh, I'll tell him," she says.

"Stop." I laugh. "Keep that sexy voice for when it's just the two of you. Ick," I say, pretending that I'm grossed out. We both know that's not the case. Sex is natural, and they're in love. Do I want to think about it? No. Absolutely not, but I'm not grossed out knowing that they have sex. It's human nature.

I close my eyes and can feel myself drifting when I hear a squeal. One that's very much that of a little girl. Turning my head, I watch as every woman's fantasy walks out the back door of the house and toward the pool.

Declan is holding his daughter's hand, his brothers Orrin, Brooks, and Rushton beside him. I refocus and see my brother leading the pack. Blakely is bouncing on the balls of her feet, excited as hell to go swimming, and I find myself smiling while watching her excitement. It's palpable.

I'm thankful for my sunglasses as my eyes take in Brooks. His dark shaggy hair, the skintight T-shirt, and swim trunks. Memories of our night together, of my legs wrapped around his shoulders, his face buried—yeah, I can't go there.

"Daddy, can we go in now?" Blakely asks.

"Give me a second, squirt. I need to get your swimmies blown up," Declan tells her.

"Let Uncle Rushton do it. He's good with his mouth." The guys crack up laughing, and Blakely, with her four-year-old innocence, has no idea why. She just grins, knowing that her words make her dad and her uncles laugh.

"Always got my back, kiddo." Rushton holds up his hand for a high-five, and Blakely delivers.

The guys start pulling off their shirts, all except for Rushton, who is in the process of blowing up his niece's arm floaties. It's as if we're at a swimsuit photo shoot for me. They're all cut and drop-dead gorgeous, but my eyes still stray toward Brooks. It's not just me looking at him and dreaming. This time I know what it feels like to have those strong hands gripping my thighs. I know how it feels to have his lips molded with mine. I know that he's talented in many facets.

"Damn," Ramsey mutters. "I'm related to them, and even I can appreciate how hot they all are," she whispers.

"Yep." There is no point in denying it. The Kincaid brothers are all damn sexy. Hell, even my brother can hold his own with them. Every woman in Willow River would give up salon visits for a year to be in our place right now.

I watch as Rushton and Declan make sure Blakely has her

swimmies on her arms. She's bouncing on the balls of her feet, eager to go swimming. Declan gives her a nod, and she takes off running and jumps right into the deep end. I know she can swim, but still, my heart lodges in my throat until I see her breach the surface, splashing water at Brooks, Orrin, and Deacon, who are already in the water. She swims after them, and they let her catch them. Her laughter is infectious.

"They're so good with her," I say.

"Yeah. They really are. That little girl holds all of their hearts in her hands."

"They're going to be in some big trouble when she gets older."

"Right? Can you imagine when it's time for her to date? She's got her dad and nine uncles, because you know that Deacon is going to be right there as well to intimidate her date."

"Ramsey!" Blakely calls out. "Palmer!" She calls for me too. "Come swim with us."

"How do we say no to that?" Ramsey asks.

"We don't." Together, we stand and make our way to the pool. I'm glad I kept my sunglasses on. It's going to make it easier to look at Brooks without being obvious. The only downfall is that all the guys are also wearing sunglasses, so I won't know if he's watching me.

I make my way down the steps into the water and walk toward my brother, who is leaning against the edge of the pool. Rushton grabs Ramsey, causing her to squeal as he lifts her into the air and carries her to Deacon.

"Delivery," he tells my brother, making him laugh.

"Thanks." Deacon slides his arm around Ramsey's shoulders and pulls her close, pressing his lips against the top of her head.

I smile at the two of them, and focus on not looking at Brooks. I was wrong. Just because he's wearing sunglasses doesn't mean I won't know when he's watching me. I can feel his hot and steady gaze.

"Now, Palmer." Rushton rubs his hands together. "What shall I do with you?"

I point at him. "You behave."

"Nah, where's the fun in that. Hey, Blake?"

"Yeah?" she calls back.

"Do you think Uncle Rush should dunk Palmer?"

"Yes!" Blakely cheers, and with that one word from the adorable little girl, my fate is set.

"Rushton," I warn. He doesn't care about my tone, and he advances on me anyway. He grips my hips and tosses me over his shoulder. His hands grip the backs of my thighs while I try to squirm out of his arms. He walks toward the deep end of the pool, and when he's satisfied that we're deep enough, he grips my hips and tosses me up in the air as if I'm the same size as Blakely.

I'm sputtering with laughter when I come up for air and swim toward him to retaliate. He smirks because we both know he outpowers me.

"I'll help you, Palmer." Blakely starts swimming in my direction, so I slow my advance on Rushton to give her time to get here.

"Ready?"

"Yeah. I'll dunk him for you." She latches her little arms around Rushton's neck, and he falls under the water as if she weighs a thousand pounds.

"High-five, my friend." I hold my hand up for Blakely, and she slaps at my hand much harder than needed but not hard enough to hurt.

"Oh, now you're both going to get it." I don't know how he manages to do it, but Rushton grabs each of us under one arm and pulls all three of us under the water. When I emerge, Ramsey is there helping us gang up on him.

That's pretty much how the next hour goes. Just playing and goofing off in the water. The entire time I can feel his stare, but I pretend like I don't notice. I don't know if our agreement was a one-time thing, but regardless, it's a secret, and I intend for it to stay that way. If this little deal of ours extends to more than one time, I don't want their pity when it eventually ends.

## BROOKS

SHE WON'T LOOK AT ME. I've been watching her all afternoon, and not once has she looked my way. I felt her gaze when we first walked outside, but since then, nothing. She has no issue letting my brother toss her around in the pool, laughing and living it up like they're the best of friends. I want to punch him and tell him that she's mine, but she's not mine.

She wants this to be a secret, and I'm fine with that. But I need to add a rule of my own. One time wasn't enough for me so, while we're doing this, whatever this might be, there is no one else. Not for me and not for her. That also means she needs to not let Rush toss her around like she's a ragdoll in the water. Okay, fine, he's being easy with her. I'm just jealous as hell that it's not me gripping those slender hips and feeling that soft wet skin. It could be, but I can't get past the fact that if I touch her, I won't be able to hide that I've seen her naked. I'm barely maintaining control as it is.

I've wanted to reach out to her so many times this week, but work was hell. I worked Monday through Wednesday and then picked up eight-hour shifts both Thursday and Friday for a coworker who has a sick kid. Another coworker took the other four hours of each shift. Together we got her covered, but it was draining. We were slammed every day due to the emergency room in Harris being on diversion. One of their doctors was out sick, and another on vacation, and they've barely been able to keep their heads above water. Luckily, we're fully staffed, but the extra load kept us all hopping the entire shift. There is no downtime. Hell, there's hardly time to stop and use the bathroom.

Anyway, when I got home, by the time I showered and ate, I was crashing. It was a long-ass week, but I still thought about her. Every single time I lay in my bed, I thought about having her here with me. Even at work, there was a woman her age who came in for a cut on her hand from cooking, and she made me think of Palmer. Every fucking thing makes me think of her.

I thought that we would get our fill of one another. Get a taste, expel some of the chemistry between us, and my thoughts would be my own once again.

I was wrong.

In fact, I've never been more wrong in my entire life. It's as if my mind is no longer my own. It's the Palmer show, and I'm just a spectator.

"Jade just pulled in," Orrin says.

"Oh, I'll go greet her." Palmer is already swimming to the edge of the pool and climbing out.

I watch as the water slides down her body just before she's wrapping a towel around herself and hiding from me. Fuck me. She's beautiful.

"Don't hog all of her time!" Orrin calls out.

Palmer laughs. "Relax, big guy. I need to grab myself a drink while I'm in there too. I'm parched. Does anyone else want anything?"

Everyone passes, and she's off, disappearing into the house. I count to one hundred slowly in my head five times before I move from my perch on the side of the pool and head for the steps. "I'll be back. I gotta take a—" I suddenly remember my niece is here, and I try to clean up my mouth when she's around. "I have to use the restroom," I amend. "Anyone need anything?" I offer just as Palmer did before me.

"Uncle Brooks, I'm thirsty," Blakely calls out.

I point at her. "I've got you covered." She smiles a smile that melts my heart. Grabbing my towel from one of the lounge chairs, I dry off and wrap it around my waist, much like Palmer did, and casually head inside. I take my time when all I want to do is run to her. As soon as I reach the door, Jade is there.

"Hey, Brooks." She waves.

"Hey. It's a good thing you're going out there," I tell her. "Orrin already threatened Palmer not to steal all of your time."

She grins and shakes her head. "He's ridiculous."

"Nah, he's just in love." Her face pinks, and it's cute as hell, but that's not the blush I want to see. I close the door behind her and go off in search of Palmer.

I hear the water running in the bathroom, so I post up outside the door waiting for her to exit. When she does, she gasps, and her hand covers her heart.

"You scared me."

I take a step toward her. "I'm sorry." I push her wet hair back off her face and take another step closer. "Do you know how hard it is to watch you out there? Laughing and having fun with my brothers, and know that I can't touch you?"

"No one said you couldn't join us, Brooks."

"You're right. But we agreed to keep this a secret."

"What does that have to do with anything?"

I lean in close, pressing a kiss just below her ear. She shivers, and goose bumps break out across her skin. I want to trace them with my tongue. "I know what your lips taste like when they're pressed to mine. I know what your pussy feels like when you're losing control. I know what it's like to have your legs locked around my head, and last, I know how it feels when you take my cock deep down your throat. I can't just pretend to play with you out there and not touch you the way I want to touch you."

She whimpers, and the sound goes straight to my cock. "I

want to pull you in my arms and feel your skin next to mine." My lips move, trailing kisses down her neck. When I lift my head, her eyes are heated, and she's rubbing her thighs together. "Tell me what you need, Palmer."

"You can't just come in here and corner me in this dark hallway and say those kinds of things."

"Are you aching?" I ask softly.

"You know that I am."

"Can I help you?"

"I'd be pissed if you didn't. That's what this arrangement is for, right?" she asks.

I hate and love that statement all at once. I hate that it's an arrangement at all. I love that I'm the one who gets to fix this for her. "While we're doing this, it's just us."

"I thought that was a given."

"Just making sure."

"Brooks." My name is a whispered plea.

She's holding the towel that was once around her waist, and I'm suddenly thankful for mine. It's helping to contain my cock. Sliding my hand beneath the wet strands of her hair, I grip her neck and bring her lips to mine. Her familiar taste hits me in the chest and causes my already racing heart to pound double time.

Breaking the kiss, I rest my forehead against hers as I use my index finger to trace down her jaw, the long slender length of her neck, and down to the valley of her breasts. Her bikini top slides from her skin easily and allows me to tweak her already hard nipple.

Continuing my trek, I glide my hands over her belly, and when I reach her bikini bottoms, I slip my finger beneath the waistband and trace the skin beneath.

"You're teasing me."

"I'm enjoying you. There's a difference."

"Can you enjoy me a little lower?"

A chuckle breaks free from my lips. "Ask, and you shall receive, beautiful," I whisper before claiming her lips with my own. She meets me stroke for stroke, and when I slide my entire hand into her bikini bottoms, she bites down on my bottom lip, which only drives me crazier.

When my fingers slip through her folds, I groan into her mouth at the feeling of her wetness coating my fingers. My thumb lightly presses against her clit, causing her to dig her fingers into my biceps, her nails biting at my skin. Knowing that's going to leave a mark that I won't be able to explain, I advise her to move them. "My hair, baby. I won't be able to explain the marks on my arms."

"That's what you get for teasing me," she huffs but moves her hands to my hair. "You said you would make this ache go away."

"I wanted to take my time with you."

"We don't have time, Brooks. Someone could find us. Please." She's begging me, and it's hot as fuck.

"Move the towel between us." She does as I ask without question. "Bite down on it."

"What?"

"Trust me."

She does as I ask, and that's when I slide one long digit inside her. I repeat the process a few times before adding another while curling my fingers. I alternate pumping in and out of her to making a come-here motion with my fingers, and if her grip on my hair is any indication, she likes it all.

I need to get her there and fast. We've both already been gone far too long. Using my thumb to massage her clit, while my fingers are curled inside her, she shoots off like a rocket. Her arms and legs quiver as she comes down from the high of her release, and my cock is stone.

"Took you long enough," she sasses.

I laugh and kiss her lightly on the lips. "I wish I had more time."

"What would you do with me if you did?"

"I'd drown myself in this," I say, lazily running my fingers through her wet pussy. "Then I'd lift you onto my cock, and let you milk me dry."

"When can we do that?" she asks, smiling up at me with a happy dopey smile.

"Not tonight while we're in your brother's hallway. You need to get back out there. Don't forget you were going to get a drink. Maybe brush out your hair or something and tell them I've been in the bathroom."

"You think they're going to believe that?"

I shrug. "I'll tell them I had the shits, that it must have been something I ate."

"You're awful," she says, swatting at my chest.

I capture her hands and bring them to my lips, kissing the palm of her hand. "Go before I haul you into this bathroom and fuck you. Trust me. I won't care who hears us when that happens."

"Come home with me tonight?" she asks.

"We can hide your car in my garage. You should come to my place. Plus, there are no close neighbors like there are in your building that we can't trust to snitch us or worse, blow our cover."

She points at me. "Good thinking." She looks between us where my hard cock is beneath the towel pressing into her belly. "What about you?"

"I'm going to take care of it."

"Now?"

"I have to. I can't go out there like this, and after what we just did, having you come all over my fingers? I need the release."

"I can help." She reaches for the towel, but I stop her.

"No. We're going to get caught. Go on out. I'll handle this and be out soon."

"Tonight?" she asks.

"Tonight," I agree, kissing her one more time before stepping back and letting her walk away from me. I watch her until I can no longer see her before slipping into the bathroom and turning the lock.

With a flick of my wrist, I'm able to remove the towel, letting it fall to the floor. I work at the strings on my swim trunks, tugging at the fabric, letting it pool at my ankles. My cock juts out, slapping my stomach. Gripping it in my hand, I squeeze hard.

It's easy for me to pull up the memory of my cock in her mouth, hitting the back of her throat. The way she swallowed every drop and licked her lips afterward. I pump faster, replaying every second of my night with her in my head. My balls tighten, and a familiar tingle races down my spine. It's not the same as if she were here with me, but the pleasure is building.

My fist grows tighter. Each pass along my cock increases in speed, and then it hits me. Fire races through me as I spill into the sink. I sag against the counter, spent and not nearly satisfied.

*Tonight.*

I just have to get through the rest of the day. Dinner with my brothers and friends, and then when I go home, it's with the knowledge that she's coming too. I'm going to get to take my time with her, and that's the only thing that motivates me to clean up and right myself before grabbing Blakely a bottle of water, and joining everyone back at the pool.

"You get lost, man?" Orrin calls out.

I rub at my stomach. "Must have been something I ate." My brothers and everyone else start cracking up laughing. I ignore them and go the edge of the pool to hand Declan the bottle of water for Blakely. To keep up with the ruse, I choose a lounge chair on the other side of the pool. I take a seat and place my hand on my belly. My glasses are covering my eyes, and I tilt my head back as if I'm sleeping.

I'm not sleeping.

I'm watching Palmer. She's back in the water with Ramsey and Jade as they play with Blakely. My niece is loving the attention of the three women, and my heart squeezes for her—at losing her momma before she got to know her. My mom and Ramsey were the only women in her life until Jade came along. I guess Palmer, too, by association. I know she's hung out with Ramsey and Blake several times over the last couple of years.

As if she can feel my gaze, Palmer glances over at me. It's just a quick glance, but her eyes on me has my cock twitching. I'm glad I'm sitting over here on my own—knowing that if I keep staring at her, things are going to get worse for me. I close my eyes and listen to the sound of everyone around me.

"You just going to sit over here and pretend to be sleeping the rest of the day?" I open my eyes to find my brother Declan now sitting in the lounger next to mine. He's two years older than me and two years younger than Orrin, our oldest brother.

"Just relaxing."

"She's having a blast," he says, and he doesn't need to tell me who he's talking about. I know it's his daughter.

"She is. I'm glad you brought her."

"She's going to be begging me to come back every day now." He laughs.

"You brought her a few times last year."

"Yeah, but it was just us guys at the time. Ramsey and Palmer were never here when we were, and now we have Jade."

"How long until you think until he proposes?"

"Soon."

"Yeah," I agree.

It's weird to think that one of us might be married soon and that Blakely could have little cousins to play with. I know it's a part of life, and it will happen hopefully for each of us, but we've all been single for so long that it's going to be different. Good, but different.

"Daddy! Watch me!" Blakely calls out.

He waves, and we watch as Ramsey lifts her to the edge of the pool. She holds her arms in front of her as if she's a professional diver and falls into the water. Jade and Palmer are there next to her, cheering her on as soon as she surfaces.

"She loves their attention," Declan says, voicing my earlier thoughts.

"You're doing great with her, Dec."

"I know, but she's getting older, and she's going to need a woman to go to for advice."

"She has Mom and Ramsey, and I'm sure Jade."

"I know. I just feel like I'm failing her."

"Declan, you bust your ass for that little girl. You give her all your time other than when you're working, and a lot of the time she's there with you. She knows she's loved, and she knows that you would move mountains for her. You are not failing her."

"Let's eat!" Deacon calls from where he's standing on the back porch at the grill.

"Come on, let's grab our girl and get some food." What I don't say is that the sooner we eat and this little get-together ends, I get to take my girl home. Well, she's not my girl, but while this agreement is in session, she is.

She's all mine.

I don't share.

## PALMER

TODAY'S MY HALF DAY, AND I've been marking items off my to-do list left and right. So much so that everything I wanted to get done today is finished. It's a satisfying feeling. Staying busy has been my motto for the last week and a half. It helps me keep my mind off Brooks.

I didn't end up going to his house that night after he got me off in the hallway of my brother's house. Ramsey decided to have a sleepover with Blakely, and that included Jade and me. So, we all stayed there. We camped out in the basement, all of us sleeping on the huge sectional couch he has downstairs. We did our hair and painted our toenails, and I swear Blakely was smiling so big I was fearful her face might crack.

So, yeah, I didn't get to go to his place. Last weekend was his weekend to work, and even if it hadn't been, I worked all weekend. I had a wedding to shoot, which consisted of the rehearsal and rehearsal dinner on Friday night and all-day Saturday as the bride and groom got ready for their big day, the wedding, and the reception. It was a long-ass weekend, and I was exhausted, falling into bed and fast asleep as soon as my head hit the pillow.

We've texted a few times trying to find a time to see each other, and there just hasn't been one. We probably could have tried harder, but the middle-of-the-night booty calls seem to cheapen it. Besides, we both had to work the next day, and he's a nurse. He saves lives for a living. A good night's rest is important.

So here we are a week and a half later, and I'm craving his touch like people living in the desert crave rain. It's a constant humming in my veins that I'm certain only Brooks can cause. I've thought about texting him to see if he wants to get together tonight, but he already told me he was helping his brother Archer today. He's working on an outdoor pizza oven for their parents. As a brick mason, Archer is definitely the man for the job. I guess Archer had a dentist appointment this morning, so he took the rest of the day off and wanted to get a head start on the oven. Brooks offered to help him since it was his day off.

Instead of calling him and begging him for his time, I get in my car and drive to Harris. The food trucks are at Sunflower Park again today, and if I can't spend time with him, I can visit a place that will forever remind me of him and have some dinner.

The drive is nice. It's about twenty minutes from Willow River and an easy drive. When I get to the park, it's not nearly as busy as I anticipated it would be at this time of evening.

After parking my car, I climb out and head toward the row of food trucks. There aren't as many here as the night when Brooks and I were here, but the smells still have my belly growling. I take in my options and decide on pulled pork, deep-fried pickles, and a sweet tea. I grab my tea first. That way, my food doesn't get cold or soggy. My next stop is the pickles, and last, the pulled-pork sandwich.

I had planned to eat in my car, but there are several open picnic tables, so I decide to do that instead. It's a nice night, warm for Georgia summer, but not so hot I'll melt to death while I eat either. It helps that the sun is setting. The food trucks will be closing up soon, so I made it just in time.

Peeling back the wrapper on my pulled pork, I take a big bite and moan as the taste explodes on my tongue. So damn good.

Digging beneath the container for a napkin, I wipe at my mouth just as I feel a presence behind me. Don't ask me how, but I know it's him.

"I bet you that doesn't taste as good as you do." Brooks's deep voice greets me.

I turn to look over my shoulder. "Hey. What are you doing here?"

He takes a seat facing me on the bench of the picnic table. "Archer needed some more materials. I volunteered to pick them up for him so we'd have them this weekend to finish up the project. He has to work tomorrow, and I'm off, so I volunteered. I was stopping to grab something to eat. I saw you sitting here."

"Go get you something. Eat with me."

He smiles, leans in, and pecks my lips. "I'll be right back." He stands to move toward the food trucks. I glance around, looking to see if anyone we know is here and could have seen him kiss me.

I can't believe he did that in public. Then again, he got me off in the hallway at my brother's when anyone could have come in the house and caught us. This kiss, though. It was soft and sweet and almost felt like something he would do if we were a real couple. Something I know I can't let my heart wish for.

I spend too much time in my head, because before I know it, Brooks is back and taking his place next to me at the table. "I grabbed a large bucket of fries so we could share."

"Are you trying to put me into another food coma?" I ask, stealing a fry from the large bucket.

"Maybe just sweeten you up to convince you to come home with me?"

"Hmm, and you think fries will do that?"

He shrugs. "Not sure, but I'm pretty sure the promise of orgasms will." He takes a huge bite of his pulled-pork sandwich.

"Plural?" I ask, knowing damn well that's what he said.

"The night's still young" is his reply.

"I don't know. That's a big challenge to fulfill." I'm trying to keep the banter going, so maybe he doesn't notice what his words do to me. So that maybe he doesn't realize my panties are already ruined.

For him.

He reaches over and grabs my hand, pulls it beneath the picnic table, and places it over his cock. His very noticeably hard cock. "Challenge accepted." He laces his fingers through mine and rests them on his thigh, which leaves us both with just one hand to eat with. I'm fine with it. And sure, it looks obvious, but our hands are not out in the open where anyone can see us.

"What are the chances that we'd both be here for dinner again?" I ask.

"I was driving by, and this reminded me of you and our day together." He shrugs. "I hadn't had dinner, so I stopped. I had plans to call you on my way home and see what you were doing."

"I wanted to call you," I confess. "I knew that you were helping Archer, and I didn't want to interrupt. I knew the trucks were here again, and yeah, they reminded me of our day here, so I got in the car, and here I am."

"You should have called. You could have ridden with me."

"Next time I will."

"What are your plans after this?"

"Following you home."

He chuckles. "Good answer."

When I pull into his driveway, he parks on one side of the garage, and I park in the other just like he advised when he called me a few minutes ago when we turned onto his road. No one will know I'm here. My belly swirls with anticipation of what's to come. It's as if this night has been in the making for almost two weeks, and we're both live wires ready to spark.

Before I have the chance to, he pulls open my door and offers me his hand. He helps me from the car, shutting the door behind me and pushing my back against the warm metal. His hands land on either side of my face as he kisses me.

This isn't just any kiss. This is longing and passion, and need. So much need. I grip his wrists as we stand here in his garage and devour one another. There's an urgency between us, and it has nothing to do with a time constraint but the fact that this moment is long overdue. It's been a week and a half of constantly thinking about what we missed out on that night. The coals have stayed hot, and now that fire has sparked yet again.

I couldn't tell you how much time has passed. We're lost in one another, in the fact that behind these walls, there is no time limit, no rushing to not get caught. It's just the two of us and this crazy intense chemistry.

Brooks slows the kiss and stands to his full height. "You make me lose my head."

"Where are we again?" I ask, making him laugh.

"Come on, beautiful. Let's get you inside." With his hand on the small of my back, he leads me into his house.

I kick off my shoes in the laundry room and set my purse and keys on the dryer, holding onto my phone, following him into the kitchen. "It smells good in here."

"Thanks. That's all Mom. She buys us all candles saying that she doesn't want to visit her sons' houses and smell sweaty socks. It's as if she thinks we can't manage cleaning without her. I blame the twins, as the only two still living at home, they're spoiled rotten, and she cleans up after them. She's already forgotten what it's like to live with her other sons who did that shit on their own."

"I'm sure she did it for all of you, and they are the babies. I couldn't imagine raising nine boys and being down to the last two at home. It's probably a coping mechanism for her. She's not going to know what to do with herself when they move out."

"I don't know that they ever will if she keeps spoiling them as she does."

"Aw, do I detect a hint of jealousy?"

"Nope." He winks, and my reply is a wide smile. He grabs my hand and leads me to the living room, where he takes a seat on the couch and pulls me into his lap. "How have you been?"

I'm shocked that he's asking. I assumed I was here for one thing and one thing only. His interest has my heart fluttering in my chest. "Busy. I had a long list of things to do this afternoon, but I was able to work through them all. Now all I need to do is get caught up on photo edits, but I only have one shoot, and it's in the studio tomorrow, so I should have lots of time to get caught up there too."

"How was the wedding last weekend? That was a lot of hours."

"You're one to talk, Mr. 'I work twelve-hour shifts that turn into fourteen plus.'"

"Yeah, it's been a rough one, but I don't have kids, so I pick up for those who do when I can. One day, when I'm a father and need to alter my schedule, I'd like to think they will remember all the times I picked up for them and do the same for me."

My belly gets all fluttery thinking about Brooks holding a baby, and of course in this visual the baby is ours. His and mine. I shake out of the thought. "The wedding was good. It's always long days when I'm the photographer for the entire weekend. I took thousands of images that I need to sift through and edit."

"Your eyes light up when you talk about it."

"What?"

"When you talk about your job. You get this sparkle in your eyes."

"I really love it. It never feels like work for me."

"Do what you love, and you'll never work a day in your life."

"Kincaid wisdom?" I ask.

"Nah, saw it on a social media post."

"I should have known," I say, laughing lightly.

He pulls me closer, and I move around until I can rest my head on his chest. "Archer kicked my ass today," he says, his voice low.

"Yeah? I'm sure your mom is excited about her pizza oven."

"She really is. She's wanted one for a long time. Her birthday is in a few weeks. We all pitched in for the materials. Well, everyone except for Archer because he's doing the majority of the work, and the rest of us are helping when we can. We're all going to be at my parents' this weekend to hopefully finish it up."

"That's nice of you."

"Blake is pumped. She can't wait for Papaw to make her pizza outside." He laughs.

"She's adorable."

"You're adorable," he says, kissing the top of my head.

I turn to look at him, and he kisses me softly. "Lie with me?"

I nod and stand from his lap. I expect him to take us to his room, but he surprises me when he stretches out on the couch and pats the spot in front of him. I lie down facing him, and he wraps his strong arms around me.

"Better," he says softly.

Lifting my arms, I run my hands through his shaggy hair. I love the way it feels between my fingers. He pulls me closer, which I didn't think was possible, and burrows into me, letting me have better access.

"You're going to make me fall asleep."

I don't say a word. I just keep running my fingers through his dark locks. Part of me wants to ask about all those orgasms he promised me, but there is another part, a bigger part of me, that craves this even more. It's intimate, and yet we're both fully clothed. It's a moment I never thought I'd have with him, so of course, I'm going to take it.

Brooks lifts his head, and his big blue eyes bore into mine. I don't blink, meeting his gaze. "I wish I knew what you were thinking." I wish I could read his mind.

"I'm thinking I want to kiss you."

"Then kiss me."

That's all the push he needs before he leans in and gently caresses my lips with his. His hand slides up the back of my shirt, and to my surprise, he just rests it there. His thumb makes small circles, but he makes no move to take things further.

I still have one hand buried in his hair, while the other arm is wrapped around his neck, holding onto him as if my life depends on it. He takes his time kissing me. His tongue lazily slides against mine as if he has all the time in the world. His hard length presses against my belly, but he doesn't seem to mind, and to be honest, neither do I.

I don't know how much time has passed, but my lips are swollen, and my heart, well, it's in dangerous territory. I never expected a night like this with him, and it's damn hard to keep my emotions out of the moment.

He eventually pulls away and guides my head to his chest. I hold onto him, soaking up every moment that I get to be here with him in his arms. We don't speak, but then again, the moment doesn't need words. My heart is galloping in my chest, and from the sound of it, his is too. Does he feel this? Is he having a hard time keeping feelings out of our arrangement too?

Eventually, his breathing evens out. I peek up at him and realize he's asleep. He worked hard today helping his brother, and he still wanted to spend his night with me when we both know he could have very easily come home and crashed.

My eyes find the clock on the wall, and it's just before eleven. I need to be at the studio in the morning at eight. I should leave, but I can't seem to make myself stand. I tell myself I'll stay until eleven thirty. Then I'll force myself to go home and sleep in my own bed.

Alone.

I spend the next thirty-plus minutes watching him sleep. His jaw is covered in a couple of days of stubble, and even that makes him sexier. It's just Brooks, the man. He's the whole package, and no matter how hard I've tried, I know that when this ends, I'm going to be crushed. I'm going to have to find a way to move on and not let our friends and family know that my heart is shattered into a million pieces that only one man can put back together. I knew this would happen, but I jumped in feet first anyway.

I'll deal with the fallout when it gets here. All too soon, the clock hits the eleven thirty mark, and it's time for me to head home. Carefully, I try to detangle myself from him, but his eyes pop open.

"What's wrong?"

"Nothing. I'm heading home."

"No." He holds me tighter. "Stay over."

"I need to be at the studio early. I really should go. Thank you for having dinner with me and for the cuddles."

"I owe you orgasms," he says, covering a yawn.

"Don't worry, big guy. I'm going to hold you to that."

He leans forward and kisses me softly. "I'll walk you out."

"You don't have to."

"I do. I'm going to bed anyway." We both stand, and he walks me out to the garage to my car. He kisses me deeply before opening my door and waiting for me to climb inside. He waves and walks toward the wall to hit the button opening the garage door.

I fight back the tears as I pull out, and the door slowly closes, holding him inside. This is going to be so much harder than I ever thought it would be.

# Chapter 13

## BROOKS

IT'S BEEN RAINING LIKE POURING piss out of a boot all damn day. I've been at Mom and Dad's along with all eight of my brothers, waiting to see if this storm is going to pass so we can work on finishing up this outdoor pizza oven my mom's been talking about for years.

"It doesn't look like it's going to let up." Ryder turns the screen of his phone so we can all see the radar. "It's supposed to be clear and sunny tomorrow."

"Well, I guess we're rained out, boys," my dad says.

"You mean I get all my boys here two days in a row? Mother nature is my new best friend," my mom teases. "I'll make Sunday lunch and Sunday dinner."

"Mom," Archer speaks up. "You don't have to do that."

"I know, but I want to. I miss having all of you here, and I know you all try to make it on Sundays, but that's for a couple of hours. I get all of you all day. And there are some Sundays when your lives make it so that you can't be here, and I understand that. I'll take the small victories with my sons when I can get them." She smiles at each of us, and damn if that doesn't hit me in the feels.

"Daddy," Blakely calls out. "Can we have Rams, and Palmer, and Jade spend the night with us? Please, Daddy?"

My dad coughs to cover his laugh. My mom looks horrified, as if Declan has been having orgies in front of his daughter. Orrin grins because he knows where the question is coming from, and me, well, all I can think is that she can't stay with you because I want her to stay with me.

"I don't think so, squirt. Uncle Orrin and Jade have plans," Declan tells his daughter. He's totally making that shit up. I'm sure they're going to be together, but Orrin hasn't said a word about plans with Jade tonight. We all left this day and night open. We wanted to get this project finished for Mom. "Ramsey is with Deacon, and I'm sure Palmer is out on a date."

"Can I go on a date too?" she asks.

"When you're thirty," Declan tells her.

Blakely nods. "Okay." In her four-year-old mind, thirty seems like a fair answer. She has no idea thirty is way off the mark of the age she's actually going to start dating.

"You ready to go?" Declan asks Blakely.

"I guess." She shrugs. "Are we coming back soon?"

"We'll be back tomorrow," he tells her.

"Dec?" Mom speaks up. "Can she stay?" she mouths. Declan nods.

"Blake, do you want to spend the night with Mamaw and Papaw?"

"Yes!" Blakely punches her little fist in the air. She runs to her dad and throws herself into his lap, where he's sitting on the couch. "Can I, Daddy? Please, can I?" she begs.

"You promise to be good?" he asks.

"Oh, I so promise."

We all laugh. "You can stay. Give Daddy and your uncles some love." She does just that. She hugs and kisses all of us goodbye, and we all head to our vehicles with plans to come back tomorrow and try again.

"What are you doing with your night off?" Sterling asks Declan.

"Sleeping." He laughs. "Sleeping in the rain is my jam, and having a night where I don't have to be on, sounds like the perfect night."

None of us give him shit because how can we? We don't know what it's like to be a dad. We do know that he's a damn good one, and if he wants a night to just chill in his own space, he's earned that.

"What about you?" Sterling asks.

"I think I'm going to do the same. It's been a long-ass week, and I need to get caught up on laundry and a few other things if I'm going to be here tomorrow." A murmur of agreement from all my brothers fills the small front porch. The twins are even claiming they're staying home tonight. Truth be told, they love spoiling Blakely, and they're all about trying to win the favorite uncle titles.

Once I'm on the road, I grab my phone and call Palmer. She answers on the first ring.

"Hey, you."

Damn, it's good to hear her voice. "What are you up to?"

"Sitting in the dark, kicking myself in the proverbial ass for cleaning house this morning and not showering right away. Now I have no power, I assume from the storm, and I'm in desperate need of a shower."

"Come to my place."

"I'm just whining. I'm sorry. How's the pizza oven coming?"

"It's not. We were hoping the rain would let up, but we gave up, and we're all going back tomorrow."

"Yeah, this weather is shit."

I laugh. "It really is. So, are you coming to my place to shower or what?"

"You're not even home. How do you know you have power?"

"How do you know I'm not home?"

"I can hear the air conditioning vents."

"Fine. I'm not home, but my security system always alerts me to a power outage, and I haven't received one. Come on. You know you want a shower. And it's got to be getting hot as hell in your apartment without air conditioning."

"It's not too bad."

"Palmer."

"Brooks," she sasses, and I can't wait to see her to kiss the sass from her perfect pink lips.

"I'm ten minutes out. Pack what you need to shower at my place. I'll be out front waiting for you."

"You don't have to do that. I can go to my parents' or to Deacon's."

"You can come to my place with me."

"Let me get some things together, and I'll come over for a little while."

"Since I'm already out, I'll pick you up. You don't need to be driving in this shit," I say as the rain starts to come down even harder against the windshield.

"You do know I'm a big girl, right? I can drive, go potty, and even feed myself."

"Haha, smartass. Let me do this for you, Palmer. Just pack a bag. I'll be there in eight minutes."

"Has anyone ever told you that you're bossy as hell?"

"You're the first to be around long enough to have the opportunity. I'll see you in seven minutes, beautiful." I end the call before she can complain, or worse, decline. I'm not taking no for an answer. There is no point in her sweating it out at her place when she can be at mine.

With me.

It takes me twelve minutes to get to her apartment with the torrential rain. I pull up to the front door and see her standing in the hallway. I smile and beep the horn. She grins, shakes her head, and makes a run for it. Leaning over, I push open her door, and she jumps in, bag and all, slamming it behind her.

"Hi." She looks over at me, and she's drenched, but the smile on her face is bright.

"Hi." I push her wet hair out of her eyes before sliding my hand behind her neck and pulling her in for a kiss. "You taste like chocolate."

"Oh." She grins. "I made these before the power went out." She reaches into her bag and pulls out a small container of what looks like cookies. "Chocolate chip. I brought them for you as a thank-you for the ride and for letting me use your shower. And your air conditioning," she adds.

"That wasn't necessary, but thank you." I release her and settle back behind the wheel. "You ready?"

"All set." She smiles, and I swear the tilt of those lips has a direct line to my heart, and it squeezes every single time she points that smile in my direction.

I pull back out on the road. Mindful of my passenger, I stay off the throttle. "So you spent the day cleaning?" I ask her.

"Yes. I had just finished the cookies and mopping the kitchen when the power went out. I got all my laundry done and the entire apartment cleaned before it happened. The only thing I didn't clean was me."

*I can help with that.* "I need to do that too. That was the plan for tomorrow, but now I'll just have to put it off."

"Brooks! If you had plans, you shouldn't be picking me up and hauling me around."

"You're more fun." I should tell her that I missed her, but I keep that to myself. I know that's not what this is supposed to be, but I missed her all the same.

"Well, I'm already a sweaty mess, so I'll help you clean before I shower."

"No. You're a guest."

"And your plans for the weekend were hijacked. Really, I don't mind cleaning. I want to help you."

"We'll see," I say.

"Nope. Either you help me, or I go home."

"What if I refuse to take you?"

"I can call Ramsey, or Deacon, or hell, one of your brothers."

"And how will you explain the fact that you're with me?" I want her to say she doesn't give a shit if they find out. I hate hiding her, hiding us, but I agreed to this ridiculous plan. What I was thinking, I don't know. It's been weeks, and we're still hiding.

"Dammit," she mutters.

"Have you had dinner?" I ask, ignoring the twinge of disappointment that she can't read my mind.

"Do cookies count?"

"No. Cookies don't count. I made spaghetti last night. There are leftovers. I think I even have a box of garlic bread in the freezer."

"You don't have to feed me too."

I reach over and grab her hand, placing it on my thigh, before putting mine back on the wheel. "I want to feed you, Palmer. Just let me, okay?"

"Okay," she agrees softly. She's quiet for a few minutes, and the rain continues to fall angrily from the sky. "It's really coming down." Her hand grips my thigh as if she's scared, and I hate that I really need to keep both hands on the wheel and can't cover hers with mine to comfort her.

"It is, but I've got this."

"I trust you."

Three words that I never really cared to hear from a woman before. There's never been a woman in my life who has been around long enough for me to care if she thought that she could trust me. For some reason, with Palmer, it's important. I like knowing that I have her trust, and I find that she has mine, which is not something I give women. At least not until her.

Finally, I turn into my driveway and hit the garage door opener. It opens with ease, and I pull my truck inside and hit the button to shut the door, closing the noise of the rain outside with it.

"We made it." I lift her hand to my lips and kiss her knuckles.

"Safe and sound." She smiles, her shoulders relaxing.

"Let's get you fed," I tell her. We both climb out of the truck and make our way into the house, kicking our shoes off in the laundry room.

"You warm up dinner while I start cleaning," Palmer says, letting her bag drop off her shoulder and land on the laundry room floor.

"Palmer, you're not cleaning my house."

"Then take me home."

"No." I stand with my feet apart and cross my arms over my chest. "I just got you here. I barely got to see you Wednesday night, and it was a long damn time before that. I'm not taking you home."

Her shoulders drop as she steps toward me. My arms fall to my sides, and she places her hands flat against my chest, staring up at me. "I want to do this for you, Brooks. I don't want to go home yet. I want to be here, but I also want to make your life easier."

"You make it better." The confession slips past my tongue before I can stop it, but I don't regret it.

"Please? The two of us together can knock it out in no time. You're clean for a bachelor," she teases.

"That's not why I invited you here."

She leaves one hand on my chest and moves the other to rest against my cheek. "I know that. That's why I want to help you. Can you honestly tell me that you wouldn't jump in to help me if the roles were reversed?"

"Of course I would."

She stands on her tiptoes and presses a soft kiss under my chin. "Then let me. Please?"

Let me tell you something about Palmer Setty and those big green eyes of hers. When she's standing so close, her hands on your body, and she turns the power of those beautiful eyes on you and follows with a please, you can't say no.

*I* can't say no.

"Fine," I concede.

"Thank you." I'm rewarded with a kiss on my lips. I wrap my

arms around her waist, holding her close, kissing her the way I've been dying to since the moment she hopped into my truck.

"Brooks," she mumbles against my lips.

"Hmm." I don't stop kissing her.

"If we start this now, we're never going to start cleaning, and I really do need a shower before this goes any further." She pulls back and wrinkles her nose.

"I'll take you any way that I can get you." I'm telling her the truth. She thinks she's a mess. I think she's beautiful.

"Go cook us some dinner, or warm us up some dinner or whatever. Give me the dusting supplies and the vacuum."

"I hate this."

"Get over it, big guy." She pats my chest and takes a step back.

"Cleaning supplies and the vacuum are in the hall closet."

"Got it," she calls over her shoulder, already headed toward the closet. I hear her rustling around, and then music fills the house. I have an open-floor plan, so I can see her as she props her phone up on the TV stand and gets to work dusting my living room and dining room area. I don't have a lot as far as decorations, so it's not like it's a time-consuming job, but I still hate that she's doing it. I wanted to spend time with her, not guilt her into cleaning my house.

Shaking out of my thoughts, I move to the fridge and grab the bowl of spaghetti, add it to a pan, and set the burner on low to warm it up. Turning on the oven to preheat, I get to work setting the box of garlic bread sticks out on a cookie sheet to bake.

Fifteen minutes later, I have place settings at the island, with two big plates of spaghetti. "Babe!" I call out to her. She lifts her head and smiles at me. "Time to eat."

"Perfect timing. I just finished dusting."

"Thank you." I stand next to the island and steal a kiss from her once she gets close before pulling her chair out for her.

"This looks great."

"Mom made sure we all knew how to cook. She said we would be good husbands one day. She still claims to this day that her future daughters-in-law are going to love her for all the training she gave us."

"I love your mom."

"I think it's safe to say that you and I both got lucky in the parent department."

"I agree with that statement. They do sometimes lecture me, but I just remind myself how lucky I am. Ramsey didn't have that until she came to Willow River. My parents are saints compared to hers."

"I'm glad she got away from them."

"You all took her in, no questions asked. Your parents, hell, you and your brothers, you all saved her. You showed her what family is supposed to be."

"You had a lot to do with that too. She didn't trust easily, but she took to you right away."

Palmer laughs. "I didn't give her much of a choice. I knew she was good people. I'm a good judge of character. When I found out she was related to all of you, I knew I was right. Now she's my person. I don't know what I would do without her."

"Don't let your brother hear you say that," I tease.

"Oh, he knows. And he's good with it. She's my best friend and the love of his life. She's made him so happy. I can't wait to watch them grow their family."

Leaning over, I press a kiss to the top of her head. "You're good people, Palmer Setty."

"What I am is sweaty and a hot mess."

"I told you…" I start, but she shakes her head smiling.

"I was all of that before I offered to help you. Let's eat this yummy dinner. Then we can sweep and tackle the kitchen together. After that we can divide and conquer the bedrooms and the bathrooms."

"The spare bathroom hasn't been used in a while. Usually, just my brothers when they stay over. I always just use the master, so just a quick dusting, and it should be good. The bedrooms, I'm not even going to touch those. I changed the sheets the last time my brothers stayed over, and no one has been in them since. So my bedroom and bathroom after the kitchen."

"Eat up, Kincaid. We have jobs to do." She flashes me a grin before biting off a huge bite of a breadstick.

I've never spent much time thinking about relationships and how it would feel to be in one. Not until this situation with Palmer. If other men got to see her like this, they'd be lining up to take her out. The idea pisses me off more than it should. I know we said this was just for benefits. I thought those benefits would be sexual, and they have been, but they're also friendship and something else I can't exactly name, but I'm ready to run toward it.

If I was ever going to be domestic with anyone, to make a go of something real with anyone, it would be Palmer.

# Chapter 14

## PALMER

"ARE YOU SURE YOU DON'T have a housekeeper?" I ask Brooks. I just finished cleaning his bathroom, and it wasn't even really that dirty.

"No. We all had chores growing up, and most of them revolved around cleaning. It's not hard to pick up after myself."

"Are you an alien?" I tease.

He laughs. "No. I'm not an alien." He finishes wrapping up the cord on the vacuum. "I'm going to put this away."

I follow along behind him, taking the small basket of dirty towels from the bathroom to the laundry room. I quickly start the washer and shut the laundry room door. It's still raining outside, but not as hard. Switching on the porch light, I stare out into his backyard. The back porch houses a grill and a set of patio furniture. Just off the porch, it looks like a fire pit and homemade benches surrounding it.

"Whatcha doing?" he asks, coming to stand behind me, wrapping me in his arms.

"Watching it rain."

"It's been a shitty day for weather."

"It sucks being stuck inside all day." I look over my shoulder at him, and he kisses my nose. "At least both of our houses are clean."

"There's that," he agrees. "But who says that we have to stay inside?"

"Did you not see the buckets of water falling from the sky?"

"I saw it." He kisses my neck. Reaching around me, he pulls open the sliding glass door and takes a step forward.

"What are you doing?" I ask.

"We're going outside to play in the rain."

"What?" I sputter with laughter while allowing him to guide us out on the back porch. The rain isn't coming down as hard as it was earlier, but there is still a steady fall from the sky.

He closes the door and takes me by the hand, twirling me around. He pulls me into his chest and dips me dramatically. My head is tilted back, and the rain pelts against my flushed skin.

"When I said I needed a shower, this isn't what I meant," I tease when he lifts me back to a standing position.

"I have to keep you on your toes." He winks, twirling me again.

"Do you always dance in the rain, Kincaid?" I ask when I'm once again pulled back into his arms.

"No. This is my first time." He bends and kisses me softly. "My parents still to this day dance around the kitchen and even in the rain. I asked Dad once why he always danced with her. He said, 'Son, you always dance with her, even if it's in the rain, and you do it like no one is watching.'"

"Ah, the musings of Raymond Kincaid," I reply.

"He has a lot of them. I asked him 'why though?' I didn't understand why all the dancing."

"What did he tell you?"

"He said, 'boys,' because my brothers were all there too. 'When you find someone you want to dance with, you'll understand.'" He presses his lips to my forehead as we sway to the sound of the rain falling against the deck.

My heart is beating so hard you'd think Thumper was taking up residence in my chest. I want to ask him if I'm that someone to him, but my heart won't let me. This is casual. Brooks hasn't let on that it could be or even that he wants it to be more. He's treated me lovingly and with respect from day one. That's just who he is. He's one of the good ones, and with each day, I fall harder for him when I know I'm not supposed to.

I can't seem to stop it.

He twirls me around a few more times before the rain starts to pick up. "Let's get you inside." With his arm around my waist, he leads me back into the kitchen. I shiver when the cool air-conditioned air hits my skin. "Fuck. I didn't think this through. I'll get you a towel. Strip." The words are barely past his lips before he's racing down the hall to grab a towel.

He's back in no time, and I'm still standing on the rug, dripping everywhere. He has a towel slung around his shoulders and another in his hand for me. "Palmer, you're supposed to be stripping."

"In your kitchen?"

"Yes. In my kitchen. Get naked, baby," he says. One might think he's being cheeky, but his tone is more serious than I've ever heard it. His eyes are locked on mine and not my body.

"I'm fine," I tell him.

"You're shivering. Dammit, I should have thought of that." He grumbles something about his dad being wrong about dancing in the rain as he reaches out and lifts the hem of my shirt, pulling it over my head and dropping it to the rug I'm currently dripping all over.

With a level of care that has my heart tripping over itself, he helps me strip out of my clothes, not caring at all that they're landing in a sopping pile on his hardwood floors. Once I'm naked and still shivering, he wraps the towel around me and lifts me into his arms, bridal style.

"Brooks!" I shriek as I wrap my arms around his neck to hold on.

"We need to get you warmed up."

"I'm fine, big guy." I kiss his scruffy cheek. His worry, the way he's insisting on taking care of me, has me feeling all warm and gooey inside, despite the cold temperature of the room. His hair is in clumpy wet pieces against his face, but it doesn't seem to bother him. He only seems to be bothered by the fact that I'm cold. He takes me into his room and into his bathroom, where the shower is already running and steam is filling the room.

"Test the water," he tells me.

I reach in, and the hot water feels amazing against my cold skin. "It's fine," I tell him.

"I'll lay some towels out for you." He turns, but I reach out for him.

"Wait." He stops to look at me. "Join me?" I hold my breath, waiting for him to decide.

He gives me a stiff nod and steps away, grabbing a handful of towels from the closet, and tossing them on the closed toilet seat. Then he starts to strip. I keep my eyes on his every movement as he peels away his rain-soaked clothes. When he's finally fully naked, his hard cock standing at attention, I hold my hand out for him, and he takes it. Together we step under the hot spray, pulling the curtain around us.

My back is to the water, so I tilt my head, letting the hot water warm me. I sigh as the water instantly starts to replace the chill from the rain and the air conditioning. When I finally lift my head, Brooks is standing in front of me. His arms hang at his sides, and his hands are balled into fists. He's watching me with a look I can't describe.

"Brooks?"

He takes a small step toward me, his arms still hanging at his sides. "You're beautiful. Soaked with rain, in the shower, all dressed up, or after a day of cleaning. It doesn't matter what state of you I see. They're all beautiful."

"I'm a sure thing, Kincaid," I joke. My voice wavers, which is a dead giveaway that his mere presence is affecting me in ways I can't hide.

"Can I touch you?"

"You don't have to ask me that. We're in this together, right? Just you and me?"

"Just you and me." He nods.

"Then, while we're active with our benefits status, you never have to ask me."

"That's dangerous, Palmer," he says, stepping closer, his hands landing on my hips.

"I'll take my chances."

I stand still as he slides his hands up my sides, slowly, methodically. When he reaches my breasts, he tweaks my nipples, one then the other, before bending his head and pulling one tight bud, then the other into his hot mouth.

I brace my hands on his shoulders as he takes his time nipping and lightly sucking, which is driving me insane with desire for him.

His lips leave my breast and begin their journey again. This time it's over my chest, my neck, and finally his lips land on mine. He kisses me slowly. He takes his time, tracing my lips with his tongue.

"Brooks." His name is a plea, but I'm not sure what for. I need more of him, but at the same time, this is good too. Just him and me, and his hands and mouth anywhere and everywhere he wants them to be. It's erotic and sexy, and after all these weeks, I feel like tonight might be the night I get to feel what it's like to have him be a part of me. Something that, regardless of how this ends, he'll never be able to take from me. I'll forever have the memory of this night with him.

"What do you need?"

"You."

He pulls his lips from mine and bends so we're eye to eye. His dark blue irises study me intently. He lifts his hand and pushes my hair back out of my eyes, and I mimic the gesture to him. "You have me, Palmer." The way he's looking at me, it's as if those words mean more than they do. At least that's how my traitorous heart takes them.

"You inside me." My words are bold. That's how this man makes me feel. As if I could ask him for anything, confide anything to him, and he would give it to me if it was within his power, and those secrets, locked in a Brooks vault, kept just between us. It's heady and scary and exhilarating all at the same time.

"We didn't bring your shower stuff in with us."

"No biggie," I tell him.

He reaches behind me and grabs his shampoo. "You're going to smell like me."

"Good."

He chuckles lightly while placing shampoo in the palm of his hand before returning the bottle to the shelf and proceeds to wash my hair for me. I'm ready to ask him why he's ignoring my request, but before I can, he explains himself.

"I promised you a shower. I didn't know that I'd be privileged enough to shower with you, but now that I'm here, I'm taking full advantage of taking care of you. Something I know you don't let many do. For some reason, right now, you're letting me." He massages my scalp with his fingertips.

"That feels good," I tell him. My arms wrap around him and pull him close to me. Our naked wet bodies are aligned, his hard cock poking me. He's turned on but continues to ignore the fact.

"Are you trying to make me lose control?" he asks.

"What?"

"You've got your naked body plastered against mine, and, baby, I don't have a condom in here. I'm trying to clean you up like I promised before I drag you to my bed and dirty you up again, but you're making that damn hard." He kisses the tip of my nose. "Head back," he says, running his hands through my hair, helping to rinse out the shampoo.

"Good enough," I say, twisting to turn off the water. Pulling back the curtain, I step out and toss him a towel, then twist my hair in one, and use the other to dry off before wrapping it around my body.

Brooks steps out of the shower, running the towel I gave him over his hair. Once he's satisfied, he tosses it into the hamper and then tugs the one around my body, gripping it and tossing it as well.

"What are we doing with this?" he asks, pointing to the towel on my head.

Tilting my head to the side, I pull the towel off and hand it to him. "Where are the condoms?"

Brooks chuckles before bending over and lifting me into his arms. "In the nightstand. I bought a new box when we started this."

"Oh, you were out?" I ask. I don't really want to know the answer, but the question slips out before I can think better of it, and there's no taking it back now.

"I don't bring women here. I had a small box that had been in my truck for a while. I pitch them after a couple of months, not willing to use them if they've been damaged, and bought us a new box." He tosses me on the bed, making me laugh with each bounce, as I watch him pull open the nightstand and retrieve a large unopened box of condoms.

"Economy size? I like it." I eye the large box of condoms, and all I can think about is the places in this house we can use them. That's what this man does to me.

"I knew my usual box of three would never be enough when it comes to you."

"I don't know, Kincaid," I say, tapping my index finger against my chin. "It's been weeks."

"Palmer," he growls. "Life keeps getting in our way, but not tonight. Tonight, Mother Nature was on our side, and here you are. In my bed where you belong. Where I've wanted you for all those weeks you're going on about."

"Prove it."

His eyes smolder. He tears open the box and pulls out a strip, tossing it on the bed next to me.

"What are you doing? You need one of those." I reach for the strip and tear one off, handing it to him.

"You're not ready."

"Trust me, big guy, I'm ready."

"Prove it." He smirks, proud of himself for tossing my words back at me.

I wasn't lying. I'm ready for him. The dancing and then the shower were more than enough for me. I'm wet and aching for him. He wants me to prove it, so I do. Grabbing his hand, I boldly move it between my thighs. He handles the rest as he swipes his index finger through my folds.

"Fuck," he mumbles. Before I know what's happening, he's lifting me further up the bed, my wet hair on his pillow. His broad shoulders are between my thighs, and his mouth is on my clit. He moans as if I'm the best meal he's ever had, and the sounds cause fire to build in my veins.

"Told you," I manage to sass, making him laugh. He slides one long digit inside me, causing my eyes to roll back in my head. Reaching for the condoms, not sure where the one I tore off went, I tear off another and grip his hair, pulling him up to look at me. "Now, Brooks. Please." I hold up the single condom.

He sits back on his legs, wipes his mouth with the back of his hand, and tears open the condom. I watch his every move as he rolls it along his length. Then he's hovering over me. His muscular arms keeping his weight from my body, but I don't want him to hold back. I want him. All of him. I want his weight. I want his arms around me. I want his cock inside me. I want his mouth devouring me.

I just want him.

All of him.

Wrapping my arms around his neck, I pull him down to me. "Let me feel you."

"I don't want to crush you."

"You won't."

He nods and settles further between my thighs, reaching between us and aligning himself at my entrance. His hands are locked at the top of my head while mine grip his biceps.

"Beautiful," he whispers as he pushes inside me for the first time.

"So full," I mumble, burying my face in his neck.

"Palmer, I need to see your eyes."

I drop back on the pillow and force my eyes to open to look at him. "Hi."

"Hi." He kisses the tip of my nose. "Your eyes tell me so much. I need to see them while I'm inside you. I need to know that you're okay, and selfishly I want your eyes on me when you fall apart."

He pulls out and pushes back in, starting at a slow, steady pace. "Your pussy is going crazy."

"Told you I was ready." I grin, and he kisses me. Just a hard, quick press of his lips to mine.

"So tight and wet, you fit me as if you were made for me, Palmer."

"Maybe I was," I reply boldly. I bite my tongue. I shouldn't have said that, but he's inside me, and my heart is going crazy both from the exhilaration of the moment and because I was stupid to think I could keep my emotions out of this. My heart already recognizes him as ours, but he's not. Hot tears prick my eyes, and I blink rapidly to ward them off.

Brooks freezes. "Am I hurting you?"

"No. No." I'm quick to assure him.

"What's going on in the beautiful mind of yours?"

"I've been waiting for this. For you for a long time. Happy tears." It's not a complete lie, but not the whole truth either.

He kisses me. This time his tongue slides deep into my mouth as if he needs to be inside me in every possible way. His thrusts grow faster as he tears his mouth from mine. He reaches between us and uses his thumb to massage my clit.

"Oh, fuck." I dig my nails into his arms as my orgasm comes fast and hard without warning, crashing like a violent storm against the shoreline.

"Fuck, you feel incredible. Your pussy is milking my cock. So hot," he mumbles. A few more thrusts and my name falls from his lips. His eyes remain locked on mine as he empties inside me.

## BROOKS

I'M HAVING TROUBLE PULLING AIR into my lungs.

I just had the best sex of my life.

Hands down.

Her pussy was made for my cock. So much so that I know I need to pull out and take care of the condom, but I'm not ready to leave her heat. I'm addicted.

Knowing that I'm more than likely crushing her, I lift my weight up on my arms and stare down at her. She smiles shyly.

"Hi."

I smile and lean in, pressing my lips to hers. Her pussy squeezes my cock, almost as an aftershock, and I groan. "You're doing that on purpose."

"Maybe." She gives me a blissed-out smile, and I can't do one damn thing but return it.

"I need to take care of this." Slowly, I slide out of her and climb out of bed. I rush to the bathroom, dispose of the condom, and quickly wash my hands before rushing back to her. When I get back to the bed, she's burrowed under the covers, and I waste no time, sliding underneath them and pulling her into my arms.

"I was cold."

"I'll warm you up." I hold her a little tighter, letting her soak up my body heat. I'm still on fire for her.

"Doesn't help that my hair's still wet." She chuckles.

"I should probably apologize for being impatient, but I'm not going to. That was… hot as fuck." I can't very well tell her that it was life-changing, although, to me, it was. We have an agreement, and I need to keep reminding myself of that. With each passing day, it gets harder and harder to remember how this started and how I'd be on board for it never ending.

"Maybe it was the buildup. We've been dancing around this." She tilts her head up to look at me. "No pun intended. But we've been dancing around this night for weeks."

"Yeah," I agree. I feel raw and exposed, which is not something I'm used to feeling, and definitely not after sex. It's always just been a physical release for me, but lying here with her in my arms feels different. Maybe it's because I don't cuddle as it gives off the wrong impression, but with Palmer, I'm not ready for her to be away from me. I'm not going to dive into what that might mean. Instead, I'm forcing myself out of my head and just enjoying this time with her.

"I need another shower." She laughs.

As much as I don't want to get out of this bed, I know we have to. "Come on, lazy bones."

"That's your fault. I'm not even sure I can stand."

"No?" I ask, sliding out of bed. "I guess I'll just have to carry you." I scoop her up in my arms. Her laughter is contagious as I take my time carrying her into my bathroom and sitting her on the closed toilet. "I'll go grab your bag."

"Thank you!" she calls after me.

By the time I'm back, she's already got the water running. I hand her the bag, and she reaches inside, pulling out a smaller bag and three bottles. She steps into the shower, and in no time, the entire room smells like peaches. No wonder she always smells good enough to eat.

"You need help in there?" I ask, peeking my head around the curtain.

"If you get in here, we both know I'm not going to be getting clean."

"So that's a no?" I tease.

"Brooks," she warns.

"Fine. Kiss me, and I'll leave you alone." I can't get enough of her.

She leans over and presses her lips to mine before grabbing the curtain and pulling it closed, making me laugh. "You're lucky you're cute," I tell her.

"Flattery will get you everywhere," she fires back.

Shaking my head, I leave her to shower and decide I need one too. Moving to the bathroom in the hallway, I turn the water to hot and step under the spray. I hate that I'm washing her scent from my skin, but that thought alone makes me sound like a fucking creeper, so I lather up without further deliberation.

"Good timing," I say, walking back into my room wearing nothing but a towel. Her eyes roam over my exposed chest, and she licks her lips. I point at her. "Stop. We just got cleaned up."

She grins. "I know, and I really need to get going."

"What?" It feels as if she knocked the wind out of me. "I thought you didn't have power?" And I just assumed she'd stay over tonight. She never does, and wouldn't it figure the one woman I want to stay with always seems to have one foot out the door.

"My neighbor just texted me and said it's back on. I have clothes in the washer, and I'm sure every light in the place is on."

"We can run over and check it out, then come back."

"Brooks, that's not a good idea."

I want to pull her into my arms and tell her it's the best fucking idea I've ever had. Instead, I nod. "Let's get dressed, and I'll take you back."

"What crawled up your ass?" Ryder asks as I slam two more rocks down next to Archer.

"Nothing." That's a lie, and we all know it. I've been surly all damn day. I slept like shit last night. My sheets smelled like her. My entire fucking house smelled like peaches.

"What gives, bro?" Sterling asks. "You've been in a pissy mood since you climbed out of your truck this morning."

I expel a heavy breath. "I'm fine."

"Clearly," Rushton says dryly.

"Anyone need a drink?" I ask.

"No, but pick up a better attitude while you're gone," Declan calls after me.

My answer is to raise my hand in the air and flip him off. I love my brothers, but I'm not in the mood today. I know I'm being an asshole, but I can't seem to stop. Stepping into the house, the cool air hits me, and it's a reprieve from the outside temperatures this late in the summer.

"Uncle Brooks!" Blakely rushes toward me, and I know from experience that she's about to launch herself at me, knowing that I'll catch her. She does it to all of us.

"How's my girl?" I ask her, lifting her into my arms. She places her arms around my neck and gives me a sloppy kiss on my cheek.

"I'm getting ice cream!" she says with all the excitement of a four-year-old.

"You are?"

"Yes! Rams is coming to get me."

"What kind of ice cream are you going to get?" I ask.

She taps her index finger against her chin, pretending to think about it. I'll give it to her. She's always getting something different. When I asked her one time which was her favorite, her reply was "Uncle Brooks, it's ice cream. All of them." Did I mention she's smart as hell?

"I think I'll get swirl with sprinkles."

"Good choice." I press my lips to her temple as the front door opens. I hear my mom greeting Ramsey. Pushing my bad mood down deep, I carry Blakely to the living room to say hi to my little cousin. When I round the corner, I freeze. Ramsey is talking to my mom, and standing next to her is Palmer.

"Ladies," I say, my mood suddenly a hell of a lot brighter.

"Hey, Brooks." Ramsey steps forward for a side hug, tickling Blakely, who reaches for Ramsey. She doesn't hesitate to take her from my arms.

"Palmer." She waves and leans in for a hug too.

She's out of my arms all too soon, but her familiar scent washes over me. It's as if seeing her and smelling her is a balm for my pissed-off disposition. "You ladies are getting ice cream?" I ask, even though I already know the answer. I'm just trying to stall to keep them here a little longer.

"That's the plan," Palmer replies, glancing over at Ramsey and Blakely as they talk to my mom.

I lean in close to her, pretending to look behind her and whisper, "I missed you last night."

"You saw me," she whispers back.

"I slept like shit without you there." It's a confession I didn't plan to make.

"Brooks." There is so much she's saying from the tone of her voice. Longing, desire, and if I'm not mistaken, a little regret. She wanted to stay. The look in her eyes last night and here right now tells me she did.

"Ready?" Ramsey asks.

I take a step back. "Yep." Palmer's voice is way too chipper and guilty as hell, but I couldn't care less. I don't care if anyone finds out about us. I'm into her.

"Have fun." I wave.

"Kiss!" Blakely calls out.

I laugh but go to her, kissing her cheek. "Be good today."

"I will, but we're all leaving, Uncle Brooks."

"You ladies all be careful," I amend my statement.

"Not that," Blakely scolds me. "Rams and Palmer need kisses too."

"Oh, is that how this works?" I ask my niece when really all I want to do is take her to the toy store and buy her everything she wants.

"Yep. Thems the rules, Uncle Brooks."

"Well, we can't be breaking the rules. I am your favorite uncle, after all."

"For right now," she says, making my mom, Ramsey, and Palmer laugh.

"You little stinker." I tickle, and she wiggles in Ramsey's arms. "Ramsey, be careful, and have fun." I press my lips to her cheek.

"Now, Palmer. Ice cream is waiting," Blakely instructs.

I turn to look at Palmer, and her eyes are wide as if she can't believe I'm about to kiss her in front of my family. She has nothing to worry about. I'm not going to kiss her like I crave to, but my lips against her skin is enough to hold me over. For now. I step in close, placing my hand on her hip, and kiss her cheek, closer to her ear. "Be safe, beautiful," I whisper and release her all too soon. "Have fun," I tell her, my voice normal considering the desire I feel from even that small amount of contact with her.

"And be safe," Blakely reminds me.

"Be safe." I wink at Palmer, and a slight blush coats her cheeks.

"Tell Dec we'll bring her back later." Ramsey smiles like she knows all my secrets, and hell, she just might. I'm not trying very damn hard to hide them.

Not today.

"Bye, Mamaw!" Blakely waves, and then they're gone.

"How's it coming out there?" Mom asks.

"Good. Archer's killing it."

She grins. "I'm so excited. Next weekend's Sunday dinner is going to be homemade pizza."

"Sounds good, Momma." I kiss her cheek and head to the kitchen for a bottle of water. I down it in one go, toss the bottle in the recycling bin, and get my ass back to work.

"What's that?" Merrick asks, pointing at me.

"What?" I wipe at my face.

"You're smiling." Maverick's voice is accusing.

"Did Mom give you happy pills?" Orrin jokes.

A car pulling out of the driveway gets their attention. "Who's that?" Archer asks, wiping sweat from his brow.

"Oh, Ramsey picked up Blakely," Declan tells him. "She's taking her for ice cream."

Archer grins. "Blakely is all smiles, I'm sure."

"She was," I tell them.

"Jade and Piper are meeting them," Orrin says, sliding his phone into his pocket. "She just texted me."

"Palmer was with her." I work on keeping my facial expression smooth, not giving anything away.

"Was she now?" Ryder smirks.

"Girls' day, I guess." I shrug like it doesn't matter to me.

"Interesting." Sterling crosses his arms over his chest.

"What? That they're having a girls' day? Blake asks for it all the time," I remind them. "She had a blast when they all stayed at Deacon's."

"Oh, we know." Rushton laughs. "I've heard her ask Dec daily if they can do it again."

"You're in a better mood." Archer grins.

Assholes. They know they've got me, but I'm like a vault. I'm not giving them anything. "Got out of the heat for a few." It's a lame excuse, and we all know it.

"You were gone like ten minutes," Maverick points out.

"And you went for a drink that you didn't get," Merrick adds.

"I chugged a bottle of water while I was in there."

"Uh-huh," Merrick replies.

"Are we doing this or not?" I ask them.

"As much as I'd love to give you shit, I want to get this done," Archer says, picking up his tools and getting back to work.

Thankfully, they leave it alone and get their nosey asses back to work.

"I love it!" Mom hugs Archer, then makes her way to do the same with each one of us. She doesn't give a single fuck that we're covered in sweat. She's used to sweaty hugs from this brood. "Next Sunday, homemade pizza," she announces, just as she did with me earlier.

"You're making me hungry," Rushton complains.

"Well, you're in luck. Lunch is ready. I called in for a couple of subs, and Ramsey picked them up for me." Mom turns to look at Orrin. "I was supposed to tell you Jade was here." Mom chuckles when Orrin grins and jogs off toward the house.

"What about you?" Sterling asks me.

"What about me? Am I starving? Yes."

"You going to go kiss your girl?" Declan goads me.

"I gave Blakely a kiss before she left earlier." They don't need to know that I kissed Ramsey and Palmer too.

"Oh, Dec, it was so cute." Mom goes on to tell Declan and the rest of my brothers the story, spilling the beans.

"Ah, the plot thickens." Ryder rubs his hands together.

"She's not my girl."

"You sure about that?" Maverick asks.

"Yeah, I mean she let you kiss her," Merrick chimes in.

"Oh, it was just a little peck on the cheek," Mom explains. "Come on in and eat."

Mom walks away, leaving us all standing on the back porch. "Can we not?" I plead with my brothers.

"Admit you like her, and we'll drop it," Rushton states.

"Of course I like her. She's Ramsey's best friend and Deacon's little sister."

"Try again, brother." Sterling gives a look that tells me he can read through my bullshit. They all can.

We promised we would keep this a secret, and I'm a man of my word. No matter how badly I want to tell them all about her. Hell, I could use some advice on how I've been feeling, but I won't break a promise to Palmer. "Fine. There might be a little something, but it's all on me." I'm quick to keep her out of this. I can take their teasing. I don't want them harassing her. "Can we please just keep this between us?"

"We have to tell Orrin," Archer tells me. "We can't keep this from him."

"It's not like I'm dying. It's a crush. She's beautiful." I shrug.

"And we're your brothers," Declan reminds me.

"Fine. We can tell Orrin when Jade's not around, and not while Ramsey and Palmer are here. Can you keep your big mouths shut?"

"Bro." Maverick slings his arm around Merrick's shoulders and points at each of them. "Wingmen."

"I'm all set," I say, not able to hide my humor with my little brothers.

"We're not going to say anything," Sterling speaks up. "Right, fellas?" My brothers nod, and I feel my shoulders relax. "But that doesn't mean we won't encourage you to make your move."

"She's not just a hookup." I can hear the strain in my voice.

Declan holds up his hands. "No one said that she was."

"Maybe it's in the water," Rushton muses. "First Deacon, then Orrin, and now you."

"Stop." I shake my head at him. "We're keeping this between us, and yes, you blabbermouths can tell Orrin, but he can't tell Jade. Now, let's go eat. I'm starving."

Turning on my heels, I head to the house. I know my brothers are following me, and I also know they're all going to be watching me. Even Orrin, and he wasn't here for my confession.

Pulling open the door, I hear Blakely telling my parents and Orrin all about her day with the girls. Her words, not mine. Stepping into the laundry room, I wash my hands in the huge sink before going to the kitchen and making myself a plate. I move to the living room and take a seat on the large sectional. Ramsey, Jade, Palmer, Piper, Orrin, and my parents are all in the dining room, and I just can't be in there right now. I'm going to want to sit next to her. I'm going to want to touch her, and well, that's not a good idea. Not with all eyes on us, and I know Palmer would hate that.

So, instead, I get settled on the couch, and eventually, all my brothers, minus Orrin, join me. I know I'll have to talk to her in front of them before she leaves here today, but I need a minute. I need to steel my resolve and hide the fact that I'm falling hard for her.

# Chapter 16

**PALMER**

It's Sunday night, and Ramsey just dropped me off at my apartment. Today was awkward, fun, and unnerving all rolled into one. I knew that there was a good chance I was going to run into Brooks at his parents' place. I knew he was going to be there. What I didn't expect was to feel a pull to him so strong that I almost blew this little secret of ours out of the water.

It wasn't just me. I could see it in his eyes. After what we shared last night, it's hard to keep our hands to ourselves. Our chemistry is unlike anything I've ever felt before. Tossing my purse on the chair, I plop down on the couch, and of course my phone rings. Scrambling from the couch, I dig it out of my purse and quickly glance at the screen to see Brooks's name.

"Hey," I greet him. My tone is light and casual, not at all showing the storm brewing inside of me.

"That sucked."

"What?" I know what he's saying, but I want him to spell it out for me.

"Not being able to touch you.'"

"That's risky, Kincaid," I tease.

I can hear him blow out a heavy breath. "I know. That's why when we were eating, I stayed in the living room. I wasn't ignoring you. Well, I guess I was, but not maliciously. I just knew my brothers, hell, everyone there would have been able to see right through me."

"And what would they have seen?" I cover my mouth with my hand. I can't believe I just asked him that.

"How much I want you." There is no hesitation in his reply.

"You just had me."

"If you would have stayed over, I could have had you again. And then again this morning."

"So needy."

He laughs, and I savor the sound. "Apparently I am," he agrees.

"Busy week this week?" I ask.

"Yeah. I work Monday through Thursday. I picked up a shift covering for a vacation. Then I'm off Friday to Sunday. What about you?"

"I have a full week. I even have a shoot scheduled for my normal half day Wednesday in the afternoon. It's a newborn, so it should be fun."

"Will I get to see you this week?"

I bite down on my bottom lip. I want to scream out yes, but I know I need to not let myself get attached to him. At least not more than I already am. "It's a busy week. What are you doing this weekend?"

"Whatever involves you. My only request is that it be somewhere I can at least give you a proper kiss hello."

"Speaking of, that niece of yours is something else. Piper took a drink of water that went down wrong, which made her cough." I pause, my laughter already bubbling over.

"This must be good," Brooks says, humor in his tone.

"Oh, it is. Blakely was sitting next to her. She reaches over and pats her on the back and asks her if she needs a cock drop."

"Stop!" His laughter fills my ears. "Did you tell Declan that one?" he asks.

"No. We didn't want to embarrass her. We all started coughing, and she said, you all need cock drops. It was the funniest thing."

"She's a handful, that's for sure."

"Oh, and then we're standing in line to order, and she asks Ramsey how ice cream is made. She explains from milk and other ingredients, which seems to pacify Blakely. We're in the car on the way home, and she says, 'Rams, thank you for the frozen cow.'"

"She did not." Brooks wheezes with laughter through the line.

"She's a trip."

"She really is. I blame that on the fact that before Ramsey came into our lives on a permanent basis, my mom was the only female in her life. She's basically being raised by a pack of wolves, with me, my brothers, and my dad."

"Stop. You're not that bad." I chuckle.

"I guess not, but she's not used to having all this girly stuff and girl time. It's nice of you all to spend time with her."

"She's a good time."

"She enjoys it. All she's talked about for weeks is the sleepover at Deacon's."

"It was a fun night."

"So, this weekend?"

"What did you have in mind?"

"How much time do I have? Hours? A day? All weekend? What do I have to work with and I'll think of something?"

"I have no plans this weekend. I will have some grocery shopping and, more than likely, laundry if I don't get to it during the week. Save one of the two days for me to get caught up with life since I'm working my half day this week."

"One entire day. Oh, the possibilities," he croons.

"What did I just get myself into?" I ask.

His deep throaty laugh flows through the line. "You're safe with me, beautiful," he assures me.

"I'm trusting you, Kincaid." I keep my tone light.

"I've got five days. Mark Saturday off for me. My mom is pumped about using this new outdoor pizza oven next Sunday, so I can't miss that."

"I'll have to check my schedule," I tease.

"Saturday, Palmer."

"Saturday," I concede.

"It's getting late, and I have to be up at five."

"Have a good week," I tell him.

"Do I have to go another full week without talking to you?" he asks.

"I know you're busy."

"When I text you, are you going to reply?" He ignores the out I'm giving him.

"I always do."

"Good girl," he says huskily.

Just like that, my panties are ruined. "I'll talk to you soon," I tell him.

"Night, Palmer."

"Night." I end the call and climb off the couch. I need a shower after that, and I'm ready to call it a night. It's been an adventurous weekend.

Today has been a Monday for the record books. My first of two newborn shoots this week was this morning, and the studio has been a revolving door ever since. I've added new shoots to my calendar and sold a ton of prints from past shoots. For some reason, everyone decided today was the day to get images marked off their to-do list. Not that I mind. This is my career, and knowing that my business is thriving is my dream come true.

Locking up the studio, I head to my car. As soon as I open the door, my phone alerts me to a message. Sliding behind the wheel, I start the car to get the air conditioning going. It's the end of August and hot as hell here in Georgia.

Digging into my purse while the air conditioning that's still blowing warm air hits me like a tornado and has my hair flying in all directions, I retrieve my phone. I can't hide my smile when I see it's Brooks.

**Brooks:** Is it a full moon?

**Me:** Possibly. Bad day?

**Brooks:** Not bad, just crazy busy. I'm just now eating lunch.

**Me:** It's five o'clock. You get off at seven, right?

**Brooks:** I'm supposed to. It's a madhouse. We've had everything from sore throats to a bad car accident between here and Harris.

**Me:** Anything I can do.

**Brooks:** Be naked in my bed when I get home?

He follows his request with an entire row of grinning emoji.

**Me:** You and I both know you'd be too tired to handle me.

I give him my own line of emoji. Mine is a winking face.

**Brooks:** Challenge accepted.

I burst out laughing. I should have known he would come back with something like that.

**Me:** As good as that sounds, I have a ton of edits to get through. I thought I would have the rest of the week, but I added four more shoots to my schedule this week. Today has been crazy busy for me too.

**Brooks:** Fine. Can I call you later?

**Me:** Always.

**Brooks:** I need to get back out there.

**Me:** Did you even finish eating?

He sends me a picture of his empty container.

**Brooks:** Yep. You kept me company. Thanks for that. Talk soon.

I don't bother replying. I know he's already making his way back to his patients, and that's where his attention needs to be. Placing my phone in the cupholder, I put my car in Drive and head home.

**Brooks:** Good morning, beautiful.

I stare at the message on my phone that was sent at six thirty this morning. My heart knocks against my chest. I know he's trying to be the nice guy that he is, but damn him. All the sweet things he says and does is dangerous to my heart. I knew he was a nice guy, but this attraction I feel for him is on another level. I've never dated anyone who cared enough to send me a good morning text to let me know he was thinking about me.

Now, when I finally do, it's my friends-with-benefits hookup that no longer feels like we're just about the benefits. My heart is involved, and that pisses me off. Not at him. He's done nothing wrong. Hell, he does everything right, hence the reason my heart isn't doing a very good job of staying out of this little arrangement we've made.

It's just after seven, so I know he's already started his shift. I type out a reply, then erase it. It takes me three tries before I'm satisfied and hit Send.

**Me:** Have a great day.

Simple, to the point, and completely ignores the way he calls me beautiful. The butterflies in my belly, however, took notice, and they're fluttering around like crazy. I'm in dangerous territory. I know I need to either end this or just tough it out and let the cards fall where they may when he does. And by cards, I mean the shattered pieces of my heart.

Tossing my phone on the bed, I throw off the covers and make my way to the shower. I'm ready in record time, and I don't need to be at the studio until nine. I don't really want to start on edits and then have to stop. I get into the zone when I'm editing, and it goes much faster when I can sit down knowing or hoping I'll have the least number of interruptions.

With time to kill, I make a stop at our local bakery, The Sweet Side. The smell of sweet, gooey goodness hits me as soon as I open the door. As I stand in line, I ponder what I'm going to order. I'm starving, and it smells so good that I'm tempted to just order one of everything and leave some for my customers. That's when an idea hits.

"Welcome to The Sweet Side. What can I get for you?" an older woman greets me.

"I'll take a dozen glazed donuts, a cinnamon roll, and two large black coffees, please."

"Sure. Coming right up." I hand over my card, and she cashes me out before boxing up my order. I wait patiently while she gathers my order. She places a box, a bag, and a drink carrier on the counter. "Can you get that? Need some help to your car?"

"Nope. I'm all set. Thank you. Have a great day." I wave before sliding the bag onto my wrist, taking the box with one hand and the drink carrier with the other.

I don't know how he takes his coffee. I'm not even sure he drinks coffee, and me dropping by his work isn't something a friend with benefits would do, but he had a hard day yesterday. When I talked to him last night, it was brief. I could tell he was exhausted, so I made the excuse that I had laundry to fold and ended our call early. Taking a deep breath, I slowly exhale before grabbing my phone and sending him a text.

**Me:** Can I drop something off for you?

**Brooks:** Only if it's you.

**Me:** Nice try, big guy.

**Brooks:** Can't blame a man for trying.

**Brooks:** Come to the ER parking lot. Text me when you get here, and I'll run out to meet you.

**Me:** Okay. I'll be there in ten.

Placing my phone in the cupholder, I put my car in Drive and head to Willow River General. I battle internally with myself the entire drive. I'm blurring the lines. I was just thinking I was getting too attached and here I am, trumping his "good morning, beautiful" text with donuts and coffee. I'm still not certain it's the best idea, but I'm already committed. The donuts and coffee have been purchased, and he knows I'm on my way.

Parking in the emergency room parking lot like he told me, I wipe my hands on my capris before grabbing my phone to send him a message.

**Me:** I'm here.

**Brooks:** I'll come to you.

Well, that makes this easier. At least I don't have to stand in the lobby with patients and his coworkers watching me, waiting for him to come out. Him meeting me outside makes it easier on me.

**Me:** Okay.

I watch the doors, and within no time, he's exiting wearing his dark blue scrubs. Damn, this was such a bad idea. The man makes scrubs look sexy. I bet every female doctor, nurse, patient, and even the support staff drool over him on a daily basis. He makes it to the passenger side and pulls open the door. Quickly, I move the goodies and allow him room to sit.

He climbs into the car, shuts the door, and leans over, kissing me on the lips. "You did bring me you," he says, pulling away while I fight hard not to melt when he greets me this way.

"I brought you coffee and donuts." I nod to the box I'm holding. "I don't even know if you drink coffee. I brought you black and figured if you needed to doctor it up, you'd have something in the break room."

"You brought me donuts and coffee?" he asks with a bewildered look on his face.

"Is that okay?"

He nods slowly. His hand slides behind my neck, and he pulls me into another kiss. This one is deeper than the last. "It's more than okay," he says huskily, and the kiss is so good, I'm a melted puddle of goo. "I drink my coffee black, and I love donuts."

"I just got glazed because I wasn't sure and figured everyone likes glazed." I hand him the box.

"You got me a dozen donuts? Babe, this is too much."

I hide what hearing him calling me babe does to me. He can't see my heart fluttering in my chest. "I thought you might want to share."

"Palmer Setty." He shakes his head. "What am I going to do with you?"

*Love me.* Whoa, slow your roll, sister. There will be none of that. "I was grabbing some for myself, and I knew you had a rough day yesterday, and this is going to be a longer week for you than normal."

"Thank you." He kisses me one more time. "I need to get back. I'll text you later when I have time."

"Don't worry about that. I know you're busy saving lives and all that." I give him a wide smile, and he returns it.

"I'll find the time." Another quick peck, and he takes the box from my lap and grabs a coffee from the cupholder. "Thank you for this. It's... thank you."

"You're welcome. Have a good day."

"You too, beautiful." He manages to open the door without

spilling or dropping anything and climbs out. He bends to look at me through the open door. "Drive safe."

"Will do." I wave, and he shuts the door. I don't drive off right away. Instead, I choose to sit in the confines of my Hyundai and admire the man who has managed to capture my heart. I can at least admit that to myself. Now, what I'm going to do about it, I have no idea.

Once I can no longer see him, I head to the studio. I arrive ten minutes before my first appointment, making this morning's unplanned adventure more than worth it. I'm unlocking the front door when my phone alerts me to a message. I flip the sign to Open and walk to my desk.

**Brooks**: Thank you again for my unexpected treat.

**Me:** You're welcome.

The chime on the door alerts me that my nine o'clock shoot is here. I put my phone away and get to work. It's another busy day, but that's a good thing. It's good for business, and it keeps my mind off my situation with Brooks.

I need to do some serious thinking about where this is going and how deep I'm willing to let myself be invested. Heartbreak is inevitable, but the more time I spend with him, the more it's going to crush me when this is over.

## Chapter 17

### BROOKS

"ARE YOU GOING TO TELL me where we're going?" Palmer asks from the passenger seat of my truck.

"We're going to start with breakfast."

"Yum. Where?"

"There's a small diner over in Garrison. They only serve breakfast foods." I'm being evasive on purpose, knowing it will drive her crazy with curiosity. I also just want to surprise her. I want to see the smile on her face.

"Seriously? How do I not know about this place? And Garrison, that's an hour away."

I reach over and place my hand on her thigh. "I know." I can't look at her pretty green eyes to make sure she understands, but she places her hand over mine, entwining our fingers, so my guess is she gets it. I want to spend time with her. Harris is only twenty minutes from Willow River. Sure, we could run into someone we know in Garrison, but it's less likely than Harris. Short of whisking her away for the weekend, which we can't do this weekend, this is the best that I could come up with.

"What are we doing after that?" she asks.

"It's a surprise."

"I could persuade you." She lowers her voice to a sexy purr, and it's tempting me to turn this damn truck around and head to my place, but I don't. I hold strong. I want to spend the day with her. Sure, spending the day with her naked in my arms sounds fun, but just spending time with her does too. That's the plan, and I'm sticking to it.

I chuckle. "Probably, but it's not safe for you to try any of your persuasion skills on me while I'm driving. Let me have this?"

"Fine," she says dramatically, but I can hear the smile in her tone.

She fiddles with the radio and settles on a country station. Before long, we're both singing along with the radio, being silly. We talk about our work weeks and my mom's completed pizza oven. She even retells me about Blakely and her antics when they all took her for ice cream. The conversation never lulls, and there are no awkward moments. It's just Palmer and me being who we are, and I love every second.

"We're here already?" she asks as I park the truck outside the Breakfast Company.

"We are." The time flew for me too, but it always does when I'm spending time with Palmer.

"Cute name. They really only serve breakfast?" she asks.

"Yep. And it's so damn good. Come on." I grab my keys and phone and hop out of the truck. I hold my hand out for her when she meets me at the front, and there is no hesitation when she links her fingers with mine.

Together we make our way inside, and the sign telling us to seat ourselves is on display, so I pull her to a booth in the very back corner.

"Brooks, this place smells like breakfast heaven," she moans.

"Thanks," Roberta, the owner, says, appearing next to our table. "Brooks, I see you chose prettier company today." Roberta laughs.

"That I did. Roberta, this is Palmer. Palmer, this is Roberta. She owns this heavenly place."

"It's nice to meet you, Roberta. I haven't even eaten anything, and I know it's going to be amazing."

Roberta smiles and points at me. "I like this one."

*Me too.*

She turns back to Palmer. "You as well, young lady. What can I get y'all to drink?" Roberta asks.

I nod at Palmer, letting her know she can order first. "I'll take an orange juice and a glass of water, please."

"Brooks, the same?" Roberta asks.

"Yes, please. And a coffee black." She nods and walks away.

"Come here often, do you?" Palmer teases.

"I used to. I went to the Garrison School of Nursing. This place is cheap and has home-cooked breakfast like Mom makes. It was like a taste of home. My brothers would come up and visit and stay with me a lot, and this was a favorite hangout of ours."

"I love how close all of you are."

I nod. "It's a blessing and a curse," I admit. "They're my best friends, but they can also annoy the hell out of me."

"That's what siblings do. At least younger siblings." She grins.

"You're close with Deacon and Piper, right?" I ask her.

"We are close. Of course, Deac is ten years older than me, and Piper is five, so I was the annoying little sister. But you already know that."

"I never considered you annoying."

"Come on now," she prods me. "You can be honest."

"I'd tell you. I never saw you that way. Maybe it's because I lived in a house with eight other kids?" I shrug.

"Maybe, but I'm six years younger than you. Wait, you are twenty-nine, right? I just turned twenty-three earlier this year."

"Yeah, I'm twenty-nine. Six years isn't so bad."

"You think ten is?" she asks.

"I think a lot depends on the couple. When it comes to Deacon and Ramsey, no, I don't think ten years is an issue. They love one another, and their connection is something incredible to see. Almost like watching my parents. So, no, ten years for them isn't too many."

"But you do think it is for some?"

"I guess. I think a lot of factors play a role- maturity, compatibility, communication, just to name a few, but that's all relationships, really."

"Yeah, all of those things are important, age aside."

"Here you go." Roberta sets our drinks on the table in front of us. "Are you ready to order?"

"Sorry, we were talking." Palmer reaches for the menu and skims. "I want it all," she says with a groan.

"How about this: pick your top two. I'll get one, you get the other, and we can share. There is nothing on that menu that I won't devour."

"Are you sure?"

"Positive."

"Okay, well, French toast, and pancakes, oh, and bacon. You can't have breakfast without bacon."

Roberta chuckles. "You're just going to have to make Brooks bring you back to work your way through the menu."

"I like the way you think, Roberta." Palmer smiles kindly, handing Roberta her menu, and I do the same.

"I'll get this put in for you," Roberta tells us, and then she's gone.

"I bet you have a lot of haunts around here from when you were in college."

"Not many. I went home most weekends. This place was my favorite. There's a coffee shop not far from campus where I spent a lot of time consuming coffee and studying. I closed the place down quite often."

"I don't know if I could do your job. Needles, and blood, and all the nursing things." She shudders.

"I think it's just like anything else. You get used to it."

"Yeah, I guess you're right. I'm grateful for those of you who can. And EMTs, those people are rock stars. Some of those accidents..." She shakes her head. "I just don't think that I could do it."

We spend the next few minutes talking about anything and everything. "Here you go." Roberta delivers us two huge plates of pancakes, French toast, and a big plate of bacon.

"Oh my." Palmer's eyes are wide as she looks from the food to me. "How are we going to eat all of this?" She genuinely looks concerned.

"We'll figure it out," I say, patting my six-pack abs.

"You two just holler if you need anything," Roberta says, already walking away to greet another table.

"How do you want to do this?" she asks.

"Just dig in. We can switch later or just eat off each other's plates. I'm easy."

"Are you sure you're okay with that?"

I lean in over the table, and instinctively, she does as well. "Baby, I've tasted every inch of you with my tongue. I'm not worried about sharing my breakfast with you." Her cheeks instantly pink, and my cock twitches.

Palmer eases back in the booth and reaches for her glass of water, taking a big pull. "You can't say stuff like that."

"Am I lying?"

"No. But we're in public."

I chuckle and nod to her plate. "Dig in, beautiful. We have a day of fun to get to."

"Can I have a hint?" she asks, picking up her fork and cutting off a bite of French toast. I watch as she gets her first taste. She closes her eyes and moans, and just like that, I'm hard as stone in the middle of my favorite restaurant.

"Palmer." I swallow hard. She opens her eyes, and she must see the desire in mine. She covers her mouth, swallows, and then mumbles an apology before diving back into her breakfast.

"Here." I fork up a big bite of pancake and offer it to her. She doesn't hesitate to lean over and accept the offered bite.

"Wow," she breathes.

"Scoot over," I tell her.

"What?"

"Scoot over." I stand out of the booth and move to her side, sliding in next to her. I pull my plate in front of me, adjusting my drinks, and turn to look at her. "Now I'm closer. You can have as much as you want of both."

"What if I want bacon?" she sasses.

Reaching over the two plates of food to the plate of bacon, I grab a slice, biting off a huge bite and feeding her the rest.

"Thank you," she says once she's swallowed.

We both dive in, eating off all three plates. I manage to feed her a few more bites, which is not something I can say I've ever done before, other than with my niece. For some reason, with Palmer it feels intimate, and I guess it is.

Roberta stops to refill our drinks. She smiles and winks but doesn't comment. She doesn't have to. She and my mom have talked so many times about my brothers and me finding a good woman. It got to the point that my brothers and I would insist we eat somewhere new when my parents made the drive up. I glance over at Palmer.

*I'm pretty sure I've already found mine.*

"The aquarium?" Palmer asks, not able to hide the excitement in her voice. "This is where we're going?" She unbuckles her seat belt and moves closer to the edge of her seat as if those few inches are going to give her a better view of the building we just pulled up to.

"Yes. I have a few other places we can stop if we have time, but we have no schedule. We can stay here all day if you want."

"Did you know that I love the aquarium?" She turns to look at me, and her smile has my heart doing this crazy thumping thing inside my chest.

Reaching over, I tuck a loose strand of hair behind her ear. "No, I just thought it might be something fun to do."

"Man, I wish I had my camera."

"Cell phone?" I ask.

"Oh, for sure, but it's not the same." She looks kind of bummed, and I instantly want to fix it.

"I'll just have to bring you back."

"You don't have to do that."

I shrug. "You tell me when and we'll make another day of it." The thought of another day like today, when it's really only just begun, excites me too.

"You're the best." She leans over the console and places a loud kiss on my cheek.

"You ready to do this?"

"Yes." Her excitement is contagious. I wasn't sure how she would feel about the aquarium. I wanted something inside so we weren't sweating our asses off. There were a few options, some of which we might explore later, but this is the one that I kept going back to.

Hand in hand, we make our way inside to purchase our tickets. With a wave and a thank you to the man behind the counter, we start the tour. Palmer's eyes light up as she takes in all the fish, the sharks, the turtles, and all the other marine life that swim around us.

"Will you take my picture?" she asks. She steps off the conveyor, hands me her phone, and poses in front of a school of fish.

Before giving it back to her, I step beside her and hold my arm out in front of me to take a selfie. "That's a first for me," I say, handing her phone back. "Will you send me those?"

"Both of them?"

"Yes."

She nods, and her fingers fly across her screen. "You've never really taken a selfie?"

"With Blakely, but she's usually the one running the show, so I don't count that. That's the first time I've ever initiated it. How about that?"

"Aw, Brooksy, I'm your first," she teases.

"Come here." I slide my arm around her neck, pulling her into my chest. I kiss the top of her head before releasing her. "You ready to keep moving?"

"Yes." She grabs my hand and tugs me back to the conveyor belt, and we continue on. Over the next two hours, we take more selfies than I can count and share just as many kisses. Today, I wanted to spend time with her, not being worried about looking over our shoulders, and we accomplished that here.

That's not all that we accomplished. The more time I spend with her, the harder I seem to fall. With each moment between us, I question more and more why we can't make this thing between us real. We get along great. We laugh and have a good time. We have the same interests, and our chemistry is off the charts. She's never given me any hints that she wants to change the rules, but after today. I know that I want to.

"Now where to?" she asks, bouncing on the balls of her feet.

"Well, we have a couple of options. We can go see a movie, ride indoor go-karts, go bowling. We can go to the mall and shop, or we can even go home. My place or yours, but whatever you choose, just know that we're doing it together. You promised me all day, and I intend to collect."

"So needy, Kincaid."

"When it comes to you, yes, yes, I am."

She grins and pops up on her tippytoes to kiss the corner of my mouth. "I vote the mall and a movie. If that's okay?"

"It's our day. We can do whatever you want. I already told you my one rule."

"I've been wanting a new pair of tennis shoes."

"Then we'll start at the mall. Are you hungry yet?"

"No, but we have to get pretzels from that place in the mall. I don't care how full I am. I can never pass those up."

"Shoes and pretzels. Got it." I walk her to her door and open it for her, waiting for her to climb inside.

"Brooks," she says before I get the chance to close the door.

"What's up?" I ask her.

She chews on her bottom lip. "Thank you. For today I mean. It's been so much fun."

"The day's not over yet, beautiful."

"I know, but just in case I forget to tell you, it's been a great day."

How can I not kiss her after that? I can't. So I move in close, lean into the truck, cradle her face with my hand, and kiss the breath from her lungs. At this moment, I couldn't give a fuck less if someone sees me kissing her. I need to. It's not a want at this point. It's a need.

"Every day with you is a great day," I say, pulling back and pecking her nose with a kiss. I step back and make sure she's settled before closing her door and rounding the truck to the other side.

The drive to the mall is short, and we take our time holding hands and shopping. She finds the tennis shoes she's been needing and a couple of bathing suits that were on clearance. I tried like hell to get her to try them on for me, but no such luck. Maybe later when we're at my place.

I grab a couple of new shirts and a new pair of tennis shoes as well. I don't need them yet, but there were on the sale. I spend twelve-hour-plus a day on my feet. Good comfortable shoes are a must.

"Pretzels?"

"Yep." We head toward the small stand that sells soft pretzels and order a large container of the bites to share. "Who knew the aquarium and shopping would be so exhausting."

"Are you ready to head home?"

"Is that okay? We can maybe watch a movie another night?"

"It's fine. My place or yours?" I ask, pushing open the door for her as we walk outside.

"Yours."

"Done."

We chat all the way back to my place, leaving her packages in my truck for when I drop her off later. I lead her to my room, strip her down, and prove yet again why sharing a meal from the same plate isn't an issue. I trace every inch of her soft skin with my tongue before bringing us both over the edge of pleasure.

Today has been the best day.

# Chapter 18

## PALMER

I'M JUST STEPPING OUT OF the shower when my phone rings. I rush to dry off and snatch it from the bathroom counter. Seeing my sister's name, I swipe at the screen, putting the call on speaker. "Hey."

"Why do you sound like you're in a tunnel?" she asks.

I giggle at her confusion. "I just got out of the shower. I'm in the bathroom and have you on speaker."

"Got ya. You're heading over to Orrin's, right?" she asks.

"I haven't really decided yet."

"What? What else are you going to do? Ramsey and Deacon will be there. Mom and Dad are out of town."

"I was going to get caught up on some editing."

"Nope. No way, little sister. Life is too short for you to work all the damn time. We went through this with Deacon, and thankfully Ramsey brought him out of that. You are not going down that path. In fact, I'm going to make sure you come. I'll be there in an hour to pick you up."

"I can drive myself, Piper."

"And risk you not showing? No thanks. I'll pick you up. Well, Heath and I will pick you up. He's driving."

"You know I'm an adult, right?" I ask her, irritated for no real reason.

"See you in an hour, Palmer." The line goes dead. I'm tempted to leave, but I can't do that to my sister, my brother, or my best friend. I just need to pull up my big girl panties and deal. I can hang out with Brooks's brothers and family without him being there. It means nothing. But yet, the guilt still lingers in the back of my mind. It's not fair that I get to be there with his family, and he has to work. I know I sound crazy, but that's my thought process at the moment.

My phone rings again, and I answer, not looking at the screen. "Calling to pass out more orders?"

"Whoa, who do I have to handle?" Brooks asks.

I can tell from the tone of his voice he's being serious. "Sorry. I thought you were Piper."

"What did your sister do to you?"

"Nothing. She's just being bossy pants."

"Palmer?"

I sigh. "She's insisting I go to Orrin's today for the cookout."

"Do you not want to go?"

"It's not that. I just feel guilty. You're working, and I'm spending time with your family."

"I love that big heart of yours, Palmer Setty." He chuckles while I try not to choke on air at him using the word love in any type of reference to me. "That's why I was calling. I'm going to stop by after my shift. I'm hoping to get out early. One of my coworkers who I covered for her vacation needs the money to make up for being on vacation. If her husband gets home in time, she's going to come in and cover two hours of my shift and two hours of other coworkers."

"Can you all do that? Just switch around like that?"

"Yeah, as long as it's not overtime, and the department director knows who to expect to be here and when it's all good."

"So, you're going to be there?" I ask, already feeling my spirit lift.

"Yeah. I was hoping I'd get to see you. Maybe we can sneak some time together?"

"All of your brothers are going to be there, and my brother and sister, so I don't think that will happen."

"Is that a challenge?" he asks playfully.

"It's facts, Kincaid."

"Will you be there?" he asks. I can hear someone calling his name in the background.

"Yeah, Brooks. I'll be there."

"See you soon, beautiful." The line goes dead.

The call is over, but my heart is still beating erratically. I'm too attached. I can already almost feel the cracks in my heart that losing him is going to make. My phone pings with a message. Looking down, I see it's from Piper.

**Piper:** 45 minutes, Palmer!

Her threats mean nothing, but I promised Brooks that I would be there, and that means everything. Placing my phone back on the counter, I rush to my room and pull one of the new bikinis I bought when Brooks and I were shopping, and toss it on the bed. I grab a pair of cutoff shorts, and a tank, adding them to the pile. Quickly, I slip into a bra and panties, and pull my green sundress with flowers off the hanger, tugging it over my head. It's one of my favorites because it brings out the color of my eyes.

Orrin doesn't have a pool, but you always need to be prepared. You never know what you're going to encounter when the Kincaid brothers and my brother put their heads together.

Grabbing a bag from the bottom of my closet, I toss everything inside and place the bag on my bed while I go back to the bathroom to rush through doing my hair.

I finish getting ready with minutes to spare. Making sure I have my phone, purse, bag, and keys, I lock up and head outside. By the time I push open the door to my apartment building, my sister and Heath, who is her officially her boyfriend, pull up to the curb.

I make a mental note to ask her how things are between them. I know something they're not doing. They're not sneaking around behind the backs of everyone they love. It's getting harder and harder to keep this up, but I crave time with him. I feel like if we continue or if we put an end to this, we lose either way. *I* lose either way.

"I feel like I should be bringing something," I say from the back seat of Heath's SUV.

"You are." Piper turns to look at me and points to the floorboard. "I made chocolate chip cookies and brownies. One is for you."

"You rock, Piper."

"I wasn't taking any chances of you trying to back out."

Instead of replying, I sit back in my seat and stare out the window. I'm about to be with Brooks in front of everyone we care about. The last time it was a disaster. Okay, it wasn't really a disaster, but for me it was. I was a nervous wreck, and it took extreme effort to not let on how I feel about him. If he wasn't getting too close, he was ignoring me. I don't know what today is going to hold, but I feel even more lost in him than I was then. I don't know how I'm going to pretend like the man doesn't hold my heart in the palm of his hands.

"Palmer, there's someone we'd like you to meet."

I shield my eyes from the sun, cursing the fact that I walked out of the house without my sunglasses, and peer up at my sister. I'm currently sitting on a lounge chair on the back deck, just soaking up some sun.

My sister comes into view, and I see Heath standing next to her and another guy I've seen around town before but I've never formally met. "Palmer, this is John Mays. He works with Heath down at the fire station."

"Hi." I wave from my seat.

John shocks me when he moves to sit next to me on the lounge chair. "Nice to meet you." He grins.

I glance up at Piper, and she smiles. "We're going to go grab a drink. Do you need anything?" she asks.

"No thanks."

"I'll take a beer," John speaks up.

Piper waves, slides her arm around Heath's, and they move to the other side of the house, where the coolers are in the shade.

"So, Palmer," John leans in close, "we should go out sometime." His eyes are staring directly at my chest when he speaks.

"Palmer!" My name is called in a loud, boisterous voice. I turn my head to see Archer walking my way with purpose. He holds out his hand for me. "You said we could dance."

I open my mouth to ask him what the hell he's talking about, but he gives me a look that tells me he's here to save me. "Sorry, I forgot." I place my hand in his and allow him to pull me from the lounge chair.

"Where's this taking place? I think I need your dance card." John's eyes are once again trained on my tits.

"Sorry, bud. There are nine of us and her brother. Her card's full." Archer doesn't spare him another glance as he slides his arm around my waist and leads me away from the back porch.

"Thank you," I tell him. Archer and I graduated together, so we know each other pretty well.

"Yeah, well, I'm just trying to prevent a war."

"A war?"

He laughs. "Is that how you're going to play it?"

"I don't know what you're talking about?"

"Let's just say, I saved John from getting his ass beat, and I saved you and your tits from being fondled and ogled and whatever else that jackass tried on you tonight. Make sure one of us is with you at all times."

"He works with Heath. He can't be that bad."

"He's probably not, but I don't want to deal with the aftermath. It's a chill night."

"Has anyone ever told you you're confusing as hell?" I say the words with as much light and humor as I can, but inside I'm freaking the hell out. Does he know about us? That's what he's alluding to, right? That if Brooks were to have seen, he would have been pissed off? Would he have been? I mean, I know we said no one else while we were together, but we were just talking. Maybe he's talking about my brother? Deacon can be super protective, and if he saw John's salivating while staring at my chest, he'd definitely be ready to throw hands. Toss out a few words at the very least.

"It's my charm," Archer says with a throaty chuckle. "For the rest of the night, you keep your brother, me, or one of mine close. I don't like that guy."

"My sister introduced us."

"Well, she's been ill-advised to the kind of man he is."

"Who knew you had this protective streak," I tease. "But in all seriousness, he was making me uncomfortable. Thank you for rescuing me."

"Rescuing you from what?" I hear his deep voice behind us.

"Dammit," Archer mutters. Slowly we turn to face Brooks.

"Hey, I thought you had to work?" I ask, pretending like I didn't know he was getting off early.

"Got off early." His eyes bore into mine. "What were you being rescued from, Palmer?" He crosses his strong arms across his chest, and I can't help but swoon just a little. He's wearing a gray T-shirt that I know he wears under his scrubs. His hair is messy, and he's still wearing his scrub pants. He's all kinds of sexy, and it's making it hard for me to concentrate.

"Oh, it's nothing. Archer is just being dramatic."

Brooks steps closer. "Arch?" He doesn't look at his brother.

I hear Archer sigh from beside me, and I know he's going to tell him. "I handled it. Just some guy was hitting on her."

"We're all family here." Brooks finally turns to look at his brother.

"Not all of us." Archer gives a subtle nod to where John is now talking to Jackie, Jade's cousin.

"Did he touch her?" Brooks's voice is calm, but you can hear the underlying threat.

I need to defuse this situation. "Hey." I place my palm flat against his chest. His eyes snap to mine, and they soften. He runs his gaze over me. Not in a creepy way like John, but in a "are you hurt" kind of way. "I'm fine. He was just asking me to get together sometime."

His eyes flash with anger.

"Guys, why don't you step around to the side of the house?" Archer suggests. "I'm going to cause a distraction. You've got maybe five minutes before people know you're missing." He drops his arm from around my shoulders and takes off, running toward the homemade slip and slide. When he gets close, he lets out a loud yell and launches himself down the slide.

Maverick and Merrick yell out and follow him, and suddenly, there's a crowd.

Not caring where we are, Brooks takes my hand and leads me to the side of the house. "You're okay?" he asks, his voice gruff.

"I'm fine. Archer was just being protective."

He nods. His eyes hold mine, and I would give anything to know what he's thinking. "Good," he finally says.

"Does he know about us?" I ask.

He shrugs. "It's hard for me not to watch you when we're in the same room together. My brothers might have caught on to that. I didn't tell them about us. Just told them that I have a crush." The corner of his mouth tilts in a grin, and he reaches out and pushes my hair over my shoulder. "You look beautiful."

I step closer to him. "I'm glad you were able to make it."

He takes another step and places his hands on either side of my back. We're so close I need to do something with my hands, so I wrap them around his neck. My heart is racing because I know anyone could walk around the corner at any time and catch us.

Brooks lowers his forehead to mine. "Can I kiss you?" he asks, his voice low and gritty.

"You never have to ask me that."

He moves in and presses his lips to mine. It's a soft press at first, and then he takes it further, his tongue sliding past my lips and gliding against mine. We could be standing here six seconds, six minutes, or six hours, I'm not really sure. I've lost all track of time. Nothing exists in this moment but the two of us.

This kiss feels different from all the others before it. I wish I could explain how, but I can't seem to find the words in my Brooks induced fog I've suddenly found myself in. He slows the kiss and places his forehead back against mine.

"We should get back out there."

"Yeah," I agree, but neither one of us make an effort to move.

"How long do we have to stay?" he asks me.

"What?" I pull back so I can see his eyes.

"How long do we have to stay here? I want to kiss you and hold your hand and love on you, and I can't do that here. When can we leave?"

"I rode with Piper."

"Damn. All right, well, I guess we should go back to the party." He kisses me one more time before dropping his hands and stepping away. "You go back first. I need a minute."

My eyes fall to his scrub pants and the very obvious erection that the thin material does nothing to hide. "I'm sorry."

He huffs out a laugh. "Baby, never be sorry for making my cock hard. Hell, you do that just by breathing." He reaches his hand out, and I take it. "That's just what you do to me, Palmer. I can't control it, and fuck, I wouldn't even if I could."

"There are a lot of things women have to endure that men don't, but this is one thing we are able to hide well. That's a bonus in our column."

"What are you hiding, beautiful?" He steps closer, his hand still holding mine. "Tell me," he urges.

"I'm wet."

He growls. "Your pussy's wet for me?"

He's asking if it's him or that loser John. I can hear it in the tone of his voice. "Always. Only you," I say, giving him the reassurance it seems like he's searching for.

He pulls me into him, and his hand slides under my sundress. His fingers glide beneath my lace panties, and he groans. "All this is for me?" he asks, running his fingers through my slick folds.

"All. You." I'm already breathless, which is no surprise. This is always my reaction to him.

He slides one long digit inside me, and I grip his biceps to keep myself upright. "Brooks."

"Are you aching, baby?"

"You know I am."

"I've got you." He wraps one strong arm around my waist, holding me close, shielding me. If anyone were to walk around the house in any direction, it would look like nothing but an intimate embrace. They wouldn't be able to see that he has his fingers inside me.

I bury my face in his chest and just hold on for the ride. I know I should be worried about being caught, but the only thing I can focus on is him and how he's making me feel.

"I can feel your pussy squeezing my fingers," he says, his lips next to my ear, keeping his voice soft. "I didn't drag you to the side of the house for this, but I confess I'm not mad about it. I can't resist you." He continues to slide his fingers in and out of me, and the fire begins to burn.

"Brooks."

"Let go, beautiful. I'm right here to catch you. I'll always catch you." He holds me tighter as I explode around him. "Good girl," he says softly. "I've got you, Palmer." My head is buried in his chest, which thankfully muffles my cries of ecstasy.

"I can't believe you just did that." I laugh because, holy shit, that was dangerous.

He places his index finger beneath my chin. "I'd never let anyone see you. You know that, right?" I nod. "You're fucking beautiful. Your face is flushed, and your eyes are all glassy with desire. I want to push you up against this house and do very dirty things to you."

"You have to stop before I let you."

He chuckles as he slowly removes his hand from my panties, and I gasp when he brings them to his mouth and sucks.

"This will hold me over. For now," he adds.

"We should probably separate."

"I'm going around front to slip inside. I have to take care of this." He nods to his erection.

"You want me to?"

"No. Yes. Fuck, we can't. We've been gone long enough. Can you maybe chill on the front porch? I'll slip out the back door when I'm done. Give me five minutes, and you can return to the back."

"Five minutes?"

"That's being generous. That's how worked up I am right now."

"Thank you." I smile up at him. I can only imagine the dopey look on my face.

"We've talked about this. Don't thank me for something that we both enjoy."

We hear voices, and with a shared look, we take off running to the front of the house. I rush up the steps to the porch swing. He leans over, kisses me one more time, and disappears into the house.

# Chapter 19

## BROOKS

I'VE ALWAYS LOOKED FORWARD TO this annual trip with my dad and my brothers. It's been a tradition for as long as I can remember. It's always a good time, but this year it's hitting a little differently. It's not that I don't want to spend time with my family. I do. However, now I also want to spend time with her.

I had to work all last weekend, and my only time with her was our quick rendezvous on the side of Orrin's house. That's not enough. She was busy all week, and we only managed dinner in Harris at the food trucks. She insisted she had to go home and get caught up on edits, and I didn't argue. I know that's her job, but dammit, I miss her.

I look around the campfire at my brothers, and I realize it's not just me who's focusing on his phone, on his girl. Orrin is smiling down at his phone. I'm sure texting Jade. Declan is talking to his daughter, which is the only woman currently in his life, saying goodnight, and then there's Deacon. He's a new addition to this year's trip. Dad insisted that since he was marrying Ramsey, he was one of us now, and guess what? He's on his phone too.

I'm man enough to admit I'm jealous of them. They're openly talking to their women, telling them goodnight and that they love them, and I'm gripping my phone like it's my lifeline, but I can't call her. Not while Deacon is talking to Ramsey and Blakely is talking to Declan.

I can't call her out in the open where my brothers, her brother, and my dad can hear me. We're supposed to be a secret. I hate that we are, but I respect her wishes. However, with each passing day, it's harder and harder not to shout to the world how incredible she is.

Last weekend we could have gotten caught at Orrin's, and although I should have cared, I didn't. I didn't want anyone to see her, but for the rest of it, I couldn't care less. My need for her is too strong to care.

"Oh, and guess what?" Blakely asks, her voice loud through the phone, and I smile. I love my niece. "Palmer's taking my picture. Rams and Piper are doing my hair and Jade's doing my makeup. It's so fun, Daddy!" she exclaims.

I knew Blakely was calling from Palmer's phone. Declan didn't recognize the number, but Blakely told him that since Rams was flirting with Deacon, Palmer said she could use hers. We all got a laugh out of that, even Deacon.

I stand and pretend to be grabbing a drink out of the cooler that's behind Declan and chance a peek at his phone. I try not to let my disappointment show when I don't see anyone but my niece smiling back at me.

"Oh! Uncle Brooks. Hi." Blakely gets closer to the phone and waves. She's so close, all I can see is her nose. I shake my head. "Did you hear that Palmer is taking my picture?"

"I heard, sweetheart," I tell her.

"We all heard you, Blake," Maverick calls out.

"It's so fun!" she says again, making us all laugh.

I stare at my niece over my brother's shoulder. I'm ready to turn and go back to my seat when my girl appears on the screen. My. Girl. My eyes take her in like a man who's been stranded in the desert for hours and was just handed a bottle of water. She hands my niece a juice box and smiles at her like she's her own flesh and blood.

"What do you say, squirt?" Declan asks his daughter.

"Thank you, Palmer."

"You're welcome." Palmer's eyes finally look into the phone, and they land on me. They soften, and she waves. "Hey," she says softly.

Declan turns to look at me over his shoulder, but I ignore him and focus on her. "You ladies having a good time?" I ask. I keep my tone even as if we were discussing the weather.

"So much fun," Blakely answers for her.

"There you go." Palmer grins. "Girls' weekends are the best, huh, Blake?" she asks, wrapping her arms around my niece and hugging her. Blakely giggles and I can't help but smile.

"Blake!" I hear someone call. "It's hair time!" Piper appears in the background holding up a can of hairspray. "Hey, guys, I need to steal the star of the shoot," Piper tells us.

"Daddy, I gots to go. It's girls' weekend. Love you lots." She hands the phone to Palmer, and then she's gone.

"Well, all right then." Palmer smiles at the screen.

"Thanks for letting her call me," Declan says.

"She's such a great kid, Declan."

He nods. "She loves hanging out with all of you. I appreciate it." There is so much he's not saying. So many emotions in that statement. Declan worries about his daughter not having a mother, but we've got her. Mom, Ramsey, and now Jade, and even Piper and Palmer. She's a happy, well-adjusted little girl.

"It's our pleasure. I can confidently speak for all of us. She's a joy."

"She can call anytime," Declan tells her.

"She's going to be fine, Declan," she assures him. "But if she asks to call, we'll be sure to let her. You guys have fun."

My heart races. I'm not ready for her to hang up yet. I haven't told her how beautiful she looks or that I miss her like a fucking limb. I open my mouth to say something, anything, but quickly close it, remembering where I am.

"Have fun, guys." She waves with a wide smile, and then the screen goes black.

Declan shoves his phone back into his pocket and takes a pull off his beer. I force my feet to move as they carry me back to my chair. I drop into it, staring into the fire. My hands itch to call her, to text her, to tell her this hiding is bullshit. I want her to be mine. I want to call her and tell her goodnight and not give a flying fuck who hears me.

I never intended to fall for her.

Yet here we are.

"Are we playing flashligh tag or what?" Maverick asks.

"Tomorrow night," Sterling suggests. "I'm exhausted."

"Pussy," Archer coughs into his hand.

"Who's up for some night swimming?" Merrick asks, tearing his shirt over his head and dropping into his chair.

"I'm in." Maverick stands and does the same. Ryder, Archer, and Rushton all agree as well.

"Y'all too old to have fun anymore or what?" Ryder teases.

"Something like that." Orrin smirks, raising his beer, and then they're off.

"I need another shower," Sterling says. "It was hot as balls today."

"That"- Declan points at him- "is a fine plan."

"Hell yes. I'm in," Deacon announces. They gather their supplies and head to the bathhouse.

"I think I'm going to call it a night," Orrin says as he stands and stretches his arms over his head. "Pops, what are we having for breakfast in the morning?"

"Bacon and eggs on the griddle."

"We've come a long way," I comment. "I remember scrambled eggs and sausage links over a campfire."

"That we have, son. That we have."

"Night." Orrin waves and disappears into his tent.

Dad and I sit in comfortable silence for several minutes when he finally speaks. "What's eating at you, Brooks?"

"Nothing, Pop. I'm good." We both know I'm lying, and I know he's going to call me out on it. I should have just come out with it.

"Bullshit." That's something I love about my parents. They've never let us get away with hiding our emotions, and they're always willing to have the hard conversations.

"I met someone." The confession is not the complete truth, but it feels good to say the words.

He nods. "All those hours you've been working?" he asks.

"I'm sorry. We're keeping it quiet. I have picked up some shifts, but yeah, that's been my reasoning."

"Why are you hiding?"

"We started out as just benefits." I cringe a little admitting that to my dad. If Palmer ever finds out, she'll be pissed.

He nods again, taking a drink of his beer. "And now?"

"Now, the lines are blurred, and hiding doesn't seem like such a strong plan anymore."

"You like her."

This time it's my turn to nod. "It might be more than that."

"Ah." He grins. "Another one of my boys has fallen."

"I'm not sure. I mean, how do you know when it's real?" This is something that's been bouncing around in my head for a few days now. Is it the sex? I mean, it's the best sex of my life. Is that what I'm feeling? Is it more? I know I miss her all the time. Anytime that she's near, I just want my hands on her. I don't care if it's just to hold her hand. I want to touch her. That's more than the sex, right?

"Let me ask you this. The women before her?"

"They don't matter. Hell, I can barely remember a time before her."

"And when those women left your life?"

"It was over. It's never been anything more than a night here or there."

"That's how you know."

"What do you mean?"

"You know it's real when you don't want to stay over. You know it's real when you want to stay. When you want her to stay, so, tell me, Brooks. Do you want her to stay?"

"Always." I think back to all the nights I've asked her to stay over, and she always declines. I've never really given it much thought, but I do want her to stay. Not just so I can wake up with her in my arms the next day. Not just so I can reach for her in the middle of the night and make love to her, although all those things I want. But I want her to stay because I don't want us to be over.

"There you go." He drains the rest of his beer. "You know, we might need to start a new Kincaid family tradition."

"Oh, yeah? What's that?"

"One where we take another trip, but the women who own our hearts get to come too."

"You missing Mom already?" I tease.

"Probably as much as you're missing your girl."

*My girl.*

"You think Mom would be up for that?" I ask him.

"As long as we kept this tradition, the guys' trip, I'd say yes. She'd love to be a part of it."

"You know Blakely's all in." I laugh.

"Don't I know it. I'd say Jade and Ramsey would be too. And what do you think? You think your girl would like it?"

"Yeah, I think she would."

"I'm going to call it a night. I'm too old to stay up this late," he jokes. "You staying up?"

"Yeah. I'll make sure they all make it back."

"Night, son."

"Night, Pop." He tosses his bottle into the tote we bring for recycling and disappears into his tent. I pull my phone out of my pocket and stare at the screen. Finally, I crack and send her a text.

**Me:** Having fun?

**Palmer:** I am. Are you?

*I miss you.*

**Me:** Yeah. The twins, Archer, Ryder, and Rushton, went swimming. I'm staying up to make sure they make it back.

**Palmer:** Such a good big brother.

She sends me a selfie, and she has bright blue eyeshadow all over her face.

**Palmer:** Blakely's handiwork.

**Me:** You're beautiful.

**Palmer:** There is zero chance of getting lucky tonight, big guy. You can save the pretty words.

**Me:** Palmer?

**Palmer:** Brooks.

**Me:** You're beautiful.

Those three dots appear and disappear five times. Yes, I counted all five times, waiting with bated breath for her reply. When it finally comes through, I smile. I know my words got to her.

**Palmer:** Night, Brooks.

**Me:** Night, baby.

Tossing my now-empty bottle into the tote, I grab another and twist off the cap. Sitting back in my chair, I tilt my head toward the sky and look at the stars above. Palmer would love this. Maybe Dad's right. Maybe we add another tradition where we take another trip and get to bring the women in our lives. There would have to be rules. Like you have to be in love with her before she can come. We don't want just anyone breaking into our circle. Kincaid family traditions are sacred.

I'd bring Palmer.

The realization of what I just admitted to myself makes me smile.

"Bro, how many of those have you had?" Sterling asks. "You're smiling up at the sky like it's a naked woman."

"Just enjoying nature."

"Did you smoke something?" Declan asks.

"Fuck you." I chuckle. "You know I don't touch that kind of shit."

"I know, but you're acting all weird."

"Can't a guy just be happy?"

Declan's eyes flash to Deacon. "Yeah, man," he says, "you can be happy. Now you can stay out here and smile at the stars. I'm going to bed."

"Me too," Deacon says. "I told Ramsey I'd call her before bed, so I'm calling it a night."

"Pussy!" Sterling calls out.

"I'll own that." Deacon nods. "I don't care what you call me. Your cousin is about to be my wife. That trumps everything."

"Didn't you just talk to her?" Maverick asks.

"Yep." He waves and climbs into his tent.

I wonder how Deacon would feel if he knew I just realized I'm in love with his sister. I'd like to think that since he's marrying my baby cousin, who might as well be a sister to me, that he'd be okay with it.

*I'm in love with Palmer.*

That's so easy for me to now admit in my head.

My smile is back. "Brooks, bro, that's creepy as fuck. Put that smile away," Sterling jokes just as the rest of my brothers come back from their swim. They gather their things to take to the bathhouse, and those of us remaining disappear into our tents.

I pull up a picture of Palmer on my phone. It's one of the many we took the day at the aquarium. Her emerald eyes are bright and smiling, and it's so clear to me now what she means to me. I don't know how I didn't see it sooner. Then again, I was trying to keep this in the friends-with-benefits category. I've hated that from the start.

It's all making sense.

Now, how do I tell her? How do I tell her that she's embedded herself so far into my heart there's not a chance in hell she's ever finding her way out? I've never told a woman who I'm not already related to that I love them. I saved that for her, and damn, am I glad I did.

"I love you." My softly whispered confession is just for me, but it feels better saying it out loud. Closing out of the image, I shut my eyes, and I can see her clearly. I can see our future as if it's playing out like a movie reel.

It's time to take this to the next level.

# Chapter 20

## PALMER

"YOU WANT TO WATCH ANOTHER one?" Brooks asks. We're in his bed watching a series we started earlier this week. "I should probably get going." I say the words, but I make no effort to move. I don't want to move. I want to stay here under his comforter and in his arms. However, I know how dangerous that is to my heart.

Yeah, who am I kidding? My heart is already screwed. We passed the danger zone weeks ago, and now all I can do is be with him yet try and keep my distance from him at the same time. It's a never-ending cycle, and it's exhausting.

"You could stay over." He pulls me closer, and I feel his lips press against my temple. "You could stay right here in my arms, all nice and warm."

"Sounds tempting." It's beyond tempting. It's what I want more than anything, other than for him to fall in love with me.

"You could wake up the same way. I can make you breakfast." He pauses as if he needs to collect his thoughts. "Your car is already in my garage. No one will know you're here."

That last line is like a dagger through my chest. "I really should go home."

"You really should stay over," he counters.

"I have a lot to do tomorrow."

"Like what?"

"I have grocery shopping, edits to finish for next week, and laundry, and the list goes on and on." That's pretty much the list, but I'm sure I can think of a few other things to keep my mind occupied and off him.

"I make a mean breakfast, Palmer," he says, trying to convince me.

I cover my yawn as I smile.

"Baby, you're dead on your feet. Stay with me. I'll give you a shirt to sleep in, and tomorrow I'll get up early and make you breakfast, and I'll even help clean or do your laundry or whatever you need to do. It's too late, and you're too tired to be driving home."

"Okay." I tell myself it's for safety purposes, but really, I just want to know what it's like to fall asleep with him wrapped around me and what it's like to wake up the same way.

"Okay?"

"Yeah. If you're sure it's okay?"

He wiggles around, taking me with him, and I somehow end up on my back. He's hovering over me, and his smile is one I want to always remember. "You're welcome here anytime. Whenever, however, I don't care."

"Thank you."

He bends his head and kisses me. It's a soft peck on my lips. "I'll get you something to sleep in and go make sure the house is locked up."

"You did that before we came to your room. Remember, you wanted to make it look like you weren't home in case one of your brothers decided to drive by or stop by."

"I know, but you're staying here, and I just want to make sure." He flashes me a grin before climbing off the bed. He makes his way to his dresser and tosses me a T-shirt. "I'll be right back," he says, and then he's gone.

Tossing back the covers, I strip down to nothing but my panties and pull his T-shirt on over my head. I walk into the bathroom just as he comes back into the bedroom. He stops at the bathroom door, lifting his arms over his head and holding onto the frame. His eyes take their time drinking me in.

"Toothbrush?"

"There are extras in the bottom drawer. I get a new one from the dentist but never used them since mine is one of those expensive rechargeable ones. I save them usually for when my brothers are here."

"Thank you for the shirt." I pull at the hem and peer up at him.

"You look sexy as fuck right now, Palmer."

I gasp. "You mean I don't always?" I tease.

"Always, baby." He drops his arms and advances on me. He spins me around and lifts me to the counter, stepping between my legs and kissing the breath from my lungs. "You're always beautiful, but there is a little something extra seeing you in my clothes."

"I mean, I do make this shirt look good," I joke. "It has to be my bedhead from lying around all day, or maybe it's my lack of makeup that really sets off the ensemble."

"You know, my dad always says, tell her she's beautiful even at her worst."

I pinch his stomach, and he laughs. He cradles my face in the palm of his hands. "You're beautiful, Palmer. Inside and out. I don't care if you're in my T-shirt or dressed for a fucking ball. No makeup, face full of makeup, messy hair, or primped to perfection. You. Are. Beautiful."

"I'm a sure thing, Kincaid."

"Just for that, no sex tonight."

"But I'm staying over."

"And that means we have to have sex? I remember telling you that I'd hold you all night and make you breakfast in the morning. Never once in that conversation did we talk about my cock and your pussy."

I blush, and he smirks. "I just assumed."

"Well, you know what they say about people who assume..." He grins, lifts me from the counter, and smacks my ass. "Finish getting ready for bed. We have snuggling to get to."

"Pass me the toothpaste," I say, tearing open the pack on the new toothbrush. He's standing in front of one of the two sinks. I watch as he places some toothpaste on his brush before passing it to me. Together, we stand in his bathroom brushing our teeth, it's very couple-ish, and I don't hate it. Not even a little. My heart, however, hurts just a little. I want so bad for this to be my reality. What am I doing? I can't keep this up, or there will be nothing left of me.

When we finish, Brooks turns out the light and, with his hand on the small of my back, leads me back to his bed. "What side do you want?"

"Um, yours?" I say, making him laugh. "I mean, I just want to be curled up next to you." I feel my face heat. "I don't care what side I'm on."

He kisses my temple and pulls back the covers. "Get in, baby." He waits for me to slide under the covers before turning off the bedside lamp and joining me. He instantly pulls me into his arms and keeps them locked around me tightly. "Why haven't we done this before now?" he asks.

"I didn't want to blur the lines."

"Yeah," he says over a yawn. "Night, beautiful."

"Night."

I'm warm. So incredibly warm, and I can't move. My eyes pop open to find bright blue ones smiling at me. "Hi," I croak.

"Morning, beautiful." Brooks leans in and kisses the tip of my nose. "Did you sleep well?"

"I did." I bury my face in his chest. I'm suddenly too overwhelmed with emotions. This is more than I ever expected and everything I ever wanted. Staying over was a bad idea. A very bad idea. I'm going to crave his arms around me every night moving forward. I let my guard down and made this worse for myself.

"I know I promised you breakfast, but I wanted you right here in my arms when you woke up. Just like I promised."

*Oh, Brooks.* He's such a good guy. His words have my heart soaring, but I have to keep reminding myself that's just who he is. He's one of the good ones, and he doesn't know any other way to be. It's not me. There is nothing special about me. He's just an all-around nice guy.

"You hungry?" he asks.

"Yes. What time is it?"

"Just after eight."

"I never sleep this late."

"You were tired."

"Yeah," I agree half-heartedly. I can't tell him it was the comfort and safety of his arms that had me sleeping this morning.

"You stay here and wake up. I'm going to go make us breakfast." He kisses my forehead before climbing out of bed and making his way to the bathroom. I hear the toilet flush and the water in the sink turn on. He peeks his head out, his toothbrush in his mouth. "Bacon and eggs?" he asks, removing the brush just long enough to ask before popping it back in his mouth.

"That's perfect." I nod. He gives me a toothpaste smile before disappearing back into the bathroom, only to appear a few seconds later. "Breakfast coming right up." He winks as he strolls out of his bedroom wearing nothing but his black boxer briefs.

Closing my eyes, I will my tears not to fall. I know what I have to do, and it's killing me inside. I need to distance myself from him. I'm already hurting, and we're still together. I love him. He owns my entire heart, and it's time I realize that I'm not as strong as I thought I was.

Forcing myself to get it together, I make my way to the bathroom, take care of business, and brush my teeth. I debate on getting dressed but decide against it. I need to make the most of my time with him today, because moving forward, there will be less and less until we are no more. It hurts to even think that way. So much so that it stalls the breath in my lungs.

"Today," I whisper as I pad on bare feet toward the kitchen.

I find him standing with his back to me, scrambling eggs in a bowl. I don't stop until I'm behind him, pressing a kiss to his bare back. He glances over his shoulder at me and smiles. "You're supposed to be resting."

"I missed you." The words flow easily from my mouth, spoken from my heart. Something I know I might regret in the coming days when the pain is too much to bear. I let my hands roam over his muscular arms, his shoulders, and around his waist, holding him to me.

Brooks stops what he's doing and turns toward me. He pushes my hair back over my shoulder before reaching for the hem of his shirt and lifting it. Without being told, I lift my arms high in the air, allowing him to remove the T-shirt. I don't pay attention to where it lands. I can't. Not when his hands grip my ass through my lace panties, and he pulls me into him. His cock is already hard and pressing against my belly. He doesn't seem to mind as he kisses me, letting his hands roam everywhere they can reach.

He kisses my neck while testing the weight of my bare breasts in the palms of his hands. I moan when he gently traces my nipples with his thumbs. His mouth is back on mine, hot and wet, demanding entrance that I willingly give him. My hands roam over his chest, across his washboard abs, and over his boxer briefs. I palm his cock through the thin fabric and feel it twitch beneath my palm.

Our kisses are urgent.

Our hands are frenzied as we grapple for one another.

It's not enough. I need more. Decision made, I drop to my knees, staring up at him under my lashes.

"Palmer?"

I don't speak. Instead, I let my actions do the talking and slide my fingers into the waistband of his boxer briefs and pull them over his thighs. He kicks them off and braces his hands behind him on the counter. I waste no time tasting just the tip.

"Fuck. Palmer, babe, what are you doing?"

My hands grip his thighs as I take more of him into my mouth. That's my reply. I take my time, taking more of him with each pass until my head is bobbing up and down his cock, and his thighs are trembling beneath my grip. Moving my hands, I grip him tightly, stroking him with each pass, enjoying the taste of him on my tongue.

"Fuck," he moans as he buries his hands in my hair. His grip is firm, but it doesn't hurt. He slowly starts to pump into my mouth, and a gush of desire rushes between my thighs. "Damn, that's fucking hot," he grits out, still guiding my mouth onto his cock. "Enough," he says, his voice gravelly. "On your feet, beautiful."

I glance up and see the desire all over his face. Doing as he asks, I stand and face him. He quickly steps around me and pushes me closer to the counter. I glance over to see what he does next, and he drops to his knees behind me. I feel a kiss pressed to one ass cheek and then the other before he lightly smacks.

"These need to go," he says, pulling at my panties. I assume he's going to help me out of them, but then I hear the material tear and know that's not the case. More heat rushes to my pussy. That was so damn hot; I'll be reliving that experience in my mind for the rest of the days I have on this earth.

He strands, trailing kisses up my back before he kisses just under my ear before he whispers, "Brace yourself on the counter." I do as he says, anticipation getting the best of me. I don't have to wait long before he pushes my back down, my tits now flat against the cold counter. I miss the heat of his body pressed to mine instantly, when drops back to his knees. He grips my ass with each hand, and then I feel his mouth on me. He's slow at first, nipping and licking, then without warning, he sucks my clit into his mouth, and I can't help the moan that fills the kitchen. It's worthy of an Oscar, but so is his performance.

Reaching behind me, I grip his hair and hold him to me. He moans, and that sound sends red-hot pleasure coursing through my veins. "Brooks," I moan as he removes his mouth and replaces it with his fingers. He stands to his feet and aligns his body with me. We're both leaning over the counter while he fucks me with his fingers.

My orgasm hits me like a fast-moving train as I grip the counter and call out his name. "Good girl," he says, his lips kissing my neck. "Fuck. I need a condom. Baby, don't move," he says, starting to pull away.

"No. Don't go. I'm on the pill."

"You sure?"

"Please, Brooks." Even I can hear the desperation in my tone.

Wrapping his fist around my hair, he aligns himself at my entrance and slowly pushes inside. "Ho-ly fuck," he pants. He pulls out and slowly pushes back in. Each stroke grows faster until he's full-on fucking me, my hair still gripped in his fist. He slaps at my ass with his free hand, and my pussy convulses, close to coming for the second time in a matter of minutes.

"Give it to me, Palmer. I want to feel you come on my cock." His dirty words are like a magic orgasm button because, not seconds later, my orgasm rips through me like a hurricane. "That's it. Milk my cock," he praises.

When he pulls out, I whine like the hussy that I am for him. He turns me around, taking a few steps back and lifting me onto the island. He slides back inside me easily while his mouth latches onto my breast. He kisses one, then the other, sucking my hard, aching nipples into his mouth. I grip his shoulders, and my legs are locked tightly around his waist, just holding on for the ride.

He slides his hand behind my neck and pulls my mouth to his. Our bodies are slick with sweat, and our breathing is labored as the stroke of his tongue matches the rhythm of his hips. When he pulls away, he keeps his grip on the back of my neck and stares deep into my eyes. I whimper from the look and the way my heart is shattering.

"I'm gonna come," he grits out and tries to step back, but I keep my legs locked around him. "Palmer," he groans. "Babe, I'm close."

I want to tell him to come inside me, but I know that's risky, and after my realization before coming out here and starting all of this, if we were to have an unexcepted surprise, that wouldn't be fair to either of us. With that knowledge, I unlock my legs, placing my feet flat on the counter, opening myself to him.

"Fuck me. You're trying to kill me." He thrusts hard. Once, twice, three times, before he's pulling out and finishing himself off all over the kitchen floor.

His body shudders, and then he's once again giving me his full attention. "You, Palmer Setty, are unexpected." He leans in and kisses me so tenderly that it brings tears to my eyes.

"I should go get cleaned up."

"Shower with me?"

I nod my agreement, and before I can move to jump off the counter, he lifts me into his arms, bridal style, and carries me to his room. He sets me on my feet once we're in the bathroom. He reaches in to turn on the water before placing our towels on the closed toilet seat.

Testing the water and feeling it's warm enough, I step under the spray and close my eyes. I feel him move in behind me and hear the curtain closing us in. "Let me take care of you, and then I'm feeding you breakfast."

I keep my eyes closed and my back to him to hide my emotions, but I nod. He does exactly what he said. He washes my hair and cleans my body with the utmost care before wrapping me in a towel, leaving me with a soft kiss before he makes his way back to the kitchen to salvage breakfast.

# Chapter 21

## BROOKS

IT'S BEEN FOURTEEN DAYS.

Fourteen days since the best sex of my life.

Fourteen days since I slid into the woman I love with nothing between us.

Fourteen days since I've seen her.

I'm going out of my mind. I don't know how to handle this separation. Our work weeks have been crazy, and then I had to work last weekend. By the time I got home and showered, she was already busy with something. She was with her parents one night, and then the next, she was dress shopping with Ramsey and my mom. My mom has seen my girl, and I haven't.

That changes today.

Palmer and I have plans to go to the food trucks at Sunflower Park. My idea is to take us back to where it all began and then bring her back to my place. We'll sit out on the back patio and stare up at the stars, my girl in my arms, and I can tell her that I'm in love with her. She's never said it, but I'm pretty certain she feels the same way. I mean, she let me inside her body without anything between us. That speaks volumes, right? She trusts me, and when she looks at me, I swear I can see love in her eyes.

She had a shoot this morning, much to my dismay. I've cleaned my entire house, done my laundry, and been to the grocery store, and I'm still pacing the floors waiting for the clock to strike six, so I can leave to pick her up. We agreed on six thirty, but I'm going to be early. I can't take being away from her any longer.

I should have told her that day. I didn't because I didn't want her to think I was professing my love because of the phenomenal sex. I want to tell her when it's just us, being us, doing nothing in particular. I want it to be real and genuine and not attached to anything involving her pussy. That's how we started, with benefits, and I don't want to tell her I'm in love with her with sex. I want to tell her I love her with my heart. So, yeah, I didn't say those three little words that day, even though I felt them in my bones.

My cell rings, so I stop pacing and pull it from my back pocket. "Hey," I greet my oldest brother.

"What are you getting into tonight?" he asks.

"Oh, uh, nothing much. What's up?" I hate all this fucking lying. Palmer and I need to clear the air, so I can tell my family that she's the one for me.

"Nothing. I just haven't talked to you in a while. You've been pretty busy lately." Guilt floods me. I hate lying to my brothers and my parents. Hell, I hate lying, but for her, I would. I did. I agreed to this mess, and it's time I make it right.

"Work's been kicking my ass." It's not a complete lie, work has been hectic, and I have picked up a few shifts for various coworkers for vacations and sick kids.

"I hear that."

"How are things at the shop?" I ask.

"Good. Business is good. Too good." He chuckles. "I don't have time for the passion project I started because we've been so busy."

"That's a good problem to have, brother."

"That's what I keep telling myself."

"What are you getting into tonight?" I ask.

"Nothing that I know of. Jade spent the day with Piper. They went shopping, so she's coming over, and we're probably just going to hang out here."

"You not taking your girl out to dinner?"

"I do, but we're just not going to do that tonight. She's had a crazy week, and I've missed her, so I kind of want her all to myself," he admits. "I know that I sound crazy, but I'm telling you, brother, when you meet the right one, you'll understand. I'd take staying in with her any night over going out without her."

"I might know a little something about that," I confess.

"Yeah? Palmer?" he asks.

"Palmer," I confirm.

"Are you finally going to man up and take your shot?" he asks.

I chuckle. If he only knew. "Something like that."

"Good for you, Brooks," he says, his voice serious. "I hope it all works out for you. Everyone should feel this."

"Feel what?" Part of me is goading him to get him to say it. The other part just wants the validation that what I'm feeling is right.

"The love of a good woman."

"Who said anything about love?" I ask.

"Come on, man," he chides. "I know you. This has been eating at you for weeks. You're not one to play games, so if you're going all in with Deacon's little sister, there has to be love, or at least something close to it."

"Why'd you say it like that? Deacon's little sister. He's marrying our little cousin."

"He is," Orrin agrees. "He was also open and honest with us about it."

"Fuck. I just... I'm going to talk to her tonight. If all goes well, I'll call Deacon."

"I think that's a good idea. He needs to hear it from you."

"Yeah," I agree.

"Let me know how it goes. If you need me, you know where to find me."

"Thanks, O."

"Love you, brother." The line goes dead before I can tell him that I love him too.

I think about our conversation, and he's right. Deacon never hid his intentions or his affection for Ramsey. I can't say the same, but it was something we agreed to, Palmer and me, and after tonight, I hope she agrees that I can call her brother and tell him before I shout it to the world.

I don't expect her to tell me that she loves me too. I am hopeful she will, but at the very least, I want her to agree that this is real. That *we* are real, and we no longer have to hide that we're together. At least, I hope not.

Glancing at the clock, I see that it's five minutes before six. Close enough. Grabbing my keys, making sure that I have my wallet and my phone, I head out to pick up my girl.

"Hey, beautiful." I lean over and kiss her lips before she can even get her seat belt buckled.

She smiles. "Hey, big guy."

"How was the shoot?"

"A lot of fun actually. It was a family of six. They have three boys and a girl, and the kids were a blast. They ranged from twelve to three, and it's easy to see that they keep their parents on their toes."

"I know how that is," I tell her. "You did the shoot at their place?"

"I did. They wanted the kids to feel comfortable to capture their personalities. We did a few formal shots where the kids were dressed up. Then they changed into whatever they wanted. The little girl, she's six, she wore a princess dress, while the brothers wore T-shirts and shorts, even though it was a little chilly out today. They were all goofing off and riding bikes in the driveway. I got some great candid shots with all of them. I can't wait to start editing."

Reaching over, I grab her hand, bringing it to my lips. "I'm glad it turned out good, but I'm also glad it's over. I've missed you." I let the confession fly free without a care in the world. No more holding back. Not anymore.

"I missed you too." Her voice is soft.

"I hope you're hungry," I tell her. "I think we need to get one of everything."

She laughs, and the sound washes over me like a cool mist on a hot summer's day. "I think you already know I can hold my own."

"Have you been dreaming about a funnel cake?" I tease her.

"No, but it's definitely on the list."

"I wouldn't dream of leaving Harris without getting my girl a funnel cake," I say with mock horror.

She doesn't comment on the fact that I just called her my girl, but that's okay. I didn't really expect her to. In just a few short hours, she's going to know where that comment originated from, and then we can make it official. I bring her hand to my lips again and kiss her knuckles to calm myself down. I'm ready to just pull this fucking truck over to the side of the road and confess all right here. Right now.

But I won't. I have a plan, and I'm going to stick to it. A few more hours of holding my tongue won't kill me. Besides, I think holding her in my arms beneath the stars is the perfect way to tell her what she means to me. To tell her that I've given her my heart and I never want it back.

"What did you do today?"

"Other than missing you? Cleaned, did laundry, and went to the store. Just adulting like a boss." I chuckle.

"I need to do all of that too."

"I can help."

She gives my hand a gentle squeeze. "I appreciate that, but you and I both know that you being parked at my apartment is a red flag."

"I can ride with you."

"You don't have to go through all of that, Brooks. My place is tiny compared to yours. It doesn't take me long."

"I don't mind. That's just more time we get to spend together."

"I'm sure you have better things to do," she says, turning to stare out the window, as I guide my truck into a parking spot at Sunflower Park.

I put the truck in Park and kill the engine before turning to look at her. On instinct, I reach out and touch her, not only because she's close but because I feel the need to be closer to her. "There is nothing better than you."

"You're full of pretty words today. What's gotten into you?" She shakes her head as if she's not sure if aliens have taken over my body.

She's not acting like herself. Rushing to clamber out of the truck, I catch up to her, sliding my arm around her waist.

"Brooks." She steps away. "We're only twenty minutes from Willow River."

"Okay?"

"We could see someone that we know."

"Would that be such a bad thing?" I ask her.

"No, but if you're holding me, it might be. How would we explain that?" she asks before taking another step away from me. "Are we going to divide and conquer again?" she asks, smiling as if she didn't just verbally slap me.

Yes, that's a little dramatic, but I'm on the verge of confessing my love for this woman, and she seems dead set on the fact that this isn't real and that no one can find out about us. She's smiling at me, and it's her smile, it's real and genuine, so maybe that's just her fear talking. Maybe it's my fear talking. I've never been this tied up in knots over a woman before. I probably should have called my dad for a few words of advice on my way over to pick her up. He always knows what to say.

"Brooks?"

"Yeah, we can divide and conquer. It's getting colder. You want to eat inside the truck?"

"That works for me. I'm going left. You go right." She grins and takes off for the fry truck.

"I'm so full," Palmer groans from the passenger seat. "I think we ate more than last time."

"You still need to get your funnel cake," I remind her.

"Oh, no. I can't. I feel like I'm going to explode." She gathers our trash and puts it all into one bag. "It was that last deep-fried pickle that pushed me over the edge."

"You hang tight. I'm going to go throw this away, and I'll grab you a funnel cake to take home."

"You don't have to do that."

"I want to." I tuck her hair back behind her ear. "You can warm it up in the oven when you're ready to eat it."

"Brooks, you don't—" Her words are cut off when I press my lips to hers.

"I'll be right back, baby." I kiss her one more time before grabbing our bag of trash. I toss it in a nearby can and get in line to order one of her beloved funnel cakes.

"Here you go," I say five minutes later.

"Thank you. You didn't have to."

"What's wrong?"

"I don't feel well."

"What can I do?"

"I think I just need to go home and lie down."

"Let me take you to my place so I can take care of you."

Her eyes soften, and she reaches over and places her hand on my cheek. "That's sweet of you, but really, I think something I ate didn't sit well. I just need to lie down for a while."

"I'll stay with you."

"It's okay. I'll be fine. I'm just going to be sleeping."

"This is the first time I've laid eyes on you in two weeks. I'm not ready to let you go just yet," I confess. I'm trying really hard not to let my disappointment show. Tonight was supposed to be the night. I get that she's not feeling well, but I want to take care of her. Doesn't she see that? I don't care if I hold her the entire time she sleeps or I just sit and stare at her. I'll be with her. That's all that matters.

"I really do think it's best if I just go home. Alone," she adds.

I sigh, defeated. "Okay. If that's what you want." I wait for her to buckle up before pulling out of the lot and heading back to Willow River. My hand is on her thigh the entire drive, and her eyes are closed. I can see she's not feeling well, and I hate that I'm irritated that my plans are shot to hell. That's selfish, and I know it.

When I pull into her apartment complex, I put the truck in Park and gently rub her arm to wake her up. "Hey, sleepyhead. We're here."

She sits up and looks around. "Thank you for tonight. I'm sorry I'm bailing on you."

"It's not too late to change your mind. I can come up for a little while, or we can go back to my place."

"Thank you, Brooks, but I'm just going to go upstairs and go to sleep."

I nod, accepting that my night is not turning out as I had hoped. "Call me if you need anything. I don't care what time it is. If you need me, or anything at all, you call me. Understand?"

That gets me a soft smile. "Thank you." She reaches for her handle and starts to get out.

"Wait, don't forget this." I hand her the to-go container that holds her funnel cake.

"You're too good to me, Brooks Kincaid. Goodnight."

"I'll walk you to your door," I tell her, but she raises her hand to stop me from getting out of the truck.

"That's risky. Thank you for the offer, but I'm okay. Night, big guy."

"Night, beautiful." She closes the door, and I watch her until I can no longer see her. I sit here in the parking lot a hell of a lot longer than I should, but leaving her when she's not feeling well seems wrong. My phone pings with a text.

**Palmer:** Thank you for the funnel cake. I'm settled. You can go home now.

I smile. She knows me too well.

**Me:** Anything for you. Feel better.

She doesn't reply, and I don't really expect her to. Knowing that I can't sit out here all night like a creeper, I put my truck in Drive and head home. Instead of holding the woman I love and telling her so, I'm going to be sitting on my back porch nursing a beer all on my own. I'm disappointed, but I also want her better. Besides, we have forever.

At least I hope we do.

## PALMER

"Sorry I'm late." Piper comes rushing into the small area of the boutique that's reserved for us today. She plops down on the couch next to me and exhales. "There was an accident that blocked the road. Heath said that everyone was okay."

"Is he allowed to give you that information?" I ask her.

"He didn't give me names or anything. Just said that everyone was okay."

I nod. "He has a tough job."

"Yeah," she agrees. "What did I miss?"

"Nothing yet," Carol Kincaid tells her. "She's in trying on her first dress."

Is it awkward to be sitting with Brooks's mom while hiding the fact that I've been sleeping with her son for months and, oh yeah, that I'm in love with him? You bet your ass it is. I'm glad my sister finally showed up to be a buffer between us.

"Did she tell you that they finally picked a date?" Piper asks.

"She did. She insisted on picking me up. She told me all about it on our way to collect Carol."

"So romantic," Carol says.

"I'm still calling dibs on naming their firstborn after me."

"What if it's a boy?" Piper laughs.

"Palmer is a universal name. I can see it going either way," I tell them, making them laugh.

"Are you ready?" Ramsey calls out.

"We're ready," the three of us call back.

Ramsey steps out from around the corner and up onto the small platform surrounded by mirrors. Instead of looking at the dress, I watch my best friend's face as her lip quivers.

"Oh, Ramsey," Carol sobs. "Sweetheart, you're stunning."

"This was my favorite one out of all of them, so I tried it first, and I—" She pauses and turns on the platform to face us. "This is the one."

"You know you have the right to be a bridezilla," Piper teases her.

Ramsey laughs. "We're getting married at Willow Park on the two-year anniversary of the day we met." She looks down at herself in the dress. "This dress is everything I imagined when I think about our day."

"It's the classic A-line V-neck with a bodice of embroidered lace motifs atop a tulle floor-length skirt." The boutique attendant rattles off the technical details of the dress.

"Deacon is going to be beside himself," I say, feeling myself get choked up. "He loves you so much, Rams. I love you. I can't believe my best friend is going to be my sister."

"And mine." Piper leans her head on my shoulder.

"I'm so proud of you, sweetheart," Carol tells her. "Thank you for letting me be a part of this process. I'd like to think that the women my sons choose as wives one day would allow me to be involved, but this might be my only chance for something like this. I love you, sweet girl."

A flash of Brooks standing at the altar while I rush down the aisle to him flashes in my mind. It causes sharp pain in my chest. I've been distancing myself from him. So much so that even last weekend, I cut our night short, claiming I didn't feel well. It wasn't a complete lie. My heart was hurting. He was being so sweet, telling me he missed me and spewing sweet words. It's like he knew I was thinking about calling off our little deal to preserve what might be salvageable of my heart, so he pulled out the big guns. My heart was cracking wide open. I went back to my place and cried myself to sleep.

"I love you too, Aunt Carol."

"So, do you want to try on the next one?" the attendant asks.

"No." Ramsey's smile is radiant. "I don't need to try on any other dresses. This is the one."

"Well, all right then. I think you might just be the easiest bride I've ever worked with," she jokes.

"It's not really about the dress. It's the man." Ramsey's eyes flash from me to Piper. "I love your brother with all that I am. I'm honored to have you both here with me today. My sisters," she says, her voice cracking.

"Now you've done it." I stand and go to her, wrapping her in a hug. I feel arms around me, and I know without looking that it's my sister.

"Got room for one more?" Carol asks. She joins us, and the four of us start to laugh.

"Well," Piper says, stepping back and wiping under her eyes, "we planned for all day, but Ramsey is a super bride. So now what?"

"Well, how about we go to my place? Deacon is there with all my boys helping Raymond put a new railing on the back deck. We can pick up some food, something easy like pizza, and take it back with us."

"Perfect." Ramsey's quick to reply. "Are you two good with that?"

Piper's phone alerts her to a message, and I watch her as she reads it. "The guys got called out to another fire. I think I'm going to go to the firehouse and make them dinner to come back to.

Heath says they went from the accident to the fire, so they're all starving. They're almost finished." She looks up at us. "What do I make a bunch of hungry firefighters?"

"Spaghetti," Carol answers. "It's cheap, filling, and it goes a long way."

"Oh, good idea." Piper looks at Ramsey. "Raincheck?"

"Of course. Do you need help?"

"No. I'm good. Thank you. And the dress is beautiful. Palmer's right. Deacon is going to lose his mind when he sees you."

Ramsey grins. "I hope so. Thank you for being here today."

"Nowhere else I'd rather be. Oh, I was supposed to tell you that Mom said she's sorry she didn't make it and she would make the next one. I guess the joke's on her." Piper laughs. "That's what they get for taking yet another cruise."

"Hey," Carol defends them. "They're retired. In fact, I need to tell my husband it's about time we take a few days away."

"If it was me, and Deacon wanted to get away, I'd be there too. I don't blame her." Ramsey smiles. "Okay, let me get out of this dress and have them ring it up, and then we're off."

"I'll order the pizzas," Carol says.

"I'm buying." Ramsey points at her. "Don't think I don't know that you're going to march over to that desk and buy this dress when you know I don't need you to. Deacon tells me that I need to let you, and you can close your mouth." Ramsey laughs. "I know you, Aunt Carol, you are a kind, loving soul, and I'm forever grateful to you and Uncle Raymond for accepting me into your family."

"You were always family, Ramsey." Carol wipes her eyes.

"You know what I mean. Anyway, if you insist on buying this dress, then I insist on buying pizza."

"Fine." Carol sticks her tongue out at Ramsey playfully.

"Those cousins of mine are rubbing off on you," Ramsey jokes, pulling her aunt into a hug. "I'll be right back."

"She's my daughter," Carol says, blinking away tears. "I will never understand the decisions of my sister, but in my eyes, and in Raymond's, Ramsey is our girl." She turns to face me. "I mean, what's one more when you already have nine rowdy boys."

"You are one hell of a woman, Carol Kincaid." It's on the tip of my tongue to tell her she's raised nine amazing men, one in particular that I'm pretty fond of, but I keep it to myself. Instead, I focus on how I'm going to get through the afternoon, hanging out with him at his parents' place. He's been begging for us to get together all week. Offering to come to my place or take me to dinner, and I've claimed to be too busy every time. I know he's not impressed with me, and well, I'm not sure how he's going to act, but we're about to find out.

I've been hiding in the kitchen for the past fifteen minutes, so basically, since we got here. I've kept myself busy with marking the pizza boxes and helping Carol with paper plates, napkins, and anything else I can think of to avoid going outside with the rest of them.

"Palmer, I've got this. Go on outside with the others."

"I don't mind helping."

"Mamaw," Blakely says, coming into the room. "I gots to go potty, and it's stuck." She pulls at the bib overalls she's wearing.

Carol smiles at me. "I'll be right back." She takes Blakely by the hand, and they rush off down the hall to go potty.

Letting out a heavy sigh, I brace my hands on the counter just as the back door opens, and Brooks walks in. He smiles, but I can see that it's not his happy-to-see-me smile. He's uncertain.

"Hey, beautiful," he greets.

"Hi, big guy." I smile. I can't seem to stop myself.

"Are you hiding in here?"

Yes. "No, I was helping your mom get set up. She just took Blakely to the potty."

He nods as he comes to stand next to me. He bends over and kisses the corner of my mouth. "I've missed you." He then presses his lips to my forehead before standing and taking a few steps back, putting some distance between us.

"I'm sorry." There is so much to that apology that he doesn't understand, but he will soon enough. I just can't keep going like this. My heart is unraveling with each passing day, waiting for the day he's done. I have to be the one to do it. I can't keep waiting and wondering. It's killing me.

"How was dress shopping?"

"Good. She found the one. The first one she tried on, actually. A bridezilla she is not."

"I could never see Ramsey being a bridezilla. She's just too nice for that."

"Yeah," I agree. "I think her upbringing put a lot of that pretentious stuff in check for her. She knows what's important. The day, the man, and their forever." I almost choke on the words because my mind once again flashes to me in a white dress walking toward him.

"I'd say you're right." He pauses, looks over his shoulder, and back to me. "Can I see you tonight?"

"I have lots of edits to work on, and I rode with Ramsey. I'm not sure how long we'll be here."

He nods. "I'm not sure either. But if it's not too late, hell, even if it is, I want to see you."

"Can we just play it by ear?" I ask him.

He opens his mouth to reply and thinks better of it, quickly closing it and nodding. "Okay."

"Uncle Brooks, we're having pizza!" Blakely rushes toward him, and he bends to catch her in his arms, setting her on his hip.

"I can see that."

"Oh, Palmer, can you spend the night with me?"

Brooks chokes on a laugh.

"Yeah, Palmer, I'm sure Declan won't mind," Merrick says, coming up behind Brooks and tickling Blakely, making her squirm in his arms.

Brooks sets her back on her feet and crosses his arms over his chest, glaring at his little brother. "Or not." Merrick holds his hands up in defense.

"I'll go ask him." Blakely rushes to the back door, pushes it open, and yells, "Daddy, can Palmer spend the night with us?"

I hear raucous laughter from the backyard, and that earns a growl from Brooks.

"He's been an ass lately," Merrick says, not bothering to lower his voice.

"Merrick." Brooks's voice is laced with anger.

"I don't think so, sweetheart." I hear Declan telling his daughter. "I think Palmer has plans."

"Palmer, do you have plans?" Blakely asks.

"I have a lot of work to do. I'll get with Ramsey and your dad, and we'll find a date that works for all of us to have another girls' night."

"Okay. Can we do it soon? I'm surrounded by boys," Blakely says, sounding fourteen, not four, and she rolls her eyes.

"I promise."

That seems to appease her. "Daddy, I'm starving. My belly has been yelling at me for a long, long time."

Declan laughs and kisses her cheek. "Well, we better feed your belly then." He gets to work making her a plate. "Merrick," Declan says. "Grab a plate, and let's go."

"I'm good here," he says, swinging his feet where he sits on the counter.

"Merrick," Brooks grits out.

"Come on, Mer, let's go tell the others it's ready." Carol appears out of nowhere and nods toward the back door.

"I miss all the good stuff," he grumbles, jumping off the counter, sliding his arm around his mom's shoulders, and following Declan and Blakely out the door.

"Palmer?"

"We can't do this here, Brooks. Your brothers, they know, and your mom? Does your mom know about us?" I hiss.

"No, but she can read the room, baby. She knew I was ready to rip Merrick's head off."

"You can't do that. We can't do this."

"What?" He steps toward me, apparently no longer worried about needing to keep space between us.

"This—" I wave between us. "We can't keep doing this."

"I'm going to need you to spell this out for me, Palmer. Say what you mean."

"I mean, I can't do this anymore." I fight hard to hold back my tears. I will not let him see me cry. I have to be strong. "We said it was for fun. You did what you set out to do and then some. Now, it's just getting way too complicated."

"Complicated?"

"Yes. Complicated. We have to stop."

"No." His voice is firm. "We don't."

"I'm not discussing this with you right now. Someone is going to come in and hear us."

"Oh, we're talking about this. Where is this coming from? Just out of the blue? Wait, you've been blowing me off," he says as the realization of my actions over the last few weeks sets in.

Did you hear that loud crack? That's my heart, shattering into millions of tiny pieces, just like I knew it would.

"So what? You've just been stringing me along?" he asks, his voice rising.

"No. That's not— This thing between us has run its course."

"Run its course?" he repeats. "Look me in the eyes, Palmer." He steps closer, and I have to bite my cheek to keep a sob from breaking free from my chest. His index finger lifts my chin so we're looking eye to eye. "Tell me now. Tell me what you want to say."

I can't. "This is over, Brooks. We can't keep hiding and lying to everyone we love just because the sex is good. We knew this day would come. It's time we go our separate ways, so we can move on. Ramsey is marrying my brother. She's my best friend. You're friends with my brother. There are going to be a lot of days like today where we run into each other. I hope that we can both be adults and be cordial."

"Cordial?" His eyes are blue flames of fury. "What if I said I'm not done?"

Oh, God. Please let me make it through this conversation without losing control of my emotions. I shrug. "We said when one of us was ready, that would be it. I'm ready." Lies. The biggest lie I've ever told. I'll never be ready, which is why I have to do this. I have to have control. I can't keep wondering when the day is going to come. I need to be able to start putting one foot in front of the other and moving on with my life.

Without him.

"Look me in the eyes and tell me you don't want to be with me." He's vibrating with what I can only assume is anger. I didn't expect it, but maybe I should have. I've blindsided him. But we both knew this was going to happen. This was what we agreed to.

Closing my eyes, I take a deep breath and prepare myself to say the words that I don't mean. My final lie to him and to myself. Slowly, I open my eyes and find him watching me. He's so handsome, and we've made so many wonderful memories together. This is going to hurt me, kill me, but I have to say the words.

"I don't want to be with you." Seven words shatter my heart to pieces.

"Hey," Ramsey says, walking into the room. "Everything okay in here?" she asks.

Brooks stares at me, his brow furrowed, and when he finally speaks, it's the final blow that has my heart splintering. "Just fucking fine, little cousin. Everything is just fine." He turns on his heel and rushes out the front door.

"Palmer?" Ramsey asks.

"I-I need to go, Rams. I need to get out of here. I don't want to see anyone. Do I need an excuse or your car or something? Please." My voice cracks as the pain begin to settle in my chest like cement.

"Are you going after him?"

"No."

"Then I'm coming with you. I'll make up an excuse. Go to my car. I'll meet you there." She hugs me tight. "You finally going to tell me what's been going on?"

I nod. I don't want to tell her, but I need to talk about this. I need to tell someone. "Best friend secrecy," I say.

"You have my word. Go. I'll be right there."

Not needing to be told twice, I rush to her car and slide into the passenger seat, sinking low so no one can see me. I turn to look out the window, and I see Brooks's truck is still here. I don't know where he went, but I'm sure his brothers will make sure he's okay. I'm pretty certain everyone here can guess that there is something between us. They might not know we've been sleeping together for months, but they definitely know that there is something.

There *was* something.

"Talk to me," Ramsey says.

We're sitting on the couch in my apartment. "What did you tell them? Why did we have to leave?"

"Oh, I said that the boutique called about my measurements and that they needed me to come back to verify."

I nod. "I'm sorry you had to lie for me."

She waves me off. "One little white lie never hurt anyone. Now, start talking."

"I fell in love with him."

"With Brooks?" she clarifies.

I nod.

"How did this happen? Start from the beginning."

So I do. I tell her how we got started, the rules of our arrangement, and how I changed them when I fell in love with him. "I had to end it, Rams. I had to." I swipe at the tears that are rolling down my cheeks, but it does no good because more keep falling. "I couldn't keep wondering when he was going to decide he was done and let my heart fall even more in love with him. I couldn't take the waiting, so I ended it."

I take a deep breath. "He's pissed because he wasn't ready or whatever, but I didn't have a choice. My heart." I place my hand on my chest. "My heart hurts, Ramsey. I know without a shadow of a doubt that I'll never love anyone the way that I love Brooks, and that's on me. I crushed on him growing up, and I told myself that I could do this. I thought that I could get close to him and not let my heart get involved, and I failed miserably. He did nothing wrong."

I take a minute to gather my thoughts. "He's amazing and so good to me. He wasn't even trying to be, you know? He just was. He'd say sweet things and open my door for me, kiss me hello, and make sure I was in my place when he'd drop me off at night before pulling away. He's just... such a good man, and I needed it to stop. I needed my heart to take a step back, and the only way I knew how to do that was to end it with him."

"Come here." My best friend pulls me into a hug and just lets me cry. Neither one of us speak while I pour my shattered heart out on her shoulder.

Finally, I sit back up and wipe my cheeks. My tears have slowed. "I'm sorry."

"You have nothing to be sorry for. I'm your best friend. You're going to be my sister. If we can't be there for each other, then who will be?"

"I love you."

"I love you too." She pauses and then asks, "Can I ask you something?"

"Sure." I shrug. I've already told her everything.

"Did you tell him that you loved him?"

"What? No. Of course not."

"Why?"

"Because. This is hard enough. I don't need him feeling sorry for me for falling in love with him. I don't want him with me because he feels guilty. He's already pissed at me."

"Palmer, he wasn't pissed at you. He was hurt."

"What?" I shake my head. "That's crazy."

She reaches over to the table and grabs her phone. "Look at this."

> **Brooks:** Is she with you?
>
> **Ramsey:** Yes.
>
> **Brooks:** Let me know she makes it home safe.
>
> **Ramsey:** Are you okay?
>
> **Brooks:** Thanks for taking care of her, Rams.
>
> **Ramsey:** She's my best friend.
>
> **Brooks:** She's a hell of a lot more than that to me.
>
> **Ramsey:** Want to talk about it?
>
> **Brooks:** Nothing left to say. Take care of her.
>
> **Ramsey:** I've got her. You take care of yourself. I'm here when you're ready to talk.

"He's just worried," I say, handing the phone back to her. "I told you. He's a nice guy."

"He cares about you. One would even hedge a bet that maybe, just maybe, he loves you too."

"Stop." I hold my hand up to halt any more words from her. "Please don't do this to me. Don't put ideas in my head that shouldn't be there. I changed the rules. I fell in love with him. This is on me. Brooks owes me nothing. I just hope that one day we can be cordial with one another."

"All right, I'll let it drop for now, but I think that you should think about what I've said. Think about his actions today."

"He could have told me, Ramsey, if he didn't want this. Suppose he wanted to be with me. He could have told me."

"You could have told him too."

I nod. She's right, I could have, but I didn't see the point, and

I didn't want him to feel guilty. It's my heart that didn't listen. My heart gave itself over to him. He's innocent in all of this.

"Let's watch a movie."

"Don't you have to get home?"

"Nah, we're good. Get something pulled up, and I'll make us some popcorn."

She disappears into my small kitchen while I surf, looking for something to watch. My heart isn't in it. Not when I knew he wanted me to be with him tonight. I'll miss his touch, his strong arms wrapping around me, his kisses, and everything else about the man.

It was easy to fall in love with him.

I just hope, with time, my heart will begin to heal with this loss that is Brooks Kincaid.

# Chapter 23

**BROOKS**

Shredded. Empty.

Missing a vital piece of who I am. That's how I feel. It's been a week since that day at my parents' when my world exploded. When I found out she was there, it killed me to wait even five seconds to rush to see her. I waited a full fifteen minutes. I could tell something was wrong, but I didn't want to push her. I figured she would talk to me when she was ready.

She was ready, but not for a shoulder to cry on or an ear to listen. She was ready to tear my world to pieces. My mind was racing with how to convince her to come to my place so I could hold her under the stars and tell her she was my entire world. At the same time, she was trying the find the right way to tell me that we were over.

I admit I could have handled it better. I should have fought for her. Fought for us. I should have told her I didn't want to hide anymore. That I wanted to march out the back door at my parents' house and tell all of them that she was mine. That she holds my heart in the palms of her hands.

Instead, I let my anger get the best of me and stormed off. I texted Orrin and asked him to make an excuse for me. I couldn't go back there and face everyone. He apparently told them I got called into work, and I hate that he lied for me, but I owe him one all the same.

My phone rings, pulling me out of my thoughts. "What's up?"

"We're headed to Willow Tavern. We're on our way to pick you up," Declan tells me.

"Not interested."

"I don't really give a flying fuck. We'll carry you to this Tahoe if we have to. You're going. Mom and Dad have Blakely."

"I'm really not good company right now," I tell him.

"When are you ever? Orrin, Sterling, and me, we're on our way. You've got about fifteen minutes to get your shit together."

"I'll lock the door."

Declan laughs. "We all have keys, asshole. Get ready." The line goes dead, and I groan, tossing my phone on the couch next to me.

I had planned to sit here and formulate a plan to win Palmer back. A week without her, and I'm miserable. Sure, we've gone longer without seeing one another, but I still knew she was mine. At least I always thought of her as mine. I guess she didn't see things the way that I did, and that's on me for not telling her. I don't want to live with regrets, and I'll always wonder what she would have said had I told her that I was in love with her.

Sure, I could be setting myself up for humiliation and rejection, but I could also be setting myself up with the love of my life. To me, that's worth everything.

*She's* worth everything.

Maybe a night out with my brothers will help. I can have a couple of beers and clear my head. Decision made, I rush off to the shower.

The Willow Tavern is packed for a Saturday night. I guess it's that time of year. The temperature is dropping as we roll into the holiday season. There's not much to do outside without freezing your ass off. It helps that Hank usually has great local bands lined up on the weekend nights.

"I'm going to grab us another round." Sterling slides out of the booth and makes his way to the crowded bar.

"You good?" Orrin asks.

I shake my head. "No. But I will be."

"Have you talked to her?" Declan asks.

"No."

"Do you plan on it?" Orrin asks, draining the rest of his beer.

"Yeah. I need to tell her, or I'll always wonder."

"Look." Declan leans in close over the table from his side of the booth. "I don't know exactly what's going on with you and Palmer. I know that the last few months you've been busier than normal, but you also seemed happy. Almost content. Then there was last weekend. We all know that something happened. We don't know what, and we know that you'll tell us when you're ready." He pauses, taking the time to finish off his beer. "Look, I'm not the advice-giver in the family. That's Dad. However, I do know what it's like to live with regrets." His eyes flash with pain, and my heart squeezes for my brother and my niece and the loss they endured. "Do what you have to do to have none. If that's telling Palmer you want to be with her, and she shoots you down, so be it. Don't be left wondering."

I nod. "Yeah. It's... more than I want to get into here. But I'll fill you all in soon. I should have told her that night, standing there in Mom and Dad's kitchen, but I let my anger get the best of me. I'd already decided I was going to lay it all out for her and see where it took us. You're right," I tell him. "Even if she's not interested, at least I'll know I did what I could."

"Jade said she's been pretty quiet. Ramsey too."

I nod. I'm not sure what I'm supposed to say to that. That I hate the thought of her hurting? That I want to leave here and go to her place and beg her to talk to me? Do I tell him that I would walk through hot coals for her if she asked me to?

"Here we go." Sterling passes each of us a beer. "Look." He turns to me as he slides into the booth beside me. "I don't know if I should tell you this. I don't know what happened, but just know that something did. I also know that if it was me, I would want to know."

"Spit it out," I tell him.

"Palmer's here."

"What?" I sit up straighter in the booth and crane my head to scan the dimly lit room.

"It's girls' night. That's what I assume since she's with Jade, Piper, and Ramsey."

I look across the table at Orrin and glare at him. "What? I knew it was girls' night, but they're supposed to be in Harris. Ramsey and Jade wanted to go to the food trucks. I don't know why they're here." He reaches into his pocket and pulls out his phone. "Wait, she sent me a message twenty minutes ago." He reads the message and then turns the screen for me to see.

> **Jade:** Hey, babe. Change of plans. No food trucks. I don't know the details, but Palmer refused to go. We decided to just drive around for a while and listen to music. We're headed back to Willow River now to eat at the Tavern. Love you. I'll text you when I'm headed to your place.

"Tone down the glare, little brother," Orrin says, sliding his phone back into his pocket after replying to Jade. "I didn't know they were going to be here."

"You said you wanted to talk to her," Declan reminds me.

"Not here," I grit out.

"Fine. Go say hi. Ask her to get together later, tomorrow, or whenever. Just acknowledge her."

Twisting the top off my beer, I take a deep pull and think

about my options. The one thing that keeps sticking out in my mind is that I want to see her. It's a deep-rooted need, and even if I don't get to talk to her tonight, and even if it takes me some time to convince her to talk to me, I can lay my eyes on her. I can see those beautiful green eyes.

"Where are they?" I ask Sterling.

"Sitting at the back corner table by the restrooms. It was just the four of them when I spotted them. I don't think they noticed me."

I nod, take another pull from my beer, and tap Sterling on the thigh. "Let me out."

"You need backup?" Orrin asks.

"No. I'm just going to say hi, or just... lay my eyes on her," I tell them. I do not really care if they think I'm a pussy.

The three of them nod. "We're here if you need us."

I knock my knuckles against the table and head for the bathrooms. I decide to actually use the bathroom before I go talk to her. It's a stall tactic, but I don't care. I need just a few more minutes. I take the time to splash some water on my face and pat it dry before squaring my shoulders and heading back out.

I glance at the table and see that Piper and Jade are the only ones there. My eyes scan, and I see Palmer and Ramsey at the bar. It's packed, so they don't notice when I walk up behind them, but their conversation stops me in my tracks.

"He did not!" Ramsey laughs.

"He did. I'm telling you, Rams, I dodged a bullet with that one. He is definitely not Mr. Right. I mean, could you imagine me having to spend the rest of my life with him?" she shudders, and my heart drops to my toes.

"Maybe it's fate that he's here tonight," Ramsey teases.

"You and I both know that ship has sailed." Palmer laughs.

Having heard enough, I stalk past them and to the table where my brothers are sitting. "Can we go?"

"What?" The three of them look at me in confusion.

"Did you see her?" Declan asks.

"Did you talk to her?" This is from Orrin.

"Come on, we can grill him in the truck." Sterling stands, nods for my brothers to do the same, and pulls the keys to Declan's Tahoe from his pocket. He's our DD for the night.

They must see something on my face because Orrin and Declan both slide out of the booth, and just like that, the four of us stalk out of the bar. I don't say one single word on the way back to my place. Sterling pulls into my driveway, and I sit staring at my house. Everything inside those four walls reminds me of her. Everywhere I look, she's there. I fucking hate this. I hate the way my chest feels as if it's caving in from the pain of losing her. I hate the way her hurtful words bounce around in my head, and most of all, I hate that I still love her.

Wholly.

Unconditionally.

"I'm sorry I ruined your night out. Thanks for the ride." I don't wait for them to reply. I climb out and slam the door. I march up to my front steps and fumble with the key in the door. My hands are shaking both from anger and from pain.

I've never known Palmer or Ramsey to be cruel. For them to be talking about me like that. I just... I was good to her. She was... *is* everything to me. How could she say those things?

*Could you imagine me having to spend the rest of my life with him?*

*I dodged a bullet with that one.*

I keep hearing her voice over and over in my head, and I just want it to stop. Her hurtful words replace the sweet sound of her laugh and that beautiful smile that makes her eyes light up. I just want it to stop.

"Fuck!" I roar, slamming my fist into the living room wall. The drywall gives way as my fist slams through it. My knuckles burn, but I don't care. Feeling anything other than the sharp broken pieces of my heart is a welcome distraction.

The front door opens and in walks my three brothers. "Get out." There is no heat behind my words. I tell them to leave, yet

I don't want to be alone. Not here where at every turn her memory haunts me.

"Sit down and tell us," Orrin demands.

I fall onto the chair and rest my elbows on my knees, burying my hands in my hair. "I've been seeing her for months."

"Seeing her as in?"

"As in, she was mine. Fuck, I guess she was never mine."

"Start from the beginning," Declan tells me.

And so I do. I start at the engagement party and don't stop talking until I catch them up to the moment they just walked in on.

"I'm in love with her." My voice is gravelly. "I planned to tell her that the arrangement was shit to me, that all I wanted was her. Every time I planned to tell her, something would happen, and I wouldn't get the chance. Then last weekend at Mom and Dad's happened. I hadn't seen her all week. I missed the hell out of her, but I could tell something was wrong. She ended it, and here we are. Well, and you know what I heard her saying at the Tavern tonight."

"How did we not know you two were actually dating?" Sterling asks.

"We didn't want anyone to know. We hid it well, but I was tired of hiding how I feel about her."

"I don't know what to say," Orrin tells me. "What you told us you overheard tonight, that doesn't sound like Ramsey or Palmer to me. Maybe they were talking about someone else?"

"Who? We've been together for months, O. Months."

"You need to talk to her," Declan speaks up. "I know it's not a conversation you want to have, especially if it was you they were talking about tonight, but, B, this shit is going to eat you alive if you don't get it off your chest. If you need to scream and yell, then do it. Lay it on us. We can take it. But you need to compose yourself and talk to her. Tell her what her words did to you. Tell her that you're in love with her. Let the cards fall where they may, but don't keep it all inside. It will fester and burn like a wildfire until there is nothing left."

"You know what Dad would say if he were here, right?" Sterling asks.

"Work hard, love harder," we all say in unison.

He nods. "Love her harder, Brooks. Something isn't adding up. You two were happy, and then suddenly, she's ending things. There is a huge missing piece to this puzzle, and you are going to have to be the one to work hard to figure it out."

"I don't know how to love her any harder than I already do," I confess.

"You fight," Declan says, his voice low and gritty. "You face the hard shit head-on. You give it all you've got, so if and when you still walk away without her, you know you did everything in your power to show her what she means to you."

"And if I can't come back from that? I've given her all that I am. I don't know that I have anything else to give, and if I did find another piece of me she didn't already own, and she still tells me I'm not who she wants, I don't know that I can come back from that. Hell, I don't know how I'm going to survive without her now. Everything in this fucking house reminds me of her."

"You dig deep, and no matter how it turns out, you have us here to help you pick up the pieces. All of us. You have eight brothers who are standing behind you. Holding you up. That's for a lifetime, brother," Orrin says. "Not just today, but today and all of the tomorrows. We're here for you."

I nod. "Love you guys."

"We love you too."

When my phone rang at six o'clock this morning, I debated on answering when I saw it was work, but then I was afraid it wasn't a work call, and something had happened to someone I love, and I swiped at the screen.

Sure enough, it was my boss, asking me if I could work a few hours today. They're shorthanded, and I agreed to work from ten to four when she was able to find alternate coverage. I didn't want to work on my day off, but it's better than sitting around my house moping.

My brothers convinced me to talk to Palmer. To tell her everything that's on my mind and in my heart. The idea of her telling me that we're still over rests heavily on my mind, but I know they're right. If I don't tell her, I'll always wonder. I know in my gut I'll never love another woman the way I love her, but if I don't know for sure, I'll never be able to start to heal from the pain of losing her.

Ready for work early, I decide to make a pitstop at The Sweet Spot for breakfast. Just another place that reminds me of Palmer and our time together. I still remember that morning. I was shocked that she brought me something and was thoughtful enough to think of my coworkers as well. No one had ever done something like that for me before that I wasn't related to. I fell a little harder for her that day, and yeah, that has a little to do with my decision to stop on my way to work.

I'm standing in line waiting for my turn when I feel a tap on my shoulder. Turning around, I see Ramsey standing there smiling. "Fancy meeting you here."

"Hey, Rams," I say, turning back to face the counter. I'm still upset with her for what she said.

"Oh, no, that's not how this is going to go." She grabs my arm and pulls me out of line. Okay, I let her pull me out of line. She doesn't stop until we reach a small table by the window. "Sit," she commands, and because I want answers, I do as she says. "What's going on?"

"Nothing." I cross my arms over my chest.

"I call bullshit. Now tell me what's going on with you and why you basically shunned me just a minute ago standing in line."

"Maybe you're dodging a bullet. Oh, wait, that was Palmer." I watch her face closely. She looks confused, and then realization dawns on her.

"We'll get to how you know about that conversation in a minute. First, I want to start with you're an idiot."

"What?" I sit up straighter in my chair.

"We were not talking about you, knucklehead. We were talking about Toby."

"Who the fuck is Toby?"

"Toby is a guy Palmer dated when I first moved back to Willow River. It was very short-lived. He was at the Tavern that night and asked her to hook up."

"What?" I say again, this time a little too loudly. "He asked her to hook up. Seriously?"

"Yep," she says, popping the *p*. "She was telling me how he was never interested in her as a person, just getting into her pants. She broke it off with him, and that night was the first night she'd seen him since. And before that brain of yours goes crazy, I can already see the smoke coming out of your ears. She never slept with him. She has more dignity than that."

I feel my shoulders relax. "She wasn't talking about me?"

Ramsey shakes her head. She leans forward and places her hand over mine. "Brooks, I probably shouldn't be telling you this, but you're both too damn stubborn, and I hate to see you both hurting." She lets that sink in before she tosses me a curve ball I never saw coming. "Palmer's in love with you."

I shake my head. I must have heard her wrong. "What did you just say?" This time it's me who's leaning in close so I can be sure to hear every word.

"You heard me the first time, but I'll say it again. Palmer is in love with you."

"No." I'm quick to dismiss her claim. "She ended things. Wait, how do you know about us?"

"Because after she ended things, I drove her home, and she spilled all the sordid details. She was a wreck. She still is."

"I don't understand." My mind is racing with what this means. She loves me. Palmer loves me.

"It's not my story to tell, and I've already said too much. All I will say is that you need to pull your head out of your ass and fix this since she won't. She doesn't even know that you overheard that conversation that was most definitely not about you."

"I... shit. I got called into work today. I'm on until four."

"She's busy today anyway." Ramsey smiles. "I talked Deacon into another photoshoot."

"Really?"

She nods. "I did, so Palmer is doing that today at our house."

"I get off at four, and then I'll meet you there. Can you keep her there until then?" I'm already forming a plan and organizing all the things I want to tell her in my mind—first and foremost, that I'm in love with her.

"I can try. If not, I'll text you and let you know where she is."

I nod. "Deal." Standing, I walk to her side of the small table and bend over to hug her tight. "Thank you, Ramsey."

"Someone had to help you pull your head out of your ass."

I laugh, and it's genuine. "I just... she's my entire fucking world, and it shattered when she ended things."

Ramsey's eyes soften. "Tell her that. Let her explain her side of things. You two could have very easily fixed all of this days ago with a little communication."

"I've learned my lesson. If I get her back, if I can convince her to be mine, I'll never hold back how I'm feeling ever again. Never."

"Good. Now, let me buy you breakfast."

Ten minutes later, I'm hugging her goodbye and climbing behind the wheel of my truck, feeling like a new man.

Love harder. That's exactly what I plan to do.

I expected today's shift to drag by, knowing that at the end of it, I would be going to get my girl, but it was the exact opposite. We were slammed all morning, which helped keep me focused and my mind occupied. However, this afternoon has been slow. I almost asked to leave early, but changed my mind. I've got two more hours of my shift, and I'm home free. "I'm coming for you, beautiful," I whisper before tossing my empty water bottle in the trash, knowing I need to get back out on the floor. Just as I'm stepping out of the break room, my phone vibrates in my scrub pocket. Quickly, I pull it out and see who it is.

**Ramsey:** Are you still at work?

**Me:** Yes. I get off at four.

**Ramsey:** I'm here. Can you meet me in the lobby?

I don't bother to ask her why she's here. I work in the emergency room, and I don't get surprise visitors, so something is wrong. Is it Mom or Dad? One of my brothers? I quicken my step, pushing through the double doors. My eyes scan the room until they land on Ramsey standing in the corner, gripping her phone.

"Rams?"

"Hi." Her eyes are bloodshot, but she looks to be okay.

"What's going on?"

"She's okay."

That's what she starts with. "Who? You're scaring me here. Tell me what's going on."

"Palmer."

My heart drops to my toes, and there is a fast-growing lump in the back of my throat. I swallow hard. "Palmer?"

"She was at our place doing the shoot, and she just fainted. Deacon was able to rush forward and catch her. She woke up right away, but we insisted that we bring her here so she can get checked out."

It takes about thirty seconds for her words to sink in before I grab her hand and pull her through the doors. My heart is beating so fast it feels as though it could beat right out of my chest. I reach the board and see *P. Setty* and the bay number next to it and pull Ramsey with me. Faintly, I hear one of my coworkers call out, asking if I need help. I don't need help. I need Palmer. I need to set my eyes on her, and I need to hold her and tell her how much I love her.

I *need* Palmer.

Pushing open the door of her exam room, I see her sitting up in bed, with Deacon at her side. I don't look at my friend as I release my hold on Ramsey. I don't hear anyone or see anyone but Palmer. My eyes roam over her, and she looks to be unharmed. When I reach her side, I bend over, placing my hands on either side of her cheeks.

"Hi, beautiful."

Tears fill her eyes. "Hi, big guy."

# Chapter 24

## PALMER

HIS HANDS ARE TREMBLING, AND there are tears in his eyes. I feel wetness coating my cheeks as I also lose the battle with my emotions. I open my mouth to speak, but he shakes his head. I quickly close it, not really sure what I wanted to say anyway. My tears have nothing to do with the fact that I'm in the hospital and everything to do with the man staring at me as if I'm his entire reason for being.

"I love you," he whispers. His voice is thick and raspy.

"W-What?"

He smiles. "I love you. I'm in love with you." He leans in and kisses my forehead. "Now that I've got that off my chest tell me what's going on with you. Are you okay? Are you hurting?"

"You love me?"

He smiles softly. "I do."

"But we said we were over." I can't process what's happening right now. We were supposed to be a fling. I ended things to keep my heart from breaking even worse when he decided he was done. I've been miserable, and all this time... he loves me?

"Baby, don't you know we could never stay over?"

A throat clearing has him turning to look over his shoulder. "Deacon." Brooks greets my brother as he settles into the chair next to the bed and moves in as close as he can. He slides his hand beneath mine and carefully brings it to his lips. He presses a kiss to my knuckles.

"What did I miss?" Deacon asks. He doesn't sound angry, just really confused.

"You missed the fact that your sister is the love of my life." Brooks looks him square in the eye, not backing down from whatever my brother decides to throw his way.

"Brooks?" I croak his name. His eyes flash to mine.

"What do you need?" He kisses my hand again. "Are you in pain?"

"No. I'm not in any pain."

"Tell me so I can fix it."

"I feel fine. I just fainted, and these two insisted that I come to get checked out."

"I'm glad they did." He kisses the back of my hand again.

There's a knock at the door, and Doctor Brown steps in. "Brooks?" he asks, surprised. "Do you know our patient?"

"She's my girlfriend." He turns to look at me. "Actually, that's a lie. She's more than that. She's the love of my life."

More tears fall, and before I can wipe them away, he's there, using his thumbs to do it for me. "Love you," he says softly.

"Well, Miss Setty, I have some preliminary test results. Are you okay with me discussing the results with the present company?"

"Yes. This is my brother, and my best friend, his fiancée, and you know Brooks."

Doctor Brown nods. "Well, your blood pressure was a little low, and I'm guessing you had a drop, which caused you to pass out."

"What caused the drop?" Brooks asks. He's in full-on nurse mode.

Doctor Brown looks at me, and I nod. "He'll probably have to put it in non-medical terms for me anyway." I laugh.

"Well, we ran some bloodwork, as you know, standard procedure, and it seems that congratulations are in order. Palmer, you're pregnant."

"What?" I breathe the word, and my hand moves to my belly, but there's already one there. Brooks's large hand is splayed out, and his eyes are boring into mine. A single tear slides over his cheek.

"Palmer." His voice cracks. He stands and leans in close. "We're having a baby." He smiles, and for the rest of my life, I will never forget the look on his face. Pure happiness and love.

"A baby?" I repeat, because I'm having trouble processing what's happened in the last fifteen minutes. The man I love professed his love to me when I thought I was nothing but a fling to him, and now we're having a baby.

Brooks closes the distance between us and presses his lips to mine. "We made a baby."

"We're going to step outside for some air." Ramsey stands and pulls on Deacon's arm. He's watching us closely, and I'm suddenly worried all hell is going to break loose.

"Deacon."

"You're happy?"

"I'm bursting with it," I say truthfully.

He looks at Brooks. "She's my little sister."

Brooks nods at Ramsey. "And she's mine." He glances back at me before he gives my brother his full attention. "We didn't plan this, Deacon. But I can tell you that this baby and your sister will be loved unconditionally. There will never be a day in either of their lives that they won't feel wanted and cherished. I'm sorry we hid this from you, but this is happening. I love her, Deac."

Deacon nods and lets Ramsey pull him from the room. Brooks turns his attention back to the doctor. "How are the rest of her numbers? Anything alarming?" He has one hand on my belly and the other holding mine.

"No. Everything looks good. I put in for an OB consult just so we can do an ultrasound and get eyes on the baby, but everything looks good. Congratulations, you two. I'll give you some privacy while you wait." With that, the doctor turns and leaves the room.

"I'm sorry," I tell him. "I didn't know. I wasn't trying to trap you or make you stay with me."

"Hey." He stands from his chair. "Scoot over, beautiful. I'm coming in."

"What?" I huff out a laugh.

"You heard me. Make room. Daddy needs to lie with his girls."

My heart does a flip in my chest. "Girls?" I ask, moving over and making room for him.

He shrugs as he climbs into bed beside me. "Just a feeling." He slides his arm under my neck, and I waste no time snuggling into his chest. "Watch your IV," he says, making sure I'm settled before he relaxes. "Damn, I've missed you," he says, pressing his lips to the top of my head. "I didn't know if I'd ever have the chance to hold you in my arms again, and now I'm here holding you and our unborn baby."

"Brooks—" I start again, but he makes a shushing sound that has me doing exactly that.

"I would never think that you got pregnant on purpose, Palmer. I was there every damn time. I lived it with you. I remember every single moment of our time together. In fact, she was probably conceived that morning in my kitchen."

"I'm on the pill," I remind him.

"Nothing is one hundred percent effective. She was meant to be."

"Oh, no. I've been taking my pills, and I had a glass of wine last night at the Tavern." My hands go to my belly. "What if that hurt the baby?" Panic fills my voice.

"It's okay. Everything is going to be just fine."

"You don't know that."

"We're going to get a look when the OB comes in. They'll do a vaginal ultrasound to get eyes on the baby."

"Today?" I ask, feeling excitement bubble up.

"Yeah, but if we're right about when we conceived, then she's going to be tiny, but we'll be able to see that everything is okay."

"My heart is full." I lift my head and find that he's watching me.

"I had this big elaborate plan to tell you that I was in love with you. Things kept happening, and I never got the chance, and then you ended us. I never want to feel that kind of pain again, Palmer. I've been a miserable bastard without you in my life."

"I'm sorry. I was driving myself insane, wondering when the hit was going to come. I was constantly wondering when you were going to end things between us, and I knew it was going to kill me. I did it before you could. The wondering and worrying were slowly killing me, but afterward, being without you, that was worse than the wondering."

"I'm right here." He presses his lips to mine, and tears start to form behind my eyes.

"I love you."

He hugs me to his chest. "I love you too, my beautiful girl."

There's a knock on the door, but Brooks makes no effort to move. "Come in," he calls out.

Ramsey peeks her head in. "Can we come in?"

"Yes," I answer. I sit up in bed, as does Brooks, but he keeps his arm around me, and I lean against his chest, soaking up his comfort.

"How are you feeling?" Deacon asks.

I smile. "Happy."

He nods and pulls Ramsey into his arms. "Congratulations." He looks at me and then at Brooks.

"Thanks, man," Brooks replies, and I can hear the excitement in his voice.

"Okay, so let's talk names," Ramsey says with a wide grin. "I mean, I did help the two of you find your way back to each other. I'm thinking naming rights to my niece or nephew is sufficient," she teases.

"You knew?" Deacon asks.

She smiles up at him. "I knew."

"Don't be mad at her. I swore her to secrecy."

"I'm not mad. I'm glad you had someone to talk to. I wish y'all wouldn't have hidden this from all of us, but that wasn't our choice to make."

"It just kind of happened," I tell him.

"Back to naming my niece or nephew." Ramsey gives me a pointed look, and I burst out laughing.

"Niece," Brooks tells her.

Ramsey shrieks, "What? You know?"

"No." I'm quick to shake my head. "He just thinks he knows."

"Gut feeling."

"Aw, we'll finally have a Ramsey Kincaid," my best friend teases.

"I love you, Rams." I smile at her.

"Love you too. We're going to head out. Brooks, can you get our girl home safely?"

"If by home you mean my place, then yes."

"That works for me," Ramsey tells him. She hugs us both, and then my brother steps up.

He hugs me. "Love you, little sister. Congratulations."

"Love you too."

Deacon pulls back and offers his hand to Brooks. They shake, nod at one another in some sort of silent understanding, and then they're gone.

"I think the bedroom next to ours is the best for the nursery."

"Ours?"

"You're moving in with me."

"Oh, am I?"

"Yep."

"Do I get a say in this?"

"Sure. If you want to move to a different place, we can."

"You really want me to move in with you?"

"Yes. I want you to move in with me. I want this baby to grow up in the same kind of loving homes that we did. I'm in this, Palmer. One hundred and fifty thousand percent, I'm in this. I love you. And I love this little girl."

"I love you too."

"We will eventually need a bigger house."

"What? Why? You have three bedrooms."

"She needs lots of brothers and sisters."

"What if we have all girls?" I hide my smile, because I'm more than on board with this life plan that he has for us. I can see it all playing out in my head. Our future.

"I hope they all look like their momma." He kisses me just as another knock sounds at the door. "Come in," he calls out.

"Hi, I'm Sabrina. Oh, Brooks. Hi." She waves.

"Sabrina, this is my fiancée, Palmer."

"Nice to meet you," Sabrina says and gets to work setting up the ultrasound machine.

"Fiancée?" I mouth to Brooks.

He grins. "Did I forget to mention that I want you to be my wife?" he muses.

"You're like a freight train without brakes on the tracks." I laugh.

"When it comes to our family, I'll own that." He winks just as Sabrina begins to explain the process of the ultrasound.

I move into position, feeling uncomfortable as hell, but Brooks can sense that, and he leans over, pressing a kiss on my cheek, and whispering in my ear, "Relax. We're about to see our baby girl."

I melt, and my body instantly relaxes. The way he just accepted this is our future, the way he openly tells me how he feels, has my belly doing flips and my heart soaring.

"All right," Sabrina says. She's moving that damn wand inside me, and I grip Brooks's hand. Sabrina rattles off measurements and medical jargon with Brooks, and then she points to the screen. "Right there. See that tiny flutter?"

I focus on where she's pointing, and I see it. "Yes," I say, my voice raspy.

"That's your baby's heartbeat. You're measuring at about five weeks, and sometimes that's a little too early to see the heartbeat, but this little one wants to show off today."

Tears leak from my eyes as I stare at that tiny flutter. That's our baby. Brooks presses his lips to my temple and clears his throat.

"Everything looks good?" he asks her.

"Just perfect." Sabrina smiles. "Congratulations, you two. Your due date is calculating at June seventeenth."

"Thank you," I tell her.

She quickly cleans up and moves toward the door. "You can go ahead and get dressed. Brooks, just crack the door when you're ready, and we'll send someone in with discharge paperwork." With a wave, she leaves, shutting the door behind her.

Brooks frames my face with his hands, and his big blue eyes swirl with emotion. "I love you. Not just because you're having my baby, because of the incredible woman that you are." He swallows hard. "I promise to love you and our children every day of forever."

"That's a long time, big guy." My heart feels like it's too big for my chest.

"And to me, it doesn't sound nearly long enough. Come on. Let's get you dressed and stop and get your prescription and get you home."

"Prescription?"

"Prenatal vitamins."

"Oh. They didn't mention that, but I knew I would need them."

"That's why you have me. Maybe they'll let me help deliver the baby," he muses, reaching over and grabbing my clothes.

"Is that something you'd want to do?"

"Bring my baby girl into the world? Hell yes."

I nod. "Then when we have our first checkup, you should talk to them about it."

"Let's get you dressed." He steps between my thighs where I'm sitting on the edge of the bed, and reaches behind me to untie my gown. He pulls it off, tossing it to the bed as he hungrily takes me in.

"Not here," I warn, making him laugh.

"Is that a challenge, beautiful?"

"Do you want your coworkers to hear me?"

"No one hears you but me." He furrows his brow.

I chuckle. "Then take me to your place."

"Not my place, Palmer. Home. I'm taking you home to our home. I was serious. I want you to move in with me. If we need a new place, we can sell mine, but I don't ever want to fall asleep again without you next to me."

"Take me home, big guy." His eyes are bright and filled with so much love. I don't know that I've ever been happier than I am in this moment.

"Fuck, I love you." He kisses me hard and then proceeds to carefully help me get dressed. When I stand to pull my leggings on, he drops to his knees and places a tender kiss on my belly. "Daddy loves you too, baby girl."

"You can't do that," I tell him, tears clogging my throat. He peers up at me. "Look at what you do to me?" I point at my tear-filled eyes.

"There will never be a day moving forward that you don't know exactly how I'm feeling. Good or bad, I'm never holding back again. I almost lost you, Palmer. Me wanting the moment to be perfect kept me silent, and I almost lost you. I will never make that mistake again. Every moment with you is the right moment."

I nod because how do I argue with that? "I love you."

"I love you too." He helps me with my leggings and then my shirt before cracking the door. I expect discharge to take forever, but apparently, I have connections with my baby daddy, and thirty minutes later, we're walking into his house with my prescription in hand that he was able to have filled at the hospital pharmacy.

"Can I get you anything?" he asks.

"Sleep."

"You're tired?"

"I haven't slept well in over a week."

"Then we'll go to bed." He takes my hand and leads me down the hall to his room, well, our room now. "Deacon texted me. He said he has all of your equipment and everything at his place. He said to text him when you're ready, and he'll bring it by."

"I can just pick it up on my way to the studio tomorrow. I have a key to their place."

"My brothers all have a key to mine as well. I'm going to have to take them back."

"What? Why?"

"Because this is your home now. I can't have them walking in on you naked in the kitchen."

"And who says I'm going to be naked in the kitchen?"

He rests his hand over my belly. "That's how we got here," he reminds me.

"Don't take their keys, Brooks. I don't want you to change your life for our baby and me."

"I don't want them seeing you."

"Are you going to tell them that I live here?"

"You know that I am."

"They're good guys. They're not going to come barging in, knowing that's what they could find. You never know when there is an emergency, and they might need to get inside. Let them keep them."

"Another reason I fell madly in love with you."

"Oh, should I start a list?"

"Not enough paper in the world, baby."

"You're too much."

"Come on." He strips down to his boxer briefs, and I strip down to my panties. He hands me a shirt, and we crawl into bed. He wraps me in his warm embrace, and in no time, we're both sound asleep.

# Epilogue

## BROOKS

TODAY WAS A GREAT DAY. We started out with lunch with Palmer's family and then ended with dinner with mine. We're ten weeks pregnant, and still, the only people who know are Deacon and Ramsey. We thought it was best to hold it to ourselves until after her first trimester.

It was a struggle not to stand up and tell everyone we love, at her parents' place and at mine, that I'm thankful for the love of my life and the mother of my daughter. No, we don't know if we're having a little girl, but I just feel like we are. Something in my heart tells me I'm going to have another little Palmer to love. Boy or girl, it doesn't matter to me, but my heart tells me it's a girl.

"I'm so tired," Palmer says from her spot next to me on the couch.

"It was a long day."

"It really was," she agrees.

She's been a fucking rock star at this pregnancy thing. She's been tired and only had a few bouts of morning sickness; otherwise, she's been very healthy, and she's fucking glowing. I've heard that before but never really witnessed it. No, that's not right. I never really cared to notice. Not until it was my woman and our baby.

"I was thinking about going out for some fresh air before bed. If I promise to keep you warm, will you join me?"

"Like... for a walk?" she asks, and I can already see she's going to turn me down if that's the case. Growing our little girl is wearing her out.

"No. Just sit out on the back patio for a few minutes."

"Sure." She shrugs and stands.

I grab the blanket off the back of the couch and tap my pocket to make sure the ring that I put there early this morning is still there. I thought maybe I'd ask her at her parents' place, then I thought, nah, I'll do it at my parents,' but then I realized I wanted it to just be us. I had a plan to tell her that I was in love with her, and well, it was a good plan, so I'm going to use it with a minor modification.

Pulling open the sliding glass door, I step out on the back patio. I take a seat on the lounge chair and pat the spot next to me. Palmer cuddles up next to me, and I cover us both with the blanket.

"It's a nice night. Lots of stars," she says, staring up at the night sky.

"You know, this was my plan."

"What?" she asks, still looking up at the stars.

"I planned to bring you out here just like this and tell you that I was in love with you. I planned to tell you that our arrangement was null and void because you owned my heart."

"You getting sappy on me, big guy?" she teases, but I don't miss the soft sigh.

"Just telling you I had a plan, and this was it."

"Well, I'm sorry you didn't get to use it. It would have been perfect." She lifts her head from my chest to look at me. "I love you."

"I love you." My hand is under the blanket, so I slip my hand into my pocket and clasp the ring that I bought her. It took me some time to find the right one, and then it had to be sized, or it would already be on her finger. I palm the ring and reach for her hand. I trace over each finger.

"What do you think about a swing set over there?" I nod toward the side of the yard. "And maybe a tree house in that old oak tree?"

"I can see it," she replies, her eyes staring out at our backyard. "Are you building both?" she asks. "I mean, I can supervise, but I'm not all that great with a hammer."

"Baby girl has nine uncles, maybe ten if Heath ever pulls his head out of his ass and asks Piper to marry him."

She laughs. "They'll get there."

"What if I told you that I want us to get there?"

She sits up and looks at me. "What do you mean?"

I stand and walk around the lounger, pulling her to her feet and dropping to one knee. "I didn't get to bring you out here under the stars and tell you that I love you, so I'm improvising. Instead, I'm asking you to marry me. I'm asking you to spend the rest of your life with me. Let me love you for eternity as Palmer Kincaid." I swallow hard. "Palmer, will you do me the incredible honor of being my wife? Will you marry me, beautiful?"

The tears coating her cheeks glisten in the moonlight. She nods but doesn't give me the words. "Let me hear you say it, beautiful."

"Yes." She screams way louder than she should for being outside this time of night. "Yes, I'll marry you."

I slip the ring on her finger and stand, pulling her into my arms. I never knew it was possible to love someone as much as I love Palmer and our unborn child. I'll spend every day showing them what they mean to me.

## PALMER

It's Christmas Eve, and Brooks and I managed to convince our families to come together for one big celebration. Ramsey and I had to go to both places, so she and I teamed up and used that as the excuse. It wasn't a hard sell.

Ramsey and Deacon are still the only two who know about the baby. We wanted to wait until we were through the first trimester before we told everyone. That was two weeks ago, and today is finally the day. I'm fourteen weeks, and I feel great. I have a small little bump that I've been able to hide with leggings and loose sweaters.

Deacon and Ramsey graciously offered to host all of us at their place. My mom and Carol both jumped in and helped with the food, as did Jade and Piper. Everything came together with ease.

We just finished dinner, which was amazing, and everyone is sitting around ready to open presents. Since there were so many of us, we all decided to draw names, except for Blakely. She gets all the things because we all want to spoil her rotten. I smile, knowing that next year, her baby cousin will be right here with her. I hope we can make this a tradition.

"Who's ready for presents?" Deacon shouts.

"Oh, Uncle Deacon, I wants pwesents," Blakely tells him, making us all laugh.

Brooks taps my thigh where I'm sitting on his lap on the couch, and I stand. He takes my hand, and we move to the front of the room. "Palmer and I have something for all of you," he says, smiling down at me.

I chuckle because he's right. This room is filled with grandparents, aunts, uncles, and a cousin, so yeah, I guess our baby is for all of them too.

"Maverick has an envelope for each of you. I'll save you the trouble of opening it." He chuckles. "Inside, you will find an invitation to join us at Willow Manor on New Years' Eve." Brooks smiles down at me. "I want you to be there when I make this beautiful woman my wife."

Cheers erupt all around us, and we are bombarded with hugs and handshakes. It takes several minutes for everyone to get their turn, and Brooks raises his hand. "One more thing." He smiles at me, and I turn to face our families.

"We're having a baby!" I cheer, and if I thought the wedding announcement was well received, this is so much more. We talked about it and we wanted a short engagement. We spent so much time hiding, we're ready to shout our love for one another to the world.

We get another round of hugs and handshakes, and then I feel a tug on my sweater. Blakely raises her hands for me to pick her up, and Brooks notices. He scoops her up in his arms. "Aunt Palmer can't lift you while she's pregnant," he explains. He's being over protective. There is no reason I can't lift her. Instead of arguing, I let him have his way. I know it's coming from a place of love for me and our baby.

Blakely tilts her little head to the side as if she's processing his words. "Can we still have girls' days?" she asks.

"Of course," I assure her.

"Can the baby come too?" she asks.

"Yes, the baby can come too."

"Palmer and I are getting married. She's going to be my wife, and our baby will be your little cousin," Brooks explains. The room is silent as they listen to us help her understand what's happening. She's been the baby for four years, and this will be a change for her.

Her little brow furrows, and she places her hands on either side of Brooks's face. "Where do we get one of those?" she asks him.

"Get one of what, sweetheart?"

"A wife?"

Brooks coughs, as does Declan, who's standing next to us. "Squirt, it's time for presents," he says to distract her.

"Yeah, one of those. A wife." She points at me. "If my daddy gets one of those, then I get a baby too. Or can I have your baby?" she asks.

Brooks chuckles. "No, you can't have our baby, but as the big cousin, you'll have to help us teach the baby all kinds of fun things."

"Daddy! I needs your phone. We hafta call Santa."

"Squirt, Santa comes tonight, remember?"

"I know that's why we hafta call him now. He needs to bring us a wife."

Declan smiles sadly, taking his daughter into his arms. "It doesn't work like that, baby. Come on, let's open presents."

Sterling takes her from her dad's arms and hands her a gift, and just like that, all is forgotten. I keep my eyes on Declan as he watches his daughter with sad eyes, and I send up a silent prayer that the two of them will find someone who brings the amount of joy into their lives that Brooks has brought into mine.

Brooks moves behind me, wrapping me in his arms. One hand rests on my belly, the other over my chest, holding me close. "Love you, beautiful."

"Love you too, big guy."

Brooks was right. We were never going to stay over. Instead, we have forever.

for taking the time to read **Stay Over**.

Want more from the Kincaid Brothers?
Pre-order ***Stay Forever*** now.
***Stay Forever*** is Declan Kincaid's story
kayleeryan.com/books/stay-over/
*Available November 1, 2022*

Want to read Deacon and Ramsey's story?
Grab ***Never with Me*** here:
kayleeryan.com/books/never-with-me/

***Never miss a new release:***
Newsletter Sign-up
Be the first to hear about free content, new releases, cover reveals, sales, and more. kayleeryan.com/subscribe/

### With You Series:
Anywhere with You | More with You | Everything with You

### Soul Serenade Series:
Emphatic | Assured | Definite | Insistent

### Southern Heart Series:
Southern Pleasure | Southern Desire
Southern Attraction | Southern Devotion

### Unexpected Arrivals Series
Unexpected Reality | Unexpected Fight | Unexpected Fall
Unexpected Bond | Unexpected Odds

### Riggins Brothers Series:
Play by Play | Layer by Layer | Piece by Piece
Kiss by Kiss | Touch by Touch | Beat by Beat

### Entangled Hearts Duet:
Agony | Bliss

### Cocky Hero Club:
Lucky Bastard

### Mason Creek Series:
Perfect Embrace

# More from KAYLEE RYAN

***Standalone Titles:***
Tempting Tatum | Unwrapping Tatum
Levitate | Just Say When
I Just Want You | Reminding Avery

Hey, Whiskey | Pull You Through
Remedy | The Difference
Trust the Push | Forever After All
Misconception | Never with Me

***Out of Reach Series:***
Beyond the Bases | Beyond the Game
Beyond the Play | Beyond the Team

## Co-written with Lacey Black:

***Fair Lakes Series:***
It's Not Over | Just Getting Started | Can't Fight It

***Standalone Titles:***
Boy Trouble | Home to You | Beneath the Fallen Stars

***Co-writing as Rebel Shaw with Lacey Black:***
Royal | Crying Shame

# Acknowledgments

*To my readers:*

Thank you for your continued support. If you've made it this far, you've devoured another one of my books, and I can't tell you what it means to me that you picked my words for your escape. Thank you for choosing Stay Over. I cannot wait for you to meet the rest of the Kincaid brothers!

*To my family:*

I could not do this without your never-ending support. Thank you for standing beside me while I chase my dreams.

*Integrity Formatting:*

Thank you for making the paperbacks beautiful. You're amazing, and I cannot thank you enough for all that you do.

*Regina Wamba:*

I love this image! I've been sitting on this one for a while. It's the perfect image to represent Brooks and Palmer. Thank you for being amazing at what you do.

*Book Cover Boutique:*

You nailed the design on this series. Thank you so much for taking my vision and bringing it to life.

*Lacey Black:*

I don't really know what I can say that I haven't already said, except I love you, my friend. Thank you for being my constant pillar of support and sounding board. Even when it's not one of our co-writes, you're there to bounce ideas and read scenes, and your friendship is invaluable. Thank you for being amazing.

*My beta team:*

Jamie, Stacy, Lauren, Erica, and Franci, I would be lost without you. You read my words as much as I do, and I can't tell you what your input and all the time you give means to me. Countless messages and bouncing ideas, you ladies keep me sane with the characters being anything but. Thank you from the bottom of my heart for taking this wild ride with me.

*Give Me Books:*

With every release, your team works diligently to get my book in the hands of bloggers. I cannot tell you how thankful I am for your services.

*Julie Deaton:*

Thank you for giving this book a set of fresh final eyes.

*Becky Johnson:*

I could not do this without you. Thank you for pushing me and making me work for it.

*Chasidy Renee:*

Thank you for everything you do. How did I survive without you before now? No matter what the task, you're always there with your never-ending support. Thank you so very much for all that you do.

*Bloggers:*

Thank you, it doesn't seem like enough. You don't get paid to do what you do. It's the kindness of your heart and your love of reading that fuels you. Without you, without your pages, your voice, your reviews, and spreading the word, it would be so much harder, if not impossible, to get my words in the reader's hands. I can't tell you how much your never-ending support means to me. Thank you for being you. Thank you for all that you do.

*To my reader group, Kaylee's Crew:*

You are my people. I love all of the messages and emails you send me. I love the little book community we've created. You are my family. Thank you for all of your love and support, not just with books but with life. No matter what I decide to write, you are there, ready to consume every word. Thank you for being the amazing group of people that you are.

Much love,

*Kaylee Ryan*
AUTHOR

Made in the USA
Columbia, SC
13 September 2022